Broken Homes

Book Nine of the Barrington Family Series

Chris Taylor

LCT Productions Pty Limited

Other books by Chris Taylor

The Munro Family Series (in order)

The Profiler
The Investigator
The Predator
The Betrayal
The Deception
The Negotiator
The Christmas Vigil (A novella)
The Ransom
The Defendant
The Shooting
The Maker

The Sydney Harbour Hospital Series (in order)

The Perfect Husband
The Body Thief
The Baby Snatchers
The Final Bullet
The Debt Collector
The Lab Test
The Stolen Identity
The Cliff-top Killer
The Likeable Fraudster

The Sydney Legal Series (in order)

An Accidental Murderer
At the Hand of her Father
A Woman Scorned
Lies and Deception
Ordinary Evil
The Ties that Bind
The Perfect Crime
A Toxic Inheritance
Malicious Love

The Craigdon Family Series (in order)

Callum
Joel
Isabella
Nicholas
Sophia
Flynn
Noah
Logan
Elizabeth

The Barrington Family Series (in order)

Broken Lives
Broken Promises
Broken Bonds
Broken Spirits
Broken Minds
Broken Vows
Broken Hearts
Broken Dreams
Broken Homes

The Fairfax Family Series (in order)

A Cattleman in Disguise
A Cattleman's Quest
A Cattleman's Daughter

A Cattleman's Secret Baby
To Catch a Cattleman
The Doctor and the Cattleman
To Rescue a Cattleman
A Cattleman's Heart
For the Love of a Cattleman

Bachelors and Brides Series (in order)

Matilda

Austin

Farrah

Benjamin

Verity

Denver

Ebony

Tyrone

Willow

Books by Chris Taylor
Writing as
Bella
Christian

This Is Where It Ends Series (in order)

Jessie's Story

Ryan's Story
Holly's Story
Sarah's Story
Veronica's Story

Love audiobooks? Check out Chris Taylor Books on audio
iTunes   Amazon   Audible

Join Chris Taylor's Facebook reader group/fan page and be among the
first to receive news of book releases, read and review books
prior to release
and other amazing offers.

Join Now!

This book is dedicated to my husband, Linden. My love, my life, my soul mate. I couldn't do this without your love and support. Thank you.

LCT Productions Pty Limited

18364 Kamilaroi Highway, Narrabri NSW 2390

ISBN: 9781925441154 (eBook)

ISBN: 9781925441161 (Print)

Chapter One

There was an elephant on his chest. Or a ton of bricks. Something hard and immoveable. Something that made it hard to breathe. He hurt all over. His chest was on fire. Every breath an agony. A white-hot knife point stabbed at his brain. Unrelenting. The pain was beyond anything he could have imagined. He couldn't think past it...except...

Ruby...?

Oh, God. I can't stand it. Please, God. It hurts too much. Please...

He wasn't sure he could endure it. Wasn't sure he wanted to...except...

Ruby...?

Ruby Ashworth clung to Vaughan Barrington's hand so tightly her fingers ached. She'd been a fixture at his bedside ever since he'd arrived at the Sydney Harbour Hospital. Frank

Barrington had arranged for his son to be medevacked from Bali and Ruby was thankful for his intervention, even if he'd ruffled a few feathers along the way, including hers. She hadn't met Frank or his wife, Evelyn, until they'd landed in Denpasar. They'd come straight to the hospital.

From that moment, Frank had taken over. Though Ruby was grateful to have some support, it was like she no longer existed. Frank didn't care that she was Vaughan's fiancée. All he cared about was his son. For two weeks, Vaughan had been too unstable to move. Everyone had chafed at the delay. Frank's temper had grown shorter with every day that Vaughan remained in the Denpasar hospital.

Frank's agitation was easy to understand. Ruby was also keen to see Vaughan moved to Australia and into more specialized medical care. After all, it was she who'd contacted Vaughan's father. But she hadn't expected the man to stomp all over everyone – nurses, doctors, technicians, her. For Vaughan's sake, she set aside her irritation over Frank's overbearing ways and fell in with his plans, but now they were back in Australia, she was done with his arrogant and domineering manner.

In response to Vaughan's serious condition, the hospital had limited his visitors. Only one person could be with him at a time. Right now, that was Ruby. As she stared down at the man she loved, her eyes filled with tears. Guilt ate at her.

"Please, Vaughan. Please, wake up. I need to talk to you. I need to tell you how much you mean to me. How sorry I am for not telling you the truth…"

Her voice hitched on a sob. She swiped at her tears with her free hand and tightened her hold on Vaughan with the other. She lifted his hand to her lips and kissed his fingers, then pressed them against her cheek. His skin was warm. He felt so alive. If only he'd open his eyes, smile at her, speak…

But he remained still and quiet, except for the rhythmic sound of the respirator that kept him alive, pumping air into his lungs. It was funny. If she overlooked the fading bruises on his face and the fact his beard had grown thicker and longer than she'd ever seen it, he looked like he was merely asleep. Like he'd wake at any moment and give her that heart-stopping grin that sent butterflies swirling through her stomach…

A quiet voice beside her startled Ruby into awareness. She hadn't heard the soft, rubber-soled approach of the nurse who hovered close by.

"I'm sorry, Ruby. Your time's up. Vaughan's father has been waiting outside for nearly twenty minutes." The nurse grimaced. "He's growing impatient."

Ruby compressed her lips against the familiar rise of irritation. "Of course he is."

"I'm sorry. I wish I could let you stay, but you know the rules," the nurse replied, not unkindly.

"Yes. The rules." Ruby glared at the nurse, even though her anger was for Frank. "Tell me, what does it matter to Vaughan how many visitors he has at one time? He's unconscious. He doesn't have a clue who's here."

The nurse held her ground. No doubt this wasn't the first time she'd had to deal with a difficult relative.

"There's a lot we don't understand about a patient's level of awareness while they're in a coma. There have been plenty of recounts from patients who recall hearing conversations around them while unconscious." The nurse shrugged. "Who knows? But our priority is our patients, and we'll always err on the side of what's best for them. It's tiring for conscious patients to deal with a constant stream of visitors. We have to assume it's that way for coma patients, too."

She gave Ruby another understanding look. "I know it's hard for you. For everyone. But patients who have suffered as much as Vaughan need all the rest they can get so they can heal. Limiting his visitors is one way to do that. Surely, that's what you want too?"

Ruby's cheeks heated with embarrassment at the nurse's pointed look. "Yes, of course," she mumbled.

Averting her gaze, she gathered up her jacket and handbag. Bending low, she kissed Vaughan on the cheek and turned away. Squaring her shoulders, she drew in a deep breath. With a bit of luck, she could slip past Frank without another confrontation.

Hannah Barrington clung tightly to her boyfriend's hand as they waited with her father outside the ICU. She and Liam had stopped by to visit with her brother, Vaughan. The last two weeks since his transfer to the Sydney Harbour Hospital had been stressful for all of them. Although he was receiving the best of medical care, he was still in a coma and no one could tell them if or when he might regain consciousness. So far, the signs were positive that he hadn't suffered any permanent brain damage, but they wouldn't know for sure until he woke. *If* he woke.

No. I refuse to believe that. He's going to wake up. He's going to get better. He's going to be fine...

If she repeated the words often enough, they might come true. She could only hope.

The door to the ICU swung open and the woman who was apparently Vaughan's fiancée came out. Ruby Ashworth barely glanced in their direction. Her shoulders were slumped and her eyes were red. Her long blonde hair hung loose, dull and lank. She headed toward the lifts without a word.

Sympathy welled up inside Hannah. It must be hard for Ruby to see Vaughan like that. They were all finding it challenging to comprehend the extent of his injuries, including the fact he might never wake up. His condition had neither improved nor worsened. They were all grateful for that.

"I'm going in," her father said, his voice gruff with emotion. Hannah nodded. "Okay, Daddy. We'll wait for you here."

Frank disappeared inside the ICU. The double doors closed silently behind him. Hannah leaned her head on Liam's shoulder and sighed.

"I hate this," she murmured.

Liam reached for her hand and threaded their fingers together. "It's tough. The waiting."

"Not only that. It's the not knowing whether he's ever going to get better. I could stand the waiting if I knew there would be a positive end to it. Poor Daddy. He's taking it especially hard. He's used to having Vaughan around. He's an integral part of Barrington Mining."

Liam tightened his hold on her hand and pressed a kiss against her hair. Silence fell between them. She was grateful he didn't offer any useless platitudes. The waiting room was quiet. Only the occasional muffled conversation from a nearby ward broke the stillness. She drew in a deep breath, filling her lungs with the smell of his cologne. His presence brought her comfort. Made her feel safe. Loved.

Though they'd only been a couple a short time, it felt right. She couldn't imagine wanting to spend her life with anyone else. She smiled. *It must be love.* She'd always thought that particular emotion overrated and had never felt the need to commit to anyone for very long. But Liam had changed all that. It was funny how life turned out.

"What do you know about Ruby?" Liam asked quietly.

Hannah shrugged. "Not much. She met Vaughan in Bali several months ago. Now they're engaged. That's it. Why?"

"There's something about her that seems familiar. I can't put my finger on it, but it's been bugging me from the moment I first saw her. It's like I've seen her before."

"Well, apparently, she comes from Sydney, so I guess it's possible you might have seen her before. Although in a city of more than five million people, I'd hate to fathom the odds of that."

"It'll come to me, don't worry. I never forget a face."

She smiled tenderly and pressed a kiss against his lips. He let go of her hand and pulled her close. She sighed softly. It felt so good to have his support, his love. Knowing he was in her corner and would be there for her, no matter what.

"Why did I spend so much time trying to avoid relationships?" she murmured against his shirtfront.

"Maybe it was because you were with the wrong guy. Not every relationship's a success. Not everyone finds their soulmate."

Her heart swelled with love. She pulled back slightly to stare up at him. "Is that what I am? Your soulmate?"

His gaze remained clear and steady on hers. "Yes."

Happiness flooded her veins. She reached up and pulled his head down to hers and kissed him once again.

"I love you, Liam Hennessy."

He smiled, his eyes filled with love and tenderness. "I love you too, Hannah Barrington." Caught up in each other's eyes, they didn't notice Frank had returned until he cleared his throat.

"If you two are done, let's get out of here."

Hannah blinked in surprise. "Daddy! You're finished?"

"Yes." Frank looked away and shuffled his feet. "I can't stand to see him that way."

Hannah's heart clenched at the raw pain in her father's eyes. She stood and went to him. "Oh, Daddy." She put her arms around him and hugged him. "He's going to be okay."

"You don't know that, Hannah," her father said.

Hannah bit her lip against a rush of emotion, too choked up to respond. Liam stepped forward.

"Hey, let's go downstairs and grab a coffee."

Hannah shot him a look of gratitude. He reached for her hand and drew her in close beside him. They walked toward the lifts.

"How was he?" Hannah managed.

Frank looked grim. "Same as always."

Over coffee in the hospital café, Frank distracted all of them with talk about the mine where Hannah worked as the chief safety officer. It was only one of several mines owned by her father, but it had always been a flagship of their holdings.

"Have you met the new investigator yet?" Frank asked.

Hannah glanced at Liam before responding. "No. Liam has a couple more days in the job before his resignation becomes effective. The Resources Regulator has advertised the position. I guess we'll meet the successful candidate soon."

"Let's hope they're a bit more amiable than the last one."

Frank's gruff tone belied the reluctant upturning of his mouth. He looked at Liam and winked. Everyone laughed and sipped their coffee. Then a speculative look filled Frank's gaze.

"What are your plans after you leave the Resources Regulator?" he asked.

Liam set his coffee cup down before replying. "I've put out a few feelers with some private companies. Right now, it's a matter of wait and see."

Frank eyed him steadily. "Would you be interested in working for Barrington Mining?"

Hannah started in surprise. "That's a great idea!" She glanced at Liam. "I mean, is that something you might be interested in?"

To her relief, Liam's expression remained open. He shrugged. "Maybe. I'd really like to stay in the Hunter Valley region if possible." He smiled at her before turning back to face her father. "What did you have in mind?"

Hannah's heart raced at the idea. Though she'd never given any thought to Liam working for her father because of their past history, that didn't mean the idea didn't appeal to her.

"I was thinking you could come on board as one of our safety officers," Frank said. "You'd be working under Hannah, of course, but with your extensive background in safety, there's no denying you'd be a real asset to our team."

Liam grinned. "Despite the fact I used to work for the Resources Regulator?"

Frank chuckled. "*Because* of that."

Hannah laughed, along with Liam. She looked at him, her excitement at the thought of them working together too hard to contain.

"I'd love to work with you," she said.

Liam's grin widened. "I'd love to work with you, too."

"We'd make a great team," Hannah added.

Liam chuckled. "You won't get any argument from me."

"Then it's settled," Frank said, finishing the last of his coffee. He pushed away from the table and stood. "I have to get going. I'll see you later."

As her father left the café and headed toward the hospital exit, Hannah reached for Liam's hand and squeezed it.

"Did you really mean it? Do you really want to work for my dad?"

Liam leaned over and cupped her cheek. He pressed a soft kiss against her lips. "I love being with you, Hannah. And just think of the perks!"

She frowned. "The perks?"

"Yes, I'll be the envy of everyone there. I get to go home and shag the boss!"

She grinned. "You won't mind me being the boss?"

"You can boss me around all you like."

The look he gave her was so hot it scorched her. Heat flooded her veins and centered in her core. Despite her anxiety for her brother, she couldn't help but be filled with desire for the man who'd lit up her life and captured her heart.

She grinned back at him. "Careful what you wish for."

He leaned forward and kissed her. "Promise?"

It wasn't until after Hannah went in to see Vaughan that Liam remembered where he'd seen Ruby Ashworth.

"She's related to Joseph Rodriguez," he said.

Hannah frowned as they made their way out of the hospital and toward the carpark where they'd left Hannah's car.

"The earthmoving contractor Daddy fired?"

"Yes. She's his daughter."

Hannah came to a sudden halt. She stared at Liam, her heart thumping. "Are you sure?" "Yes. I came across an article online that included a photograph of them together at a function for mining executives. The article identified them as father and daughter."

"Was Daddy at the function?"

"Yes, I think so. You were too."

Hannah frowned. "I was? I don't remember seeing her. We certainly weren't introduced. I wonder whether Daddy met her?"

"I'm guessing not. He hasn't said anything about recognizing her. I assume there were a lot of people there."

Hannah nodded. "Yes. More than a thousand guests from all over Australia. It was a pretty swanky party. How did you come across the article?"

"I was doing some research into her father for my investigation. I found a photo of them together at that party, along with Nathan Garcia."

Hannah's lips twisted at the mention of the man who used to be her righthand man at the mine and who'd turned out to be Joseph Rodriguez's nephew. Nathan had betrayed her and the mine and she was still struggling to come to terms with what he'd done. Charges had been laid. No doubt everything would be stirred up once again when the case went to trial.

She shook her head, still bewildered by Liam's revelation. "That means Vaughan's fiancée is Nathan's cousin. What are the odds?"

Liam looked grim. "Exactly."

Something in his tone caught her attention. "What? You think there's more to this?"

Liam sighed and began walking again. Hannah hurried to keep up with him.

"Don't you think it's a bit too much of a coincidence?" Liam asked. "I mean, Joseph Rodriguez gets fired for continuous safety breaches. He sends his nephew into the mine for the sole purpose of causing accidents—enough to nearly get the mine closed—and about the same time, his daughter *happens* to meet your brother in Bali?"

The cynicism in Liam's tone filled Hannah with dread. "Oh, my God!" she whispered. "Do you think their meeting was planned? But for what purpose?" Then another thought occurred to her. She grabbed Liam's arm. "Don't tell me you think she had something to do with Vaughan's accident?"

Liam shook his head. "No. Of course not." He paused and then added, "I don't know what to think."

Hannah stared at him in shock. Her thoughts galloped a mile a minute. No, to think Ruby had anything to do with Vaughan's accident was ridiculous. Anyone could see how much she cared for him. She'd been practically glued to his side. Even her father had complained he couldn't get time alone with his son because of Ruby.

But still... She was Joseph Rodriguez's daughter. The same man who'd put into action a plan to get their mine closed. And he hadn't cared who got hurt in the process.

Could Ruby Ashworth have deliberately set out to hurt Vaughan at her father's request? Was her apparent devotion to Hannah's brother all an act?

She was determined to find out.

Chapter Two

After spending most of the day at the hospital, Ruby was relieved to seek refuge in her inner-city apartment. Keeping vigil was exhausting. As was her concern for Vaughan's condition. It might have taken a serious accident for her to realize she'd fallen in love with him, but seeing him lying unconscious, so pale and quiet and still... It was distressing. It reminded her how fickle life could be and how it could be taken away in an instant. It also made her realize how much Vaughan meant to her.

He was a good guy. He didn't deserve this. If anyone deserved to be punished, it was her. She was the one who'd deliberately set out to deceive him. The fact she had solid reasons for doing so didn't seem to matter anymore. If only she'd told him the truth. She should have come clean as soon as she realized he was a good man and was nothing like his father. But she hadn't. Now she might never get the chance. That real possibility was killing her.

So was having to put up with his family. In particular, Frank. She'd heard so much about the Barrington patriarch from her father. It was all she could do not to spit in Frank Barrington's face. But for now, she had a role to play, that of concerned fiancée. If his family got even a hint that her relationship with Vaughan wasn't solid, she'd be refused access to him at the hospital. That was something she couldn't bear and that had nothing to do with her father and everything to do with how she felt about the man who was currently fighting for his life. The irony wasn't lost on her.

The thought of Vaughan not pulling through made her heart hurt. Her father had placed her in what was now a terrible no-win situation, though it was what she'd wanted. She'd agreed to play a part in his revenge and he was counting on her.

A fresh wave of guilt threatened to overwhelm her. As she tossed her handbag on the hall table and toed off her sandals, she clung to the hope that Vaughan would wake. Despite everything, she wanted the chance to tell him the truth and beg his forgiveness. There was no guarantee that would be accepted, but she had to try at least.

Walking barefoot into the kitchen, she opened the fridge and pulled out the bottle of Sauvignon Blanc she'd opened the evening before. Pouring herself a glass, she flopped on the black leather sofa that took up most of the space in the adjoining living room. She reached for the remote and activated the TV and then distractedly surfed the channels. Nothing held her interest.

With a heavy sigh, she took a healthy swallow of her wine. The crisp tartness exploded on her tongue. Halfway through the glass, she began to relax. It had been another long day. Another long day of not knowing whether Vaughan would regain consciousness. Another long day of worrying whether she'd ever be given the chance to explain and apologize. She'd give anything to be able to have that conversation, even knowing how devastating the result would likely be. The alternative didn't bear thinking about.

The sound of a knock on her apartment door interrupted her thoughts. Frowning, she set down her wineglass and padded down the hall. She lived on the ninth floor. Random visitors were an oddity, and she certainly wasn't expecting anyone. Peeking through the security peephole, her stomach dropped on a gasp.

Hannah Barrington stood on the other side. She didn't look happy.

Ruby's guilty conscience immediately jumped to conclusions. *She knows... Somehow, she's discovered the truth...* Taking a deep, steadying breath, Ruby reined in her panic. Hannah couldn't possibly know about her deception. She and her father were the only two who did and there was no way he would have told the Barringtons. She was being silly, allowing her guilty conscience to get the upper hand. Given the current circumstances and everything that had gone on recently, who could blame her?

But now wasn't the time to fall apart. It was more important than ever to maintain the ruse. It didn't matter that she was really in love with Vaughan. She'd banish those feelings from her mind, if not her heart, until this was over. She was so close. So close to getting what she wanted; what her father wanted, provided Vaughan woke up. She couldn't afford to blow it now. Squaring her shoulders, she drew in another deep breath and plastered a smile on her face. Then she opened the door.

"Hannah! This is a surprise! What are you doing here? Is it Vaughan? Has something happened?"

Hannah rudely pushed past her and strode down the hall. Ruby's disquiet deepened, but she forced herself to remain calm.

"I'm sorry, but what are you doing here?" she asked again as Hannah came to a halt beside the kitchen counter.

Hannah rounded on her, eyes blazing. "Oh, no. You don't get to ask the questions, Ruby Ashworth. Or should I say, Ruby Rodriguez!"

Ruby's stomach dropped like a stone. She stared at Hannah and fought to remain calm.

She knows! She knows who I am! What else does she know? Oh, hell. What do I do now? Keep calm. Keep calm. Keep calm...

The steady mantra had the desired effect. Ruby held Hannah's gaze, grateful for her outward composure. At the same time, she curled her hands into fists to conceal their trembling. She forced an indifferent smile.

"You're right. My father's Joseph Rodriguez."

"The same Joseph Rodriguez my father just happened to sack from Strathwaylin mine more than a year ago. The same Joseph Rodriguez who got his nephew to sabotage operations at the very same mine these past twelve months," Hannah said coldly.

Ruby shrugged nonchalantly. It was all she could do to maintain the veneer of disinterest. "If you say so. I wouldn't know. I don't get involved with my father's business dealings," she lied.

Hannah shook her head scornfully. "Oh, don't you go expecting me to believe that. The contract my father terminated was worth millions. There's no way your father didn't tell his family about it."

Once again, Ruby worked hard to maintain her façade of indifference. "Whatever. It's obvious to me you've already made up your mind about what I do and don't know. Why would I waste time trying to convince you otherwise?"

She advanced a couple of steps toward Hannah, who held her ground. Though Hannah wore high heels, the two women stood eye to eye. Physically, they were fairly equally matched, but Ruby had at least a decade on Hannah. And yet the younger woman didn't appear the least bit intimidated. Ruby couldn't help the spurt of reluctant admiration.

Hannah continued to glare at her. "My brother has no idea who you really are, does he?"

Though Ruby did her best to remain emotionless, something in her face must have given her away. Hannah pounced.

"Oh, my God! He doesn't know! He proposed to you, and he doesn't even know who you are! What did you do? Cast a spell on him? I don't believe this. How could you have been so deceitful?"

Ruby fought to keep her breathing even. "Your brother doesn't care about things like that. He loves me for who I am."

Hannah glared at her. "Would he love you if he knew the truth? What are you playing at, Ruby Rodriguez? What the hell are you doing with my brother?"

It took all of Ruby's courage to maintain eye contact, but she managed it. "I'm not playing at anything. Your brother and I met by chance in Bali. We fell in love. He proposed. I accepted. Then he was injured. That's it. End of story."

But Hannah wasn't buying it. "Vaughan didn't get to be forty years of age and still single by being reckless with his heart. I don't know how you got him to fall in love with you. What I do know is that my brother's lying in a coma, and no one can tell me who's responsible. Given your father's history of using family to cause accidents for the Barringtons and the things they hold dear, I've got you firmly in my sights."

Ruby gasped, outraged. "How *dare* you say that about my father! He was innocent in all of that. Your father was the one in the wrong. He fired my father for no reason!"

Hannah's eyes gleamed with triumph. "Ha!" She pounced on that. "So, you *do* know about all this. Why did you lie? Or does dishonesty come so easily to you, you're not even aware you're doing it?"

Ruby clenched her jaw to prevent herself from saying something she'd later regret. It was hard to remain silent when fury pounded through her veins. She wanted nothing more than to slap the arrogant expression off Hannah's face and tell her a few hard truths about the high-and-mighty Frank Barrington. Instead, she drew in a deep breath and fought for calm.

Hannah glared at her. "You owe me an explanation."

Ruby glared right back. "I owe you nothing."

"You know—"

"What I know is that my father was treated abominably by yours," she spat. "I don't expect you to believe that because that would mean you'd have to admit your father isn't the paragon of virtue you seem to think."

While Hannah sputtered with outrage, Ruby continued. "As for Vaughan, believe what you want. We're in love and we're getting married, just as soon as he's well enough. Come to the wedding, or not. That's your decision. It makes no difference to me."

Hannah's gaze turned icy. "We only have your word that Vaughan proposed. He never said anything to his family. Don't you think that's strange? Then again, perhaps your family isn't as close as ours. And as for your father, why don't you ask your cousin about who put him up to sabotaging operations? He caused several serious accidents. People were hurt." Her gaze narrowed threateningly. "You be warned, Ruby Rodriguez. I'm watching you."

With that, Hannah flung her long hair over her shoulder and stormed past Ruby toward the front door.

With fury still burning through her veins, Ruby couldn't help one last parting question. "How did you know where I live?"

Hannah slowed and turned around. "I asked someone at the hospital to check your contact details. I wanted to make sure they had them right. You being Vaughan's fiancée and all."

Her smirk filled Ruby with fresh anger. With fists clenched, she strode toward her. "You had no right," she said coldly.

Hannah merely shook her head. "Save it. If what I suspect is true, a so-called invasion of your privacy is the least of your worries." With that, Hannah pulled open the door and slammed it behind her.

The apartment fell silent. Ruby's shoulders sagged. She trembled all over, both shocked and shaken by the confrontation. Hannah knew who she was. She probably shouldn't be surprised. The mining industry was a small one and most of the big players were known. She wondered how many other Barringtons knew the truth. The control on her panic slipped. Everything was unraveling at warp speed.

The doctors were quietly confident Vaughan would regain consciousness. The minute he did, she needed to come clean;

to tell him the truth before he found out from someone else. That would be disastrous.

With her hands gripped tightly together, she prayed silently for Vaughan to wake up.

High above him, the sun shone brightly in a cloudless blue sky. It was the kind of perfect summer day Vaughan loved. He floated on his back in the warm salt water, utterly relaxed. Gentle waves broke over him. Their swaying movement lulled him into a half slumber. In fact, if he closed his eyes, he'd almost certainly fall asleep.

It reminded him of the perfect days spent with Ruby, lazing on Bali's beaches. Swimming in the surf. Kissing, making love. Falling asleep in each other's arms beneath a chandelier of stars, the air heavy with the scent of salt and frangipani.

Ruby...

His heart clenched with love. He turned his head this way and that, hoping to see her. He was disappointed to discover he was alone. He shifted position, treading water instead of simply floating. There was nothing but deep blue ocean as far as the eye could see. And then his gut tightened, and fear rushed through his veins.

Where am I? What am I doing out in the middle of the ocean, alone? Where's Ruby?

He pulled at the oxygen mask on his face. "Ruby!"

The sound of his voice in the stillness frightened him. Croaky and rough, he barely recognized it as belonging to him. He tried to shout again, but it took too much effort. His voice was barely above a whisper. And then a soft, cool hand pressed against his cheek. Slowly, he opened his eyes.

"Ruby..." he croaked.

"Yes, it's me! Ruby! Oh, Vaughan! You're awake! Thank goodness you're awake!"

He heard the joy and relief in her voice and couldn't hold back a smile. "Ruby..."

She was there. Beside him. Holding tightly to his hand. Tears filled his eyes. His chest went tight. He was so in love with her.

"Ruby..."

He tried to move, to touch her. Pain, sharp and immediate, hammered through his head. He gasped. "Fuck."

"It's all right," Ruby soothed, brushing back the hair from his forehead. "Don't move." She settled the mask back in place. "Take it easy, Vaughan. It's going to be all right."

He frowned. "What...? What happened?"

Ruby's forehead creased. "You don't remember?"

"A truck. I tried to swerve. Too late."

"Yes. You were hit. You've been unconscious for almost a month. You gave us all a big fright."

"Us?"

"Yes. Me. And your family. They've all been by to see you."

"They're in Bali?"

"No. You're in Sydney now. Your parents came over to Denpasar and arranged to fly you out."

Vaughan nodded slowly. "You met them?"

Ruby smiled. "Yes."

"Did you tell them about us?"

She held out her hand and waggled her fingers. The impressive solitaire diamond he'd given her flashed brilliantly beneath the light. "Of course."

He wished he'd been awake to see it. Their engagement would have come as a surprise to his family, but he was certain they'd embrace Ruby wholeheartedly and welcome her into the fold. Once again, he reached out to touch her. The pain in his head wasn't quite as severe this time, but it was there all the same. Everything was still foggy and thinking about anything other than how thrilled he was to be alive and to have Ruby by his side was beyond him.

With a sigh, he closed his eyes and gave in to the exhaustion that gripped him. He fell asleep with a smile on his face.

Ruby clung to Vaughan's hand, her heart pounding. He was awake and he'd recognized her! His head injury didn't appear to be as bad as she'd feared. The doctors had warned her there might be brain damage, memory loss—anything could happen with a brain injury as severe as his. But he'd recognized her and remembered that they were together. It was enough to send joy rushing through her veins. She could only hope he still wanted to be with her after she told him who she was.

The time to do that was now. She'd explain what she'd been planning and why. That after what her father had told her, she hadn't been given a choice. Her brother, Kyle, was dead at the hands of Frank Barrington. He might not have slipped the noose around Kyle's neck, but he was the reason her brother had fallen into such despair that he thought death was the only way out. She just hoped Vaughan would understand...and forgive her.

There was no doubt he'd be shocked. Hannah's reaction was testament to that and Hannah didn't know the half of it. But she owed Vaughan an apology and an explanation. No matter how much she dreaded the coming confrontation, it would be much more palatable if the truth came from her. But first, she had to call for the nurse and give her the good news.

Vaughan's awake! Now the hard part begins.

Chapter Three

Hannah paced the length of her father's city office, unable to stand still. The morning sun poured through the floor-to-ceiling wall of glass that formed one side of the room. It was normally a view she enjoyed. The corner office overlooked Sydney's lush Botanical Gardens. In the distance was a glimpse of the sparkling blue Pacific Ocean. But today, Hannah was blind to the impressive view. Though it had been twelve hours since her confrontation with Ruby, she was still agitated.

"I can't believe she didn't tell Vaughan who she is!" she exclaimed, her voice reflecting her irritation.

Her father sat composed behind his carved walnut desk, his fingers steepled beneath his chin. He regarded her steadily.

"What makes you think knowing who Ruby's father was would make any difference to Vaughan? We still don't have any proof Joseph Rodriguez was involved in Evan Wilson's death and Vaughan fled to Bali before the other mess with Nathan Garcia came to light. He knows nothing about the recent spate of accidents that almost got the mine closed. At the very most, he might be surprised at the coincidence of meeting Rodriguez's daughter overseas."

"But why would she keep her identity a secret? Claim to be someone else?" Hannah exclaimed. "What's she got to hide?" Hannah folded her arms across her chest and narrowed her eyes. "When I mentioned Nathan, she only grew more outraged. There's something fishy going on."

Frank nodded. "I agree. Of course, we don't know why Ruby Rodriguez was in Bali. She could simply have been there on holiday, like so many thousands of other young Australians who flock there every year, including Vaughan."

"So, why wouldn't she offer me an explanation? You should have seen her, Daddy! She looked like she was going to die of shock when I told her I knew who she was. Why the concern? Why the subterfuge? She meets a cute guy in Bali, and she gives him a false name. Why would she do that?"

"Maybe she wanted to see how trustworthy he was before disclosing too much personal information," Frank said in a reasonable tone.

"Okay, but why not tell him the truth later? Apparently, they're engaged. Surely there was plenty of time to come clean about her real name."

Frank nodded. "You're right. If she got to the point of accepting a marriage proposal, she should have trusted him enough to disclose who she was."

Hannah pounced. "Exactly! And yet she didn't. I could tell from the look on her face that she hasn't told him."

"Did you ask her why?"

"Of course, but she refused to answer my question."

Frank looked grim. "I've been a little suspicious of her from the start. For Vaughan to be engaged and not tell any of us, not even me or your mother… It all seems a little strange. Especially given what we know about her father. He's a crook. I'm not suggesting Ruby is too, but something is awry. I can understand why she kept quiet about who she was in the early days, but this is the man she agreed to marry. It's not unreasonable to expect she'd be more forthright about her family with him."

"Especially since she knew you'd sacked her father, although she seems to have a different interpretation of the facts." Hannah grimaced.

"What do you mean?"

Hannah propped a hip against her father's desk. "She seems to think her father was treated poorly by the Barringtons; that *we* were the ones in the wrong. Who knows what she was told about all that. No doubt her father slanted the whole sordid incident in his favor," she muttered.

Frank's eyes narrowed. "That sounds exactly like something Joseph Rodriguez would do. If that asshole's been using his daughter to get at my son somehow…" He let the thought hang for a moment and then made a sound of frustration in the back of his throat. "It's too bad Vaughan can't shed any light on all of this."

Hannah nodded. "Let's hope he wakes up soon and can tell us everything himself. Then we won't be forced to take Ruby's word for anything."

Frank's phone began to ring. He pulled it out of his pocket and checked the screen. He glanced back at Hannah, his expression tense.

Her heart skipped a beat. "Who is it?"

"The hospital."

Vaughan's head thumped. He was sore all over. Everything ached. But still, he was alive and from what Ruby had told him about the accident, he was thankful for that. He was also grateful that there appeared to be no lasting effects from the head injury, apart from the headache that put all other headaches to shame.

A bevy of doctors had been in to see him, called by a nurse as soon as Ruby had alerted them he was awake. They'd put him through a truckload of neurological tests. He'd passed them all with flying colors. He couldn't be more relieved. Or happier.

He looked at Ruby. She was perched on a chair that she'd pulled up to his bed and now she clung tightly to his hand. They'd already shifted him out of the ICU and onto another ward, convinced he was on the mend. Things were looking up.

So why did Ruby look so uncomfortable? And why wouldn't she meet his eye?

Please, God. Don't let it be over between us... I couldn't bear it if she's come to say goodbye... I love her so much...

"What's wrong?" he asked quietly, taking his courage in his hands. He was determined to face whatever was going on with her, head on. No matter that she might be about to break his heart; life was too short for games.

The color left her cheeks, further fueling his sense of foreboding. She let go of his hand. He immediately felt bereft. She glanced at him and then looked away.

"There's something I have to tell you," she murmured.

His gut clenched. He fought to keep his breathing steady. "Okay. What is it?"

She blew her breath out on a heavy sigh. Her gaze skittered over his. "I... I told you my name's Ruby Ashworth," she said in a rush.

Vaughan frowned in confusion, not sure where this was headed. "Yes."

"The thing is... I—"

"Ruby Ashworth is Joseph Rodriguez's daughter," Hannah interrupted as she sailed unannounced into the room, their father close on her heels.

Ruby gasped at the sudden intrusion. Her skin turned chalky. Vaughan's frown deepened. The pain in his head worsened. It still felt like he was plowing through mud whenever he tried to concentrate. "Joseph Rodriguez? Why does that name sound familiar?"

"He was one of the lead earthmoving contractors out at the Strathwaylin mine. Daddy fired him over a year ago for numerous safety breaches. He was given his marching orders the very same day Evan Wilson died," Hannah said.

Vaughan gasped. "*What?*"

The past came back to him in a rush. His head thumped as blood flooded his brain. He turned and stared at Ruby. "Your father's Joseph Rodriguez?"

Her expression was one of overwhelming guilt. She hadn't even opened her mouth, but Vaughan already had his answer. Confusion coursed through him. His fists clenched. "Why didn't you tell me?"

Ruby's gaze remained fixed on the floor. Her fingers twisted in the pleats of her skirt. She squirmed in her seat and then shifted as if she were about to leave.

Vaughan's belly filled with dread. Something was awfully wrong. *Why would Ruby keep something like this from me?* He'd never told her about his family; that his father was Frank Barrington, the mining magnate. He'd wanted her to love him for who he was. As far as she knew, he was just another fun-loving Aussie hanging out in Bali, having a good time.

She'd had no reason to suspect he had any idea about who her father was or that he'd been fired from Frank's mine. In fact, she'd had no reason to suspect anything at all. They had merely been two tourists who'd hooked up and had fallen in love on holiday.

Unless...

In a sudden moment of clarity, Vaughan's eyes widened. "You knew who I was from the very beginning, didn't you?"

Ruby's cheeks turned crimson. She made a sound of distress in the back of her throat. Her hands came up to press against her mouth. When she finally met his gaze, the expression in her eyes was tortured.

"I'm sorry, Vaughan. Please, let me explain."

Shock ricocheted through him. He stared at her in disbelief. "Who are you and what the hell were you doing in Bali?"

"That's exactly what I asked her," Hannah said, coming farther into the room. Their father crowded in behind her and hurried over to Vaughan's bed.

"Vaughan! It's so good to see you awake!" Frank said, reaching down and squeezing his arm. Tears shone in his eyes.

Vaughan swallowed past the lump in his throat. His joy at seeing his father again after so long, temporarily overrode the shock of Ruby's revelations. "Dad," he croaked.

"Oh, Vaughan," Frank said again, his voice thick with emotion.

"Where's Mom?" Vaughan rasped, still overcome by seeing his family again.

"She's on her way. Hannah and I were at my office in the city when the hospital called, so we got here faster. Your mother's driving in from Broken. She'll be here as soon as she can.

We're all thrilled you're awake! You won't believe how worried we've all been."

Vaughan compressed his lips against another wave of emotion. "Ruby said you and Mom traveled to Bali and arranged to have me brought home."

"Of course," Frank replied.

Vaughan looked at him. "Thank you," he rasped.

His father merely nodded, his lips tightly pressed together. Vaughan could see how hard he was struggling to maintain his composure. Vaughan had never felt so loved. Then his gaze fell on Ruby. She stood with her back to him, her arms wrapped around herself, her shoulders slumped in defeat.

Anger and hurt warred inside him. She'd tricked him. Their so-called chance meeting hadn't been so coincidental after all. She'd known all along who he was and had made it her business to introduce herself. The question was, why?

He looked at his father and his sister. "Dad. Hannah. It's so good to see you, but if you don't mind, could I ask you both to step outside for a moment? I need a few minutes alone with Ruby."

Though Hannah looked like she was about to argue, she didn't object when his father took her by the arm and led her toward the door. Once they were alone, Vaughan pushed through his hurt and anger and spoke.

"I've lived under the shadow of my family's success most of my life. Don't get me wrong. I love them dearly and am grateful to have them in my life, but everyone in Sydney knows the Barrington family name and what it represents." He paused.

"Before I left for Bali, I found out something that turned everything I'd believed about myself on its head and by the time we met, I was still confused about so many things. That's why I never told you my last name. On top of that, I wanted you to like me for myself. I wanted to be plain old Vaughan, an easy-going guy who worked behind a bar on the beach."

A coldness settled in his heart. He smiled humorlessly. "But the joke's on me, isn't it? All this time, I thought you'd fallen in love with a stranger. Me. Now I find that's a lie. All this time, you've known exactly who I am. The only thing I want to know is why you approached me at all. Why did you give me a fake name? What were you hoping to achieve?"

His anger rose with each question. His head began to thump. Ruby looked like she was about to cry. He refused to feel guilty over her obvious distress. He glared at her. "I deserve answers, Ruby."

"Ashworth isn't a fake name," she said tightly. "It's my mother's maiden name. I use it sometimes when I'm traveling overseas."

"Why were you in Bali?" he demanded, his harsh tone enunciating each and every word.

She winced and tightened her arms across her chest. "You're going to hate me," she whispered.

His gut clenched with foreboding. Fighting off a wave of pain that came from more than just his injuries, he locked his eyes on hers. "Tell me."

Chapter Four

*O*h, God. I'm going to be sick. Right here, on the hospital floor...

The shock of Vaughan discovering her true identity before she'd had a chance to tell him herself still ricocheted through her mind. She should have told him right after he woke. She should have known Vaughan's sister would tell him the truth.

She snuck a glance in his direction. Her stomach sank. His expression was hard and cold. It was like staring into the face of granite. And he didn't know the worst of it yet.

He's never going to forgive me. This is it. As soon as I tell him everything, we're over...

Her heart clenched in protest. It was so unfair. She'd finally given herself permission to fall in love with him and now they were done. And it was all her fault. The only thing she could do now was to get this over with and get the hell away before she broke down completely. Steeling herself for what was to come, she drew in a ragged breath.

"You're right. I did know who you were. I knew before I left for Bali."

Surprise and hurt flared briefly in his eyes before it was concealed by a blank mask. "How? You and I had never met."

"That's true. But I still knew who you were. I work in the contracts department for my father. You work in the same department for yours. We actually exchanged emails while negotiating my father's contract with Barrington Mining. During our time in Bali, I was deliberately vague about my work. You probably recall me only telling you I was employed as an EA in a busy professional office in the city. That's partly true. I'm also a lawyer. Lucky for me, you didn't express too much curiosity about my job."

Vaughan's expression remained closed. "More lies. Did you deliberately follow me to Bali?"

She forced herself to hold his gaze. "Yes."

"How did you know I was there?"

"My brother, Matthew, happened to be at the airport in Sydney and saw you. He overheard a conversation between you and the attendant checking in your baggage. You were on your way to Bali because apparently, you needed to escape for a while. Matthew, who also works for my father, recognized you and passed on the news."

Vaughan's stare intensified. "Why?" he rasped. "Why did you follow me to Bali?"

A shiver of dread ran down Ruby's spine. This was the part she'd been fearing the most. But she'd made up her mind to tell Vaughan everything. He deserved nothing less.

"I don't know how much you know about what happened between my father and yours. You've been in Bali for almost a year. You must have taken off just after my father's contract was terminated."

Vaughan nodded briefly. "I remember. Your father flagrantly refused to follow safety procedures. He flaunted the rules every opportunity he got. My father had no choice but to fire him. Your father brought that on himself."

Anger blazed through Ruby. She might have fallen in love with this man, but there was no way she was going to sit there and take that.

"You have to be kidding!" she exclaimed. "My father did no such thing! That contract was wrongly terminated for no good reason at all. As a result, my brother, Kyle, took his own life. That's on you and your family." She spat the words out.

Vaughan's eyes widened in shock. At the same time, his cheeks flushed with anger. "I don't know where you got your information, but you're way off base. Your father was an accident waiting to happen. On a mine site, safety's paramount. When rules aren't followed, people get hurt. Sometimes they get killed. I don't know what nonsense you're sprouting about your brother. I'm sorry that he died. But that had nothing to do with me or my family and if you think it does, you're crazy."

Ruby's fury ignited. "Oh, right. So, the fact my brother committed suicide over the loss of a multi-million-dollar contract that your father just happened to terminate without just cause has nothing to do with the Barringtons. Of course. I should have expected as much from the almighty Barringtons. Your family have always lorded it over everyone else. How could I expect any of you to take responsibility for my brother's death? You won't even admit the contract was unfairly terminated, let alone anything else."

Vaughan glared at her. "I stand by everything I said. And need I remind you, I'm not the only one who pretended for almost a year to be someone else. You still haven't told me what you were doing in Bali and what you hoped to achieve by getting close to me."

Ruby stared at him, her breath coming fast. As much as she wanted to continue to rail against him at the injustice served upon her family, she'd come there to tell him the truth. She drew in a steadying breath and lowered her tone.

"My father was angry over the wrongful termination of his contract. He was also devastated over what had happened to Kyle. We all were. Kyle had a lot riding on that contract. Daddy told me Kyle had used it to leverage against increased amounts from investors, bringing in a serious amount of money for expanding the family business. When he learned of the canceled contract and realized the serious financial difficulties the company was about to face, it pushed him over the edge."

Despite her best intentions, her anger flared back to life. Her nails bit into her palms as she glared at him "That's why I hold your father responsible for Kyle's death. When Daddy suggested I follow you to Bali and do whatever I could to help him and to avenge my brother's tragic death, I agreed. After the abhorrent way your father had treated my family, I was more than willing to do my bit to honor Kyle's life and lessen my father's humiliation and financial ruin. If that meant pretending to be someone else in order to get close to you and maybe elicit a few in-house secrets, then that's what I was prepared to do."

Vaughan's expression turned icy. His nostrils flared as he slowly shook his head back and forth. "You really are something. How could I have been so blind? I've always prided myself on being a good judge of character, but I never saw through you. Not once. I believed every word you said, every smile, every touch. I fell head over heels in love with you and all the time, it was a lie. *We* were a lie.

His breath came faster. A vein pulsed in his neck. "You never loved me at all, did you? You were only there for revenge. Out of curiosity, just how far were you prepared to go? You were obviously willing to sleep with me. You even agreed to get engaged. Tell me, were you ever going to marry me, or was that where you drew the line?" He paused, his chest rising and falling in quick succession and then comprehension flooded his face.

"Oh, now I get it. That's why you didn't want to get married in Bali. You kept putting me off with some stupid excuse that you wanted to tie the knot in Sydney where your family could be present, but that was just another lie, wasn't it? You never intended to get married. You were never even in love. It's all been a lie."

Ruby almost doubled over from the rush of pain that clutched at her heart. "No, Vaughan! No! You're wrong. My feelings for you are real. I'm in love with you! Yes, I went there at the behest of my father. I was prepared to do what I could to help. But then I met you and you were nothing like I expected. You were nothing like your father, at least the father my dad told me about. I hadn't counted on you being so nice. Or that I'd like you so much. That I'd fall in love with you... It made going through with the plan that much more difficult."

Vaughan's lips twisted into a bitter parody of a smile. "And yet you continued down that path, lying to me every day we were together. If Hannah hadn't realized who you were, I might never have found out."

Ruby wanted to argue against that, but there was nothing she could say. Even if she told him she'd already regretted her decision to deceive him and had decided to come clean, the chances he'd believe her were slim to almost none. She'd lied to him over and over by not telling him who she really was and what she'd been doing in Bali. She'd broken his trust. He might never believe her again.

She inched closer to the bed, desperation and panic nipping at her heels. "Vaughan, you don't understand. It isn't what you think. My father was angry. After the way your father treated him, he had a right to feel like that. And then for Kyle to take his own life as a result of what happened... We were all shocked, bewildered, hurting. Daddy asked for my help..."

Her voice faded. Her chest was so tight, she could barely breathe. Tears threatened. She blinked hard and fought back a sob.

Vaughan's expression turned glacial. "Quit trying to defend the indefensible. You were in on it right from the start. I only have your word it wasn't your idea and right now, your word means shit. You lied to me. You deceived me. You pretended to fall in love with me. You've broken my heart."

His beautiful green eyes were cold. The fury that laced his voice could have cut through glass.

"I have no one but myself to blame. I fell for you, hook, line, and sinker. I didn't once question how this beautiful woman had come into my life or how it was that we got along so well. It was like you knew me. Knew exactly what to say to make me feel good about myself. To make me fall in love. And it was all a lie. A fabrication cooked up for no other reason than for some twisted act of revenge."

His voice was harsh with pain. She hated that she was the cause of that. She wanted desperately to explain to him and to tell him that not everything had been an act. She opened her mouth to speak again, but with a savage slice of his hand through the air, Vaughan cut her off.

"Don't," he rasped. "Don't bother trying to explain. I've heard all I can stand. There's nothing you can say to make this better. You're a lying, deceitful witch. I can't believe I was taken in by you."

Ruby began trembling. Panic and fear left her weak. Though she'd braced herself for the probability that he'd never forgive her, now that reality was staring her in the face, she couldn't bear the pain.

I'm going to lose him... He hates me... Oh, God, we're over... It hurts so much...

Her heart beat a frantic tattoo in her chest. This was going even worse than she'd expected. She stared at Vaughan in desperation, hoping to convince him through the intensity of her gaze.

"You're wrong, Vaughan! Yes, I knew who you were, and yes, I followed you to Bali for a reason, but the more I got to know you, the more that reason no longer mattered. You were so warm and funny and wonderful. Kind and generous. A man I could fall in love with. A man I *did* fall in love with."

Vaughan regarded her scornfully. "You expect me to believe that now?"

Sweat popped out on her brow. "Yes! Because I'm telling the truth!"

His expression turned bleak. His shoulders slumped in defeat. "I'm tired of being lied to by people who are supposed to care. If this is what you call love, I want no part of it. We're done. Please, leave."

Ruby gaped. The panic inside her intensified. "Vaughan! No! Please, don't do this! I love you! You love me! We're getting married!" She flashed her ring finger in his face. "See! You picked this out yourself. You gave it to me. You told me you'd love me forever."

Her tone had risen, along with her distress, but there was nothing she could do about that. Vaughan was slipping away from her, one clipped, icy word at a time. She noticed the dark circles under his eyes and reminded herself that he was far from being back to full health. No doubt he hadn't been sleeping well. That's why he was being so cold, so unyielding. She clung to the hope he would thaw toward her.

As if he could read her mind, he spoke again in a tone that was so final it chilled her. "We're over, Ruby. I'm done. I'm physically and emotionally exhausted. I can't do this anymore. Please don't make me call for the nurse to toss you out."

Ruby's stomach clenched with despair. She'd never felt more hopeless. She hated that she had no control. That she was no longer in charge of her destiny.

"Vaughan, please!" She tried again. "You have it all wrong! I love you! Okay, so maybe my feelings weren't as strong as yours in the beginning, but when you were hit by that truck and I didn't know if you were going to live or die, everything became crystal clear. I knew without a shred of doubt that I love you with everything that I am. I still do."

His gaze turned even colder. It was like looking into the eyes of a stranger. His voice pitched low and was rough with hurt and bitterness.

"Oh, so now you admit you weren't even in love with me until just the other week. For all those long months we were together, you let me believe you were just as in love as I was. Yet another one of your lies. You're quite an actress." His mouth twisted in pain. "Get out! Now! And don't come back. I never want to see you again."

His words cut her to the quick. She didn't want to leave him like this, but he hadn't given her any choice. When he deliberately turned his head away from her to face the wall, she bit back a cry of anguish.

It's okay. I get it. He's upset. I need to give him some space, some time to cool off... He said he'd love me forever. Surely, he can't switch off those feelings, just like that...?

She clung to the comforting thought. It was better than the alternative. With her jaw clenched tightly against the pain of unshed tears, she collected her handbag and left.

Ruby stumbled out of the hospital. Her chest was so tight, she struggled to draw breath. Tears ran down her cheeks. She hadn't seen Hannah or Frank as she'd made a hasty retreat out of Vaughan's room and for that at least, she was grateful. She couldn't have borne seeing the smug expression on Hannah's face. No doubt she'd be pleased her brother had seen the light.

The sudden blast of a car horn startled her. She looked up and realized she'd stepped out onto the road and had almost been run over. Shaken, she pulled herself together enough to make it back to her Mazda in one piece.

Her hand trembled as she unlocked the car with her remote. Throwing herself into the driver's seat, she held her head in her hands and gave in to the emotions she'd been trying desperately to keep in check. Her shoulders shook with the force of her sobs. She loved him and he loved her, but she'd thrown it all away. And for what? A chance at revenge? To please her father? The way Vaughan had looked at her... She'd destroyed any love he had for her, and she had no one to blame but herself.

Still, she was shocked at Vaughan's reaction. She'd known he'd be upset. She'd braced herself for a difficult conversation. But to call it quits on their relationship... And to do it so coldly, as if she meant nothing to him. That was unexpected and cut deep. She hadn't been prepared for how much it would hurt.

Stupid heart.

She'd been prepared to admit her father had sent her to Bali to befriend him and get on his good side, even if that meant he might never trust her again. She cared for him too much to continue to lie to him, no matter the motivation.

I'm sorry, Kyle. I'm so sorry...

She didn't know how long she cried, but by the time she lifted her head, she was exhausted. Her blurry features stared miserably back at her in the rear vision mirror. Her eyes were red and swollen. Her nose dripped. She grimaced.

Fumbling in her handbag for a tissue, she did what she could to repair the damage. When she felt more in control, she braced herself to call her father. It wasn't like she could pretend the confrontation with Vaughan hadn't happened. She had to tell him Vaughan knew everything now. Might as well get it over with.

Drawing in a ragged breath, she took another moment to compose herself. With a knot of dread heavy in her chest, she dialed his number. He answered on the third ring.

"Ruby, what's up?"

"I'm sorry, Daddy. It's over."

"What are you talking about?"

"With Vaughan. He knows everything."

"What do you mean, everything?"

"He knows I'm your daughter. He knows about your plan for revenge."

"How the hell would he know about that?"

She gulped. "I... I told him."

"What the fuck, Ruby? How could you betray me like that?"

"I'm sorry, Daddy."

"You're *sorry?* That's all you have to say? You were my last chance, Ruby! Now what am I supposed to do! What about Kyle? Don't you care about what happened to your brother? Frank Barrington destroyed our lives! He has to pay!"

"You're right, Daddy. He should pay. But I'm afraid I can no longer be part of it. At least as far as Vaughan's concerned. I... I've fallen in love with him. That's the reason I couldn't continue to deceive him. I had to tell him the truth."

"Ruby! You stupid girl! What were you thinking? You were never meant to develop feelings for him! How could you fall for the son of a man who's destroyed me? You don't seem to understand how close we are to going under. Everything I've worked for. Gone. And what about your brother? It's because of Frank Barrington that Kyle couldn't face the world anymore."

"I know, Daddy. I'm sorry. But I'm stepping away from your plan. Vaughan and I are over."

"His father's responsible for your brother's death! How can you live with yourself, knowing you didn't do everything possible to get revenge for that? Apart from that, it's Frank Barrington's fault that we're on the verge of bankruptcy. The prick canceled my mine contract. Then he spread rumors around the industry that everyone involved in Rodriguez Contracting was a safety risk. Now no one wants to hire us. He's cost us millions! You call yourself my daughter? Best you get over this little infatuation fast and do what I told you."

Then his voice lowered to a threatening growl that was even more frightening for its softness.

"Don't forget who pays your salary, Ruby. One snap of my fingers and you're on the unemployment queue. A quiet word in the right ear and no law firm in the country will employ you. And don't think I won't do it if you don't do this for me."

The dressing down and threat to her job was so harsh and unexpected, it left her breathless.

"I never meant to like Vaughan so much," she said in a small voice. "He's not like his father, Daddy. He's good, kind. He has ethics. I know what Frank Barrington did to you and how that affected Kyle, but it's not fair to punish Vaughan for what his father did."

"You're not listening to me Ruby. Your mother and I, your remaining brother—we're your family. We're far more important than some childish infatuation. I don't care how good and kind and *ethical* Vaughan Barrington might be. You were meant to persuade him to hire you as his executive assistant, infiltrate his inner sanctum, steal company secrets... Not fall in love with him. Focus on the only thing that's important. Your job is to make Frank Barrington pay."

"But—"

"No buts. Think of Kyle. He was as much the face of Rodriguez Contracting as I am. When that prick Barrington tore up our contract and started blackening our name in the industry, Kyle took it hard. I don't need to remind you that he wasn't the strongest of men. Or even as strong as you. He battled emotional issues all his life. He let that asshole Barrington get to him. It didn't matter that the accusations weren't true. Poor, Kyle. I miss him every day."

Ruby swallowed against the lump of emotion that had lodged in her throat. "I miss him, too." She paused. "I don't understand why Frank Barrington would do that, Daddy. It seems so strange. Why would he take such a dislike to you and Kyle for no reason?"

"Who knows? Maybe he doesn't like the fact that I'm an immigrant and that my English isn't as perfect as his. I wouldn't put it past him to be a racist! Many of his kind are. Maybe he's just nasty and malicious and doesn't need a reason to destroy someone's life. All I know is that your brother's dead and Frank Barrington is responsible."

Ruby gasped. Though her father had told her about his financial woes at the hands of Frank Barrington, this was the first she'd heard about a possible racist attitude. It surprised her.

"Vaughan's such a decent guy," she said, dazed. "I can't believe his father is everything but."

"Yeah, well you'd better believe it. Your cousin, Nathan, has been working out at the Strathwaylin mine. Somehow, Frank Barrington got wind of our connection and now he's been fired. If that asshole Barrington has his way, Nathan might even face criminal charges."

Ruby gasped, incredulous. "Nathan! Oh, my God! Criminal charges? How could that happen? Poor Nathan! Have you called a defense lawyer? Does he need me to look into organizing one for him?"

"No, at the moment, I'm dealing with it. But I need you to do your part, more than ever. You need to step up your game. Patch things up with Vaughan. Stay by his side for as long as it takes for him to trust you enough to bring you on board, but don't go giving him your heart. He doesn't deserve that, and it will only cloud your judgement. Vaughan Barrington is not your friend, Ruby. He might be squeaky clean on the surface, but he's still a Barrington. All of them are lying snakes. Don't ever forget that."

"You're not listening to me, Daddy. Vaughan hates me. There's nothing to patch up. We're done."

Unwilling to listen to another one of her father's rants, Ruby ended the call. She leaned back against the seat and sighed. Her life was a mess. She'd gone to Bali with one thing in mind. Falling in love hadn't been part of the plan. But it had been easy to forget why she'd been sent there after she'd met Vaughan in the flesh.

He'd been so easy going, funny, sexy, charming. Her pulse had beaten faster from the moment she'd set eyes on him working behind the bar on the beach outside her resort. It hadn't seemed to matter to her heart that she'd orchestrated their meeting for a matter of revenge.

The more they got to know each other, the more she'd wanted to dismiss her father's claims that Vaughan was the enemy. She didn't believe in punishing the son for his father's sins. It wasn't Vaughan's fault his father was an asshole. It wasn't fair to hold that against him.

She'd been so sure she'd safeguarded her heart against him. After all, falling in love with him hadn't been part of the plan. But when his life had hung in the balance, that subterfuge had come crashing down around her. She'd been forced to face the truth. She loved him with every fiber of her being. Now, knowing how much she'd hurt him, how she'd single-handedly destroyed their love, her heart was torn to shreds. She wasn't sure she'd ever get over the pain.

She'd ruined the only good thing in her life. Now she had to live with that and somehow cobble her shattered life together and keep moving forward.

How am I supposed to do that?

She wished she knew. If her father carried through on his threat, she might not even have a job to return to. That possibility was yet another blow to her already over-burdened heart. She wasn't sure how much more she could bear.

Chapter Five

E lizabeth Craigdon put an end to the call that had just turned her life upside down and dropped her phone on the couch beside her. She trembled all over.

"What is it, Lizzie?"

She heard the question put to her by her husband, Archie, but it was like he was speaking through a barrel of molasses. Everything was distant and distorted. In a daze, she saw the concern flood Archie's face. And then he stood and came toward her.

"Lizzie? Talk to me, honey. What's wrong?"

She swallowed hard and tried to collect her thoughts. "That...was Christopher," she said, referring to her stepson.

"What is it? Is Lexi okay? The children?"

She hurried to allay his concern. "Yes. Nothing like that." She paused and looked up at him, her stomach tied up in knots. "It's Vaughan. He's awake."

Archie's face filled with understanding and compassion. He sat down beside her and drew her in his arms. Overwhelmed with emotion, she cried out and took refuge in his broad chest.

Her husband was the only other person who knew about her son. When she and Archie had declared their undying love for each other, she hadn't wanted there to be any secrets between them. So, she'd told him about how she'd been a pregnant teenager and had given birth to a son. How she'd been forced to put him up for adoption. How recently, she'd searched for him.

Then she'd found him and written to him and he'd run. At least, that's what she'd assumed. He hadn't answered her letter. Now he was back and awake. She desperately wanted to go to him, but she was terrified by the thought of how he might react. It had been ten long months since she'd sent the letter and he hadn't contacted her once.

She lifted her head and stared at Archie. "God help me. I don't know what to do."

Her voice broke on a sob and once again, she buried her face in Archie's shirt. His arms tightened around her and he whispered words of comfort against her hair. She cried quietly until she was spent. Slowly, gently, Archie tilted her face up to his.

"I love you so much, Lizzie. You bring me so much joy. One day, Vaughan's going to be thrilled that you're his mother."

He tenderly brushed the hair back off her face. "We don't know why he hasn't contacted you. We don't even know for sure he got your letter. But now he's back in Sydney and he's awake. I know you want to go to him and I fully support you in that, but I think you should wait just a little bit longer, at least until he's fully recovered. The man's been in a coma for the best part of a month. You've waited so long already. Another week or two won't hurt, don't you think?"

Elizabeth's heart filled with love. How had she gotten so lucky with this wonderful man? He was so different from her first husband. Henry Craigdon had been selfish and arrogant. She'd given him the best years of her life and had only been freed from his clutches upon his untimely death.

She'd found true love and happiness with Archie and she thanked God every day that he felt the same. She relied on his wisdom and counsel and, as much as she chafed to see Vaughan, Archie was right. She'd waited nearly forty-one years already to speak with him. What was another two weeks?

Vaughan stirred restlessly in his hospital bed. Though he was in a single room that boasted a view of a sunny park, it wasn't enough.

I need to get out of here...

He'd been there long enough. The doctors were pleased with his progress. The headache had subsided to a dull thud. Apart from two cracked ribs, he had no broken bones. From what Ruby had told him, that was a miracle in itself.

Ruby...

It had been three days since he'd seen her. Three days since his world had been torn apart. Three days filled with outrage and hurt that had served to resurrect his anger over his birth mother, Elizabeth, and her deception of more than forty years. A lying, deceiving woman who was determined to destroy his life. After forty years of silence, she'd chosen to contact him with the truth. Now he was expected to jump for joy that she'd finally come forward and claimed him as her son.

The very thought infuriated him all over again. His anger at Elizabeth was one of the reasons why he'd reacted so harshly to Ruby's deception. It had hit too close to home. He hadn't yet come to terms with the lies and revelations Elizabeth had outlined in a letter. She hadn't even had the courage to reveal them face to face.

Now he was expected to deal with the sham relationship he'd had with Ruby. More lies from someone who purported to love him. As soon as he was well enough, he'd confront Elizabeth. He should have done it months ago, instead of running away. Then again, if he hadn't fled to Bali, he wouldn't have met Ruby. That had culminated in the greatest hurt of all.

Ruby...

Pain ricocheted through him. She'd lied to him, deceived him. She'd broken his heart.

He hated that he missed her. He hated even more that he wanted her back.

Ruby lay curled up in a ball on her expensive leather couch. She'd never been more miserable. She couldn't stop thinking about Vaughan. Thoughts of him consumed her every waking hour and most of her nights. She dreamed they were still in Bali, living a carefree existence, with her loving him with her body – if not her heart. The sex between them had always been amazing. That was one of the things that had made it so easy for her to stick around.

She could have left Bali months earlier. Vaughan had been anxious to return so they could get married. But she'd put him off. Mainly because she knew their idyllic time together would come to an end once they arrived in Sydney; things wouldn't be the same between them again.

Returning, she would have come face to face with her father who would have demanded to know what kind of progress she'd made. She'd kept him updated in Bali via email and the occasional phone call, but that wasn't the same as an in-person confrontation with nowhere to hide.

So, she'd put off leaving for as long as she could and had enjoyed her time with Vaughan. The only shadow over that period had been the specter of him discovering her true identity and finding out the real reason she'd travelled to Bali – constant reminders she was only one slip-up away from disaster. Fortunately, that hadn't happened. She'd even begun to think that maybe they could stay there forever.

It was fanciful and unrealistic, but once the idea had taken hold, it had been hard to ignore. She'd wanted to forget the promise she'd made to her father. Allow herself to fall completely and utterly in love with this wonderful man. Make their life in Bali. Never go home... But then she'd reminded herself of what was at stake, of what had been done to her family, and she'd put her heart on ice.

Then he'd been injured in the accident and the ongoing struggle to decide to stay or leave had evaporated. And here they were—hurt, broken, and over. Her dream of happy ever after in ashes.

Vaughan slid across the hospital bed and slowly got to his feet. He'd been trying to walk around as often as he could. He planned to build up his strength enough to convince the medical staff he could get out of there. He walked cautiously toward the bathroom. The movement pulled at his injured ribs, but the pain was bearable. Too bad he couldn't say the same thing about his sorry mess of a life.

He groaned aloud at the reminder. He'd spent more than nine months in Bali trying to escape the drama that had become his life in Sydney. He'd been so happy with Ruby. He'd even asked her to be his wife. But now he knew what they'd had together was a lie. Just like with his biological mother. He'd lived the past forty years believing his biological mother died birthing him. Now he knew that wasn't true. In fact, she was alive and well and lived in Sydney. He'd even met her once.

He remembered the time. He'd gone to the hospital to visit his half-brother, Christopher, after Christopher and Archie Craigdon had been involved in a terrible fire. They'd both been lucky to survive. Elizabeth Craigdon had been there. Christopher had made the introductions.

Vaughan had thought nothing of it at the time, but now he realized that Elizabeth must have known then that he was her son. He'd received the letter from her only a short time later. And yet, she hadn't said a word.

Okay, so to be fair, they were in a hospital ward visiting Christopher, who'd been injured in the fire and it wasn't the time or place to start such a sensitive conversation, but that was beside the point. She'd had forty years to make inquires. To put the wheels in motion with the adoptions office and take steps to find him.

Where was she when I was five and so sad and lonely, I cried myself to sleep every night? What about when I was ten and was being beaten up by older boys in the foster home? Where was Elizabeth Craigdon then? If it hadn't been for the Barringtons, who knows where I'd be. They saved me.

His chest went tight with pent-up emotion. All his life, he'd battled to overcome odds that were often stacked against him. He'd succeeded most of the time. But right now, added to the residual effects of a serious accident, the barrage of lies and deceits overwhelmed him.

So much drama. So many lies. The dull ache in his head began to throb. If only he was well enough to travel. He could disappear again. The doctors had been by earlier and were happy with his progress. They'd even mentioned that he might be well enough to go home in a couple more days, provided he took it easy.

Oh, I can take it easy, all right. I'll go home to Bondi, draw the blinds, turn the phone off and hide out on my own. How easy is that?

He needed time to heal. He was heartsick and angry. He mourned the loss of the woman he'd thought was his soul mate, but at the same time, he was angry that he hadn't seen through her deception. He'd been blinded by her movie-star good looks, her charm and easy smile. She'd said all the right things, stroked his ego, made him feel good about himself. Still reeling from Elizabeth's revelations, being around Ruby had been like a balm to his troubled soul.

She'd been so sexy and carefree; so fun to be around. They'd laughed so much and loved so passionately. She'd made him forget about the sordid secrets he'd left behind. He'd fallen head over heels in love with her and he'd been happy about it. Ecstatic. He'd found the woman of his dreams.

But it had all been a lie. She'd been there under false pretenses. She'd been sent there by her father to get close to him in order to carry out a bit of espionage. Hannah had filled him in on the problems she'd had at the Strathwaylin mine over the past year and how they'd recently outed her open cut examiner as the culprit. Nathan Garcia had deliberately and systematically caused serious accidents at one of the

Barrington-owned mines. The same Nathan Garcia...who just happened to be Joseph Rodriguez's nephew. Surprise, surprise. Exacting revenge seemed to be a family enterprise.

Enter Ruby...

A fresh wave of pain almost doubled him over. He was gutted by the depth of her betrayal. But surging anger and determination fortified him. He was done with being a victim. It was time for him to draw a line in the sand. To put the debacle of his relationship with Ruby behind him and get on with his life. Starting with leaving the hospital.

He made it to the bathroom and then turned and walked slowly back to the bed. He'd been making decent progress with his recovery and even though he still felt sore and ached all over, the headache was now only a dull thudding. He was satisfied he could do the rest of his healing at home. In his own bed. Home, where he could better control his visitors. Where he could begin the process of rebuilding his life—without Ruby.

With that thought in mind, he pressed the buzzer for the nurse. When she appeared in the open doorway, he instructed her to prepare the paperwork required for his discharge. She instructed him she'd first have to notify the doctor and seek his consent. While Vaughan chafed at the delay, he spent the time packing the few things he had in an overnight bag and waited for the nurse to return.

He thought about calling a family member to drive him home, but he didn't want to face all the questions. The only one who knew what had really happened was Hannah and she'd already left for her home in the Hunter Valley, a two-hour drive north, confident she'd saved him from Ruby and her scheming.

With a sigh of resignation, he picked up his phone and ordered a cab.

Ruby toed off her sandals inside her front door and padded down the hallway toward the kitchen. It had been a long day at the office and she was tired. She'd finally pulled herself together enough to return to work. She'd been a little apprehensive when she'd first stepped out of the lift onto her floor, but thankfully, no one in the office had questioned her presence or given her so much as a sideways glance.

Her father must have kept quiet about his threats to her, at least with the other staff. Thank goodness he'd been out all day. She couldn't avoid him forever, but the longer he stayed away, the better for her peace of mind.

Tossing her handbag onto the kitchen counter, she headed straight for the fridge. The bottle of wine she'd opened a few nights earlier was still half full. Unfortunately, her belly hadn't stopped churning since her fallout with Vaughan. A glass of wine might not be the best thing in that moment.

In fact, she'd been feeling nauseous most of the week. She'd also been finding it difficult to sleep. The spectacular toss-over by Vaughan and the dressing down by her father hadn't helped her insomnia. She couldn't stop thinking about everything that had happened and those thoughts overwhelmed her with regret. How ironic that she'd spent all those months pretending to be in love with the man, only to discover too late that she actually was...

God, what a mess.

Opting for a bottle of soda water instead, she unscrewed the top and took a couple of gulps before flopping onto the couch. She closed her eyes and tried to forget about her awful week. It had seemed so easy, agreeing to her father's plan. He and Kyle had been treated so abominably. Cozying up to Vaughan with the view to obtain a few company secrets her father could use against Frank Barrington seemed the least she could do to try and even the score.

But what had begun as a simple exercise in deceit in order to obtain her goal had ended up being much more complicated. Vaughan himself, had been the first complication. He was just so nice. And cute. And sexy. And funny. And sweet. So easy to talk to. Too many good qualities to enumerate. She couldn't believe someone so open and caring could be related to the Barringtons. Then he'd shared with her that he was adopted and things made more sense. Still, he was a Barrington in every other way and that made him the enemy.

And now I'm in love with him and he wants nothing to do with me. He hates me. He never wants to see me again...

With a sigh, she sipped her soda water and thought about pulling something out for dinner. A microwave meal for one. Not the most nutritious offering, but an easy option none the less. Only, the fatigue that had been pestering her lately made preparing even a microwave dinner seem like an insurmountable task. The persistent nausea didn't help.

Instead, she reached for a cushion and stretched out full-length on the couch. She closed her eyes on another weary sigh and folded her hands over her belly. And then she was struck by a thought that paralyzed her.

My period's late… Three weeks overdue… Oh, God. Am I pregnant?

She'd been taking oral contraception for years without a hiccup. Surely it hadn't failed her now. Then she remembered the flu she'd battled for more than a week and how she'd taken herself off to the doctor for some antibiotics. She'd forgotten that they could interfere with the pill's effectiveness. They hadn't used other forms of contraception… *Oh, God.*

No. She was panicking over nothing. One late period didn't automatically mean she was pregnant. It was just that she was overwrought about what had happened these past couple of days. Her thoughts were scattered, her emotions a rollercoaster. And she was tired. A lack of sleep could be blamed on a lot of things, including crazy thoughts about a pregnancy that likely had no basis in reality.

But now that the thought was planted in her mind, she couldn't let it go. No matter how hard she tried to push it away, it kept coming back to taunt her. *Can I be pregnant?*

On a groan of irritation, she pulled herself upright. There was a pharmacy that stayed open late on the corner a block away. She'd go and buy a pregnancy test. Then she could put her runaway thoughts to bed and maybe, just maybe get some sleep. Mind made up, she pulled on her sandals, collected her handbag and keys and left.

Twenty-three minutes later, Ruby stared down at the two pink lines on the pregnancy test, numb with disbelief. She'd done two tests, but the results had been the same. She was pregnant with Vaughan Barrington's baby.

Great. Now what?

Chapter Six

His fists clenched around the top railing of his balcony as Vaughan stared out at the beginning of a new day. The sun, in all its splendor, had just peeked above the horizon, sending shards of rose-pink, orange, and gold light sparkling across the Pacific Ocean. He never tired of the view from his Bondi Beach apartment, but even that morning's spectacular light show didn't ease his pain.

Pockets of joggers dotted the paved walking track that snaked around the headlands. It was a track he knew well. Too bad his injuries had kept him from maintaining his usual level of fitness. As soon as he was up to it, he intended to change that. The sooner he reestablished his old routine, the better.

It had been nearly a week since he'd discharged himself from the hospital. Nearly a week of moping around the house, drowning his sorrows, eating crap food and generally feeling sorry for himself. He'd thought being back in his apartment, surrounded by his things, after spending so much time away, would help him forget Ruby, Elizabeth and all the things that had caused his depressed mood.

But that hadn't happened. He'd been consumed by loneliness. Worse still, was the feeling of being out of place in the home he'd chosen and furnished himself. The home that had once been his refuge, now only served to make the pressure in his chest more acute. It wasn't that he felt uncomfortable in the physical space. It was that for months he'd believed when he returned to his little piece of paradise, he'd have Ruby to share it with, as they planned for their future.

His dream homecoming had turned into profound loss. And despite what she'd done to their relationship, to *them*, he missed her. He hated himself for that, though he knew the self-loathing was illogical. Love didn't just switch off because the object of his affection had destroyed its foundation.

Relaxing his grip on the balcony rail, he took a step back and picked up his coffee mug. The steam curled slowly upward in the early morning air. He took a sip of the hot brew and sighed. He hated feeling like this. Lethargic, hopeless, like a rudderless boat, drifting without direction. He'd never been that type of guy. He'd always looked at life with a glass half-full kind of attitude, even when things got tough.

Except when he'd found out Elizabeth Craigdon was his mother. That shock had been too much for him to shrug off. He'd taken off to Bali without a word to anyone and hid out there for the best part of a year, only emailing his father periodically to assure him he was okay.

Now he was back; it was time to face the truth he'd been avoiding. It was time to confront Elizabeth and demand some answers. He needed to gain control again and seek the necessary closure so he could move on with the next chapter of his life. The fact it wouldn't include Ruby was devastating, but he'd get over her. One day at a time.

Somewhere out there was a woman who would love him for who he was. All he had to do was to find her. *Simple, right?* Or maybe he should avoid seeking a permanent relationship for the foreseeable future and go out and have some fun?

He didn't know what Elizabeth's intentions were in claiming him after all this time. He sure as hell didn't need another mother. He wondered fleetingly how his mother would feel about Elizabeth and how he'd break the news. He needed to ensure that she understood she was the only mother in his life.

Finishing the last of his coffee, he hurried inside to shower and dress. It was a bit early yet to make house calls, but by the time he drove out west to Craigdon Manor, it would be late enough that he likely wouldn't wake Elizabeth. But if she were a late sleeper and he ended up dragging her from bed, so be it. She'd dropped a forty-year-old bombshell. She could deal with him arriving unannounced on her doorstep. It might have taken him awhile to get his head around it, but he was finally ready for answers.

Elizabeth spread strawberry jam over her freshly buttered croissant and took a generous bite. The flaky pastry melted in her mouth. Amy, their housekeeper since the children had been young, was a marvelous cook.

"You've outdone yourself this morning, Amy," Elizabeth said, smiling indulgently.

The older woman glanced up from where she'd been stacking dirty plates on a tray. Her face transformed into a myriad of wrinkles as she smiled. "Thank you, Elizabeth. I do my best."

"You do better than that. Why do you think my seven adult children keep turning up here at dinnertime?"

Though technically, Elizabeth had only given birth to six of her late husband Henry's children, she'd long since stopped thinking of her stepson, Christopher, in that way. He was as much her family as any of them, as were his adopted and foster children. She was so glad he'd found love with Lexi and was pleased for her other children who'd all managed to find their significant others. As far as she knew, they were all happy. Having spent more than thirty years in an unhappy marriage, she couldn't be more grateful that they hadn't suffered the same fate.

"Where's Archie?" she asked, savoring another delicious bite.

"He ate earlier. Said something about wanting to get out in the garden before it got too hot," Amy replied.

Elizabeth nodded. "Well, it's a beautiful day for it. I think I'll join him after I finish my breakfast."

Though they employed two fulltime gardeners, both she and Archie liked to get out in the garden and get their hands dirty. Craigdon Manor stood on six hectares, with stately grounds that incorporated a full-sized tennis court, nine-hole golf course, heated pool and spa. It even had an elevator. It was an extravagant place to live and she hadn't been on board with all the improvements, extras, and additions Henry had insisted upon. His desire to have the biggest and the best was more to stroke his ego than anything else.

But even after Henry's death, she'd remained. Some of her family had expressed their surprise, given the unhappy state of her marriage, but this was her home, the place where she'd raised her family, and she wasn't going anywhere. She was just lucky her new husband, Archie, had been understanding of her need to stay. It also helped that a good deal of his home had recently been destroyed by fire. He was still dealing with the insurance claim.

The sound of the doorbell ringing intruded on her thoughts. She glanced up, but Amy was already making her way down the hallway to answer it. Elizabeth finished off the last of her croissant and brushed the crumbs from the tablecloth and onto her plate. She looked up as Amy re-entered.

"Who is it?"

"A man. He's asked to see you. He said his name's Vaughan Barrington. Could he be related to Christopher, do you think?"

Elizabeth felt the color drain from her face. She became lightheaded and thought she might faint. Amy regarded her curiously.

"Would you like me to tell him to go away?"

"No! No!" Elizabeth managed, trying desperately to get control of her thundering heart. She drew in a deep breath and eased it out. "No. I'll see him. Please, show him into the music room."

On feet that weren't quite steady, Elizabeth made her way to the room she'd claimed for her own the first time she and Henry had inspected the mansion with a view to buying it. A lifetime ago, she'd wanted to be a famous concert pianist. She'd even studied at the world-renowned Sydney Conservatorium of Music. The limited edition, shiny, black, baby grand piano that stood in pride of place in the music room, a gift from Henry. Aside from her children, it was one of the few things she cherished from their marriage.

She perched on the edge of a soft blue chaise lounge she'd purchased to suit the new color scheme. Matching drapes hung at the windows. In the distance, the raucous call of a kookaburra floated over the air and in through the open window. She sighed. The day had held such promise for some work out in the garden. Now she sat rooted to the couch, filled with dread, as butterflies swarmed in her stomach.

And then he was there. Her son. Filling the open doorway. Her heart skipped a beat at the sight of him. Emotion tightened her chest. She catalogued his features like a starving person catalogued a table laden with food. Tall, broad-shouldered, muscular. With caramel-colored blond hair, rather than the white-blond locks of his father. But with those eyes. Brilliant green. The generous mouth, the strong nose, the chiseled jaw. He looked so much like his father.

Vaughan's physical appearance was the reason she'd had no doubt he was her son the first moment she'd set eyes on him in the hospital after the fire. She'd been duped once before by an interloper pretending to be her long-lost child, and though she'd believed Ashton Walker in the early days, she'd secretly had her doubts. With Vaughan she had none.

When her family proved beyond doubt Ashton Walker was a fraud, she'd been devastated and embarrassed, but that experience had catalyzed her determination to find her biological son. It was long past time.

This son was now forty. Her late husband, Henry, was dead. She no longer had any reason to keep her first-born a secret, and the more she'd investigated, the more she'd needed to see him, touch him, beg him for forgiveness. Tell him how much she loved him. How much she'd always loved him.

Now he was there, in the flesh, aware he was her son and wanting to see her. She was so nervous about his reaction, she thought she might be sick.

"Hello, Elizabeth."

Her heart sank at his cool tone, but what had she expected? He'd known now for almost a year who she was and not once had he sought her out. Still, she was glad she'd finally have an opportunity to explain. She hoped that was why he was there.

She struggled to her feet. "Hello, Vaughan. It's wonderful to see you."

She took a step toward him. He took a step back. Rebuffed, she hid her hurt and indicated the matching armchair that stood opposite the chaise. "Please, take a seat."

"I'd prefer to stand."

She nodded. "That's okay." The nerves continued to flutter inside her belly. She went to wring her hands but caught herself just in time.

"Would… Would you like some coffee? I can have Amy bring us in a pot." Without waiting for his response, she called out to Amy. The housekeeper must have been hovering nearby, as Elizabeth had suspected, and promptly stepped into the room.

"Yes, Elizabeth?"

"Please bring us a pot of coffee and maybe some of those muffins you baked this morning."

"Of course."

Amy disappeared the way she'd come and Elizabeth sighed quietly again. "If you don't mind, I'd like to sit. My legs aren't as good as they used to be." She perched back on the edge of the chaise and smoothed the folds of her dress. She'd waited so long to have this conversation and now that it was upon her, she didn't know where to start.

"You're looking well," she murmured.

"Thanks, but how would you know how I normally look? We only met once before, and briefly at that."

Vaughan's tone was curt. He shoved his hands into the pockets of his jeans and looked away. Her stomach nosedived. He wasn't going to make this easy for her. Then again, he had every right to be angry, to be confused, to be filled with questions...

"I heard you were involved in an accident in Bali," she said.

He nodded briefly. "Yes. I was lucky. I'm mostly recovered now. I understand I gave my family a bit of a fright."

She was heartened by the wry smile that briefly touched his lips. She managed a wobbly smile. "You certainly did. I nearly had a heart attack when Christopher told me."

"I wasn't talking about you." Then Vaughan's expression turned harsh. "Why would you care so much? It's taken you forty years to try and find me. I could have been dead for all you knew."

She winced. He had a right to feel angry. She drew in a deep breath and nodded.

"You're right. And I'm ashamed of that. I wish I'd had the courage to go searching for you years ago. You were always on my mind. Forty years might have passed since I last saw you, but there wasn't a day that went by that I didn't think of you."

His eyes blazed. "Bullshit."

Elizabeth gasped. She held a hand up to her mouth to hold back the pain. She'd steeled herself for this confrontation, not knowing what to expect; knowing he might be angry, furious even. She owed it to him to let him work through his pain. She lifted her head and captured his gaze.

"You have every right to feel angry. You also have a right not to believe me. After all, as you say, I've had forty years to try and find you. That's a long time. Especially with the advances in technology and changes in the law. It's a simple enough matter to put in a request for information. And yet I didn't."

She drew in a ragged breath. "All I can say is that I wanted to spare others pain. You were born before I was married. I never told my husband about you. All those years we were together, he never knew about you. Neither did our children. It was cowardly of me, but at the time, it was the best decision to make. You'd long been put up for adoption. I was never going to get you back. Nor did I want to interfere with your life. I hoped and prayed every day you were happy and living a wonderful, well-adjusted life. That hope is what kept me going."

Fresh anger glittered in Vaughan's eyes. "For all you knew, I could have been having a shit of a life. In and out of foster homes. Being abused. You had no idea what kind of life I was living. And you expect me to believe you care."

Elizabeth gasped again. Listening to his accusations was like being sucker punched. "No, Vaughan! I did care. I always cared."

He glared at her. "Not enough to want to keep me. I was put up for adoption at birth. I was told my biological mother died having me. That's what my file said." He narrowed his eyes at her, his breath coming fast. "Someone altered the records. Someone lied."

She held out a hand toward him, imploring him with her gaze. Wanting to touch him, to reassure him he was wrong. The look he gave her was scathing; she let her hand fall to her lap.

"I don't know who falsified your records," she said quietly. "It certainly wasn't me." She paused and then added, "I can only imagine it was my parents. They didn't want me to keep you. They insisted I give you up. I didn't want to, but I had no choice."

"Bah!" Vaughan shouted, his expression filled with disgust. "You talk as if you were a child with no mind of her own." His gaze raked over her. "You look like a woman in her sixties. You couldn't have been that young when you had me."

"I was twenty," Elizabeth answered, her voice low and ragged with emotion.

Vaughan's expression turned scornful. "Twenty! Hardly a powerless child. You could have kept me if you'd wanted to."

Pain sheared through her heart. "You don't understand," she protested, coming to her feet. "My parents owned me. They funded my entire life. They wouldn't let me keep you."

"Oh, so it came down to money. You didn't want to be cut off from your generous allowance. Instead, you chose to give up your baby. Well, good for you."

"No, Vaughan! Oh, please. Try to understand. We were both so young, me and your father. Keeping you... It was impossible.

It was a different era. One where there was little support for unwed mothers."

Vaughan looked at her with an expression so cynical, it broke her heart.

"You were an adult, Elizabeth. Your parents were hardly in a position to force you to do anything. You could have left and taken me with you. If you'd loved me enough."

His tone remained low, but there was pain and accusation behind his words. Elizabeth's throat tightened.

He's right. I could have left. I could have tried to raise him on my own... As difficult as that would have been...

She shrugged helplessly, tears burning behind her eyes. "Oh, Vaughan! It wasn't a matter of not loving you enough. Please don't ever think that. I loved you with all my heart. But I didn't think I could support you and care for you on my own."

Wringing her hands, she began to pace, unable to stand still a moment longer. The turmoil and despair in her heart continued to weigh her down. She was panicked at the thought she might not be able to convince him that her love for him had never waned; that giving him up for adoption had been the hardest decision of her life.

"I was still living with my parents," she continued. "I had no money of my own. No skills. I wanted to be a concert pianist. I thought I'd spend my life playing the piano, traveling all over, making music in some of the grandest theaters in the world." She paused and then added sadly, "Your father, David, thought the same. He was a violinist at the Conservatorium of Music in Sydney. He was so talented... That's where we met...and fell in love. We were going to travel the world together, making music."

Vaughan's lip curled upward in disgust. "You took the easy way out. You weren't ready for a baby. I interfered with your plans. You just admitted it."

Everything Vaughan said was true. She bowed her head, unable to bear witness to his pain. There was nothing she could say that would convince him she'd taken the only option available to her. Or at least it felt that way at the time. She'd always had a sliver of doubt about her decision.

Could I have tried harder to keep him?

But she'd allowed her parents to talk her into giving him up. By then, David was long gone. He'd been as unprepared for the disruptions of a baby to his life plan as she was and though earlier, they'd promised to love each other forever, life and a baby made that promise impossible to keep. She hadn't blamed him for deserting her. It was her fault she'd gotten pregnant. He'd wanted to wait for intimacy until they could get married. She'd persuaded him otherwise.

She'd been head over heels in love; certain they'd had what it took to last the distance. She'd been young and silly, with her head full of dreams. She'd thrown caution to the wind. She hadn't wanted to wait. And then she had to live with the consequences. Only, she'd never dreamed they'd be so harsh or that she'd mourn the loss of her baby for the rest of her life.

Because that's how it had felt when they'd taken him from her, never to be seen by her again. It felt like he'd died. In some ways, it would have been easier if he had. At least then she'd have had closure, a grave to visit. Instead, she'd had nothing. She hadn't even been allowed to know where he'd gone, or who'd adopted him.

Over the years, the laws regarding adoption had undergone changes and now it was often possible to track down a child or a biological parent. And though she'd be forever glad she'd managed to find him, she prayed there would come a time when he'd be able to look at her without anger and scorn.

"Do you have any idea how many nights I cried myself to sleep?" he exclaimed. "I thought my mother was dead. There was no record of my father. I was all alone in the world with nobody to love me."

Elizabeth frowned. "So, the Barringtons didn't adopt you as a baby?"

"No! I was eleven before they adopted me. Before then, I was shifted from one foster home to another. Nobody wanted me for long. I don't know what it was about me that made me so unlovable, but there's no denying that's what happened.

"Somewhere around the time I turned eight or nine, I finally worked it out. The reason I wasn't wanted was because I'd developed such a tough skin; I wouldn't let anyone close. I'd shun any act of kindness, always suspicious of an ulterior motive.

"From a young age, I learned to fight. You had to if you wanted to survive. I was picked on and bullied by other kids in the house and I never gave an inch. I was too much trouble. That's why I was always moved on by the authorities. Foster parents complained. They wanted me gone. Like a piece of unwanted garbage. The more times it happened, the harder my shell became. It's a wonder Frank and Evelyn Barrington ever gave me a second glance."

His breath came fast. His color was high. Anger glowed in his eyes. "Where were you when I needed you? When I was crying myself to sleep? When I begged for someone to love me, to want me for their own?

"Frank and Evelyn are my real parents. The only people who ever showed me love. The only people who wanted me." He paused. "You might have given birth to me, but that's the only thing you gave me."

Every painful, angry word out of his mouth cut Elizabeth to the quick. It was like death by a thousand knives. She opened her mouth to respond, but he cut her off. It seemed he wasn't finished yet.

"You waited until I was a man full grown, with a loving, adoptive family, a career, a great life of my own to decide that the time was right to come forward and stake your claim. Whatever made you think contacting me after all these years was going to get you back the son you tossed aside?"

He drew in a ragged breath and glared at her. "I have a mother. A mother I love and cherish. A mother who's done all she can to make me feel like I'm one of her own. I'm her son. Her beloved son. You're forty years too late."

With that, he turned on his heel and stormed out of the room, almost colliding with Amy who stood open-mouthed with shock in the doorway, holding a laden tray.

On a cry of pain and devastation, Elizabeth buried her face in her hands and staggered back to the chaise.

Chapter Seven

Elizabeth couldn't have said how long she sat there, crying her heart out, but by the time she'd quietened enough to compose herself, her eyes were swollen and she was completely drained. She couldn't remember the last time she'd felt so devastated; so utterly distraught. It was like every ounce of emotion had been siphoned out of her and now she was nothing more than a husk of her former self.

Vaughan wanted nothing to do with her. He had a mother. Evelyn Barrington. She'd given him everything Elizabeth had not. Love, security, a family, their name. All the things Elizabeth had been too scared to give all those years ago. Fresh tears filled her eyes.

The door to the music room opened. Archie filled the opening. Amy must have fetched him from the garden. He wore an old pair of work pants and his sleeves were rolled up to his elbows. There was a dusting of dirt on his cheek. But the tenderness and compassion in his eyes was unmistakable. He crossed the carpet, sat beside her and drew her into his arms.

Fresh sobs came hard and fast. She thought she'd cried enough to last her a lifetime, but it seemed where Vaughan was concerned, she hadn't cried nearly enough. Fresh grief with old. Between sobs, she told him what had happened. He sat in silence and stroked her hair and whispered mindless words of comfort.

He let her cry until she quietened once again. Then he handed her a clean handkerchief he drew from his pocket. She used the linen to dab at her eyes and clear her blocked nose. She tucked the handkerchief into her bra and then shot him a grateful look.

"Thank you." She hiccupped.

Archie continued to regard her tenderly and merely shrugged. "My poor Lizzie. I'm sorry you had to go through that. I was hoping that since so many months had passed, Vaughan would have had a chance to come to terms with the fact he's your son and reached some level of acceptance."

Elizabeth's lip trembled. "He was so angry! Of course, he had a right to be, but... It broke my heart." Her voice cracked. "W-What if he never forgives me?"

Archie drew her close again and pressed a kiss against her temple. "Let's not think about that. He's had a shock. Okay, so he's had a decent amount of time to come to terms with it, but this is the first time he's come face to face with you since he found out. That's bound to bring out some powerful emotions. Give him time, Lizzie. There's always a chance he'll think differently once he calms down."

"He's had more than ten months to get used to the idea!" Elizabeth exclaimed. "What makes you think he's ever going to calm down enough to accept what happened?"

Archie regarded her steadily. "I don't know, sweetheart. But we can't give up hope. You've had forty years to make peace with yourself. You need to be patient." He kissed her tenderly on the lips. "Whatever happens, I'm here for you. Don't forget I love you."

She drew in a deep breath, her shoulders sagging on a weary sigh. "I love you, too."

Vaughan peeled away from Craigdon Manor with a squeal of tires and a head full of steam. He turned left onto the main road and floored the accelerator, headed back to the city. His only thought was to get away.

All this time, he hadn't stopped to do the math; to work out how old his biological mother had been when she'd given birth. Now he had his answer. He couldn't believe Elizabeth had been twenty when she'd had him and put him up for adoption. Twenty! And with a family wealthy enough to support her and her baby.

She hadn't said as much, but he'd read between the lines. No one with a limited income could afford to send their daughter to study music at the conservatorium. She hadn't been some homeless fourteen-year-old with no one to look after her and no one who cared. No, the only one who didn't care was Elizabeth.

Instead, she'd chosen her career. Or at least, what she'd thought would be her career. A concert pianist. And his father had been a violinist. Vaughan certainly hadn't inherited any of their musical genes. He couldn't read a note of music, let alone play an instrument. She'd offered him so many excuses for giving him up for adoption, but that's all they were. There was only one conclusion for him to draw: she just hadn't loved him enough.

Like Ruby. Who hadn't loved him at all.

His gut clenched. His throat squeezed tight with emotion. Familiar feelings of rejection, reaching all the way back to when he was a child, hovered just beneath the surface.

Why am I so unlovable?

No. He refused to think like that. He was no longer that scared, sad, lonely and depressed kid who'd been passed around through one foster family after another. Abandoned by his mother. Discarded, neglected, forgotten. No. He had a family who loved him; who treated him as their own. The Barringtons didn't care that he wasn't blood. They loved him for who he was. A part of their family.

Despite the resurfacing of hurtful memories and feelings, his adult self knew this wasn't on him. He'd had nothing to do with Elizabeth's decision to forsake him; to hand him over to someone else to raise. She couldn't have known he wouldn't be adopted until he was eleven or that he'd spend all those hellish years between, fighting for every scrap of attention. He'd protected himself by constructing an almost impenetrable inner shell.

If it hadn't been for Frank and Evelyn, he might never have allowed anyone in. He had so much to be grateful for. His mom and dad. The only mom and dad he'd ever known. The only mom and dad he *wanted* to know. The only mom and dad he needed.

Elizabeth Craigdon and her tearful revelations could go to hell.

Coming to a sudden decision, he changed direction and headed south toward Broken and the Barrington Estate. His mother was usually home this time of day. He hoped so. He needed to talk to her. He'd never asked her why they'd adopted him. In the early days, he'd been too scared to raise the question in case they changed their minds and sent him back. Later, the finding out had faded in importance. He didn't care about the why. All he cared about was that they had made him theirs, and for the first time in his life, he'd felt loved.

He found his mother in the kitchen up to her elbows in flour. That didn't surprise him. She'd always loved to bake and she was good at it. He'd lost count of the hours she'd spent with her children whenever any of them expressed even the slightest interest in baking, showing them how it was done.

She had the patience of a saint. Though Vaughan had been much more interested in being outside, riding motorbikes and climbing trees, his sister, Hannah, had been especially interested. There was a time not that long ago when the family had thought she might even open her own pastry shop. Now she was a safety manager in a coal mine. Go figure.

His mother looked up as he entered. A wide smile of surprise creased her face. At sixty-one, she was still an attractive woman. Thick white hair brushed back from her forehead. Clear blue eyes. A tidy figure with only a few extra pounds that actually suited her slight frame.

"Vaughan! It's so good to see you! I heard you'd discharged yourself from hospital. Are you sure you're well enough to be up and about?"

He leaned in and pecked her on the cheek, breathing in her familiar perfume of cinnamon, vanilla and orchids.

"I'm fine. I was going stir-crazy lying in that hospital room all day. I had to get out."

His mother nodded with understanding. "I'm glad to see you're doing so well. We were all so scared... When your father and I arrived in Denpasar and were taken to the ICU..." She shuddered. "Seeing you lying in that bed, unconscious... Tubes coming out of everywhere. Not knowing if you were ever going to wake up..." The tears of emotion that glinted in her eyes put lie to her angry frown. "Don't ever scare me like that again!"

He chuckled. "I'll try not to."

Chocolate chip biscuits were cooling on a tray on the counter. He reached over and snagged one and popped it into his mouth. It was still warm. The buttery mixture melted on his tongue.

"Yum."

Evelyn smiled. "Good?"

"As always. I wouldn't expect anything less than perfection. After all, you're the best, right?"

Evelyn flushed, looking pleased. She swatted him with a tea towel. They both grinned.

"Can I get you a cup of coffee? I just made a fresh pot."

He nodded. "That would be great. I might have another one of those biscuits, too. I skipped breakfast."

"You must have gotten an early start if you came from the city."

He compressed his lips and nodded. "Yeah. I... I couldn't sleep. Had a few things on my mind."

His mother shot him a look filled with understanding. "Ruby?"

Vaughan grimaced. "You heard about that?"

"Yes. Hannah told me. I hope you don't mind."

He waved away her words. "No, of course not. Our breakup's no secret." He drew in a deep breath and let it out on a heavy sigh. "I'm just glad I found out the truth before I married her. To think I wanted to get married in Bali. Had we done that, I wouldn't have known until it was too late." He shook his head.

"I'm sorry, Vaughan. To discover the woman you love has deceived you all this time... It must be tough." Evelyn's eyes flashed. "It makes me so angry that she took advantage of you like that! I have a mind to call her and give her a piece of my mind."

She bristled like a lioness protecting her cubs. Despite everything, he smiled. He loved that his mom was ready to come to his defense and go into battle for her kids, even though all of them were now adults.

"Calm down, Mom. I'm fine."

A thoughtful expression filled his mother's face. "You know, I never would have guessed Ruby's heart was so fickle. She was so concerned about you while you were ill. She barely left your side in Denpasar. It was the same when we got you to Sydney. Your father complained more than once how difficult it was to get a moment alone with you." She paused. "She was utterly devoted to you. I can't believe that was all an act."

Vaughan frowned. He wasn't ready to accept that Ruby might have had genuine feelings for him. And so what if she did? That didn't negate her deception or her motives. Not one bit.

His mother turned away and collected the coffee pot and two mugs. She poured and then added cream and sugar to hers. He took his black. She handed him a mug.

"Thanks." He leaned over and snagged another biscuit.

"Let's sit." His mother led the way to the breakfast nook.

"So, what brings you all the way to Broken so early in the morning? And don't tell me it's my cooking, because I won't believe you."

He shot her a wry smile. "You know me too well."

"You're my son. It's my business to know what makes you tick. Besides that, I've known you most of your life and I love you dearly. Your peace of mind has always been important to me. To all of us."

He took a sip of his coffee to hide a sudden wave of emotion. Then he cleared his throat. He'd come for answers. There was no point putting it off.

"Why did you and Dad decide to adopt? You already had Christopher. And it wasn't like you couldn't have any more. You went on to have seven children together."

His mother regarded him quizzically over the edge of her mug. "What's brought this on?"

He shrugged and averted his gaze. He wasn't ready to divulge the truth about his biological mother.

"Just curious, I guess. I've never asked you before."

She set her coffee mug down and clasped her hands together, resting them on the table in front of her.

"Believe it or not, your father and I tried for two years after we were married to have a baby. Christopher was already twelve by then. We wanted to give him a sibling and Frank wanted a child of his own. He loved Christopher, of course, and had formally adopted him when we got married, but we wanted children together. I was only in my early thirties. Plenty young enough to add to our family.

"But somehow the planets refused to align. We went to doctors. Had tests. It seemed there was nothing wrong with either of us. No one could explain why we couldn't conceive naturally. We kept trying with no success. That's when we started talking about adoption."

"But why me?" Vaughan insisted. "I was eleven. On the cusp of puberty. A difficult age. A long way from being a cute and cuddly baby or a toddler who could fit seamlessly into your family."

His mother smiled indulgently. "You're right. But we wanted a sibling for Christopher. Someone close to his age. You might not remember, but he was angry at the world back then. He had a chip on his shoulder—one the size of Ayers Rock. He felt like the world owed him something."

She sighed. "He and your father didn't always see eye to eye. We thought if he had a brother, he might feel that we were more like a family. We thought it might help him adjust to the idea and one day, he might even grow to like being a Barrington."

Vaughan smiled. "You talk about Christopher having a chip on his shoulder as if it happened a long time ago. It doesn't seem that long ago that he still hated the world and everyone in it. That had a lot to do with his biological father, didn't it?"

Evelyn nodded, her expression both sad and grim. "Yes. Henry Craigdon. Let's just say, he wasn't a very nice man. At least, not to me or to Christopher. When I told Henry I was pregnant, he immediately ended our relationship and told me never to contact him again."

Though Vaughan had been told vague details about his mother's past, he was still filled with a surge of anger at the callous way she'd been treated by Christopher's father. Henry Craigdon. Elizabeth Craigdon's late husband.

"Okay, so you wanted a kid around Christopher's age. What made you pick me? No doubt my file was filled with information on the numerous foster homes I'd been in and out of over the years. I'm sure there were notes in there that labeled me...difficult."

His mother nodded. "Yes. There were a lot of notes, but all I could see was a beautiful young boy who needed to be loved. It wasn't your fault that you'd been through so many foster homes. I took one look at you and that was it. Your father felt the same. You were the one we wanted. We couldn't wait to take you home. You completed our family."

A surge of warmth flooded through him, choking him up inside. He blinked back tears. Even after all these years, hearing her say how much he'd been wanted was a balm to his battered soul.

His mother reached over and covered his hand with hers. "I'm not sure what brought this on, Vaughan, but I'm guessing it has something to do with Ruby and the fact she obviously didn't love you like you thought she did. I know you well. You wouldn't have proposed to her if you weren't certain of her feelings."

She drew in a breath and continued in a low tone. "No doubt her betrayal's difficult to take. It cuts at the heart of you, makes you question everything. But please, don't doubt our love for an instant. Or your self-worth."

She squeezed his hand. "You're strong, determined, honest, and beautiful, inside and out. You have the kindest heart. You're sweet and generous and oh-so good looking. You'll find the right woman someday. The woman who'll love you for who you are and appreciate your special qualities. Okay, so that wasn't Ruby, but she's out there. You just haven't found her yet."

Vaughan compressed his lips on a sigh. As much as he wanted to believe his mother, right now, he was still too filled with hurt and crushing disappointment over Ruby's betrayal.

"Thanks, Mom. I appreciate the pep talk. But I don't think I'll ever trust another woman again." He shook his head. "As for falling in love, I'll leave that to my siblings. They've proven far better at making it work than I have. I don't think I have the courage to try and fail again. It hurts too much."

His mother nodded. "You're right. Love does hurt. Especially when it goes so wrong. But you can't judge all women so harshly. Imagine if I'd vowed never to give my heart to anyone again after the way I'd been treated by Henry? I'd never have been open to the possibility of falling in love with your father."

Vaughan looked at her. "After all of the heartbreak you went through with Christopher's father, it's amazing you found the courage to give love another go. How did you do it? How did you trust Dad not to break your heart?"

"I'm not saying it was easy. In fact, your father had to work very hard to win me over; to convince me his feelings were real. But in the end, I had to take a leap of faith. That's what allowing yourself to fall in love is. I'm guessing you made such a leap with Ruby, right?"

Vaughan grimaced. "Right. But that seemed so easy. She was so easy to fall in love with. I never once imagined she was harboring so many secrets; that meeting me and getting close to me had been her end goal from the beginning." He groaned. "How could I have been so blind?"

Evelyn patted his arm. "You weren't to know, Vaughan. Some people are very clever at hiding things. And none of us are perfect. We can all be duped. Look at me. Do you think I had any idea what kind of jerk Henry was when I first started dating him?"

She sighed quietly. "All I'm saying is, cut yourself some slack. You misjudged someone and now you've been terribly hurt and let down. But the measure of your character is in how you react now that you've been knocked down. You can either let it destroy you and wallow in self-pity, or you can chalk it up to experience and be determined never to be taken advantage of again.

"That doesn't mean I want you to close yourself off from love, but just remember, achieving great things usually involves great risk. In the end, if it means you find your soul mate, then that's worth all the pain, isn't it?"

He remained silent. After being so badly burned by Ruby, he wasn't convinced love was all it was cracked up to be, but he wouldn't put a dampener on his mom's sage advice by being difficult. So, he nodded and offered her a small smile. "I guess we'll have to wait and see."

Chapter Eight

R uby reached for the wad of tissues the technician handed to her and wiped away the last vestiges of gel. She sighed quietly. It had taken her a week to find the courage to make an appointment, but now the ultrasound had confirmed it. She was eight weeks pregnant.

She sat up and rearranged her clothes. She'd gone to the appointment on her lunch break. She hadn't yet told anyone about her predicament. Not even her family. One thing she was certain of, she couldn't tell Vaughan. He hated her. Had told her he never wanted to see her again. There was no way she was going to try and guilt him into being a father when he didn't want anything to do with her.

Another sigh escaped. This was one complication she hadn't anticipated. Sitting up, she slid off the gurney and stood before slipping her feet into her sandals and reaching for her handbag. She thanked the technician on her way out of the clinic.

"If you want to wait a few more minutes, I'll have your pictures ready." The woman smiled.

Ruby frowned. "Pictures?"

"Of your baby! We save them to a thumb drive. It's included in the fee."

Ruby blinked. "Oh. Okay." She looked around at the nearly empty waiting room. She wasn't sure how she felt about having pictures of her baby. Physical proof of the life that was growing inside her. It was all so overwhelming. Turning away, she stumbled toward a seat to wait.

Her thoughts were in turmoil. A pregnancy was the last thing she'd expected. If she and Vaughan were still together, she'd have been thrilled. Especially now, when she was truly in love with him. They'd be making plans for a wedding and now a baby... Life could have been so great. Now she'd never get the chance to find out.

What was she going to do? There were so many things to consider. Having the baby and raising it on her own. That was one option. She was sure she could do it. Plenty of women were single moms. Not an ideal situation and certainly not the way she'd ever imagined raising a child, but it was possible.

There was also abortion. Though everything inside her rebelled against the idea, she had to be practical. She wasn't with the father. She might never even tell him about the pregnancy. The last thing she wanted was for Vaughan to feel obligated toward her. That was one thing she couldn't bear.

Then there was adoption. Though that didn't seem to be as common these days, surely there were still couples who couldn't have children of their own and were happy to adopt.

At least then the baby would be given the chance to have a life. Provided it was adopted by someone who treated it right, loved it. She hated the thought of her child being raised in an abusive home.

The problem was, she didn't want to think about adoption, either. In fact, she didn't want to think about the baby at all. Period. It made her head hurt. And her heart. But the clock was ticking. She was already eight weeks pregnant. She needed to make a decision soon. That knowledge weighed her down like lead.

Every time she thought about Vaughan she was flooded with guilt. The calmer, saner part of her felt that he deserved to know. He was the father. It was only right he have some input into whether or not she brought a baby into the world. But her hormonal side, that had her feelings topsy turvy and all over the place, wasn't quite so sure. It was her body. She alone had the right to make the decision.

In fact, the more she thought about it, the more she was convinced she would be better off if he didn't know. That way she could make the decision without him trying to influence her, one way or the other. She didn't know how he felt about having children. It was a discussion they'd never had. They might have been engaged, but until the accident, she'd never seriously contemplated going through with the marriage. That she felt so strongly about wanting to be with him now was the ultimate irony and left her feeling sadder and more depressed than ever.

"Here you go."

She looked up in time to see the technician handing her a small envelope. She felt the thumb drive inside.

"Thank you," she murmured and shoved the envelope inside her handbag.

She stood abruptly. The technician blinked in surprise, but Ruby was beyond caring about her lack of manners. She had to get out of there. After mumbling something that passed for a goodbye, she flung her handbag over her shoulder and hurried out of the clinic.

Vaughan's feet pounded the pavement as he jogged the final mile to his apartment. The early morning sun beat down on his head. Sweat ran down his face and into his eyes, stinging them. The muscles in his calves were screaming, along with the pain in his barely healed ribs. It had been too long since he'd pushed himself so hard. He hated that he'd lost so much of his fitness.

The jogging path wended its way along the edge of the cliffs overlooking Bondi Beach. Noisy seagulls squawked on the beach, fighting over tidbits thrown their way by tourists. This time of the morning, joggers crowded the path, trying to get their run in before work.

Vaughan was no different. He'd returned to the office a couple of weeks earlier, determined to get his life back on track. He'd spent far too long lounging around in Bali. Though at the time, he'd relished the ability to hang out and have fun in a place where no one knew him or knew what he was going through, it was time to roll up his sleeves and get back into the day-to-day running of Barrington Mining.

He'd already confronted Elizabeth Craigdon and though his conversation with her had been less than satisfactory, it was one less demon he had to conquer. Forging a future without Ruby was the next challenge, but he was determined to get there—and be happy about it.

After showering and dressing for the office, he took a bus into the city and rode the lift to the top floor of the building that housed his father's empire. Busy executives, secretaries, assistants and office juniors filled the sleek, glass-and-chrome offices, scurrying to do his father's bidding. The sound of phones ringing was almost continuous. Vaughan didn't know who the hell was on the other end of the incoming calls, but it seemed there were plenty of people who wanted to talk to someone at Barrington Mining.

Spying Frank's executive assistant seated behind her desk, Vaughan raised a hand in greeting. "Good morning, Casey. How are things?" he asked.

She smiled. "Good morning."

He noticed almost for the first time how attractive she was. In her late twenties, with shiny black hair, blue eyes and a figure that would capture any man's imagination, not only was she physically appealing, but she was also smart to boot.

She'd worked for his father for about three years and he'd always sung her praises.

Frank was a hard task master. Fair, but tough. He demanded excellence from all his staff. He expected even more from his EA. And yet, it seemed Casey was more than up to the job. That told Vaughan a lot about her strength of character.

Maybe I should get to know her better? Maybe she's just what I need. A distraction from my heartache...

No. That wasn't the way to get over Ruby and he had more respect for Casey than to treat her as a rebound lover. Besides, an office relationship would unnecessarily complicate matters and right now, he wanted as few complications as possible.

"Is Dad in yet?" he asked.

Casey nodded. "Yes. He's in his office."

"Thanks,"

Vaughan made his way past the reception area and down the short corridor to his father's office. Frank was on the phone. Vaughan took a seat in one of the two chairs opposite his father's desk and waited for him to finish.

"You're in bright and early," Frank said as he ended his call.

Vaughan shrugged. "No point wasting time lounging around at home when there's work to be done."

Frank nodded in approval. "It's good to have you back, son."

"It's good to be back,"

Frank picked up the newspaper that was on his desk and tossed it to Vaughan. "Take a look at that."

Vaughan scanned the front-page headline. A large, colored picture of Nathan Garcia being led away in handcuffs covered a good deal of space. After reading the story, Vaughan folded the paper and dropped it on the desk.

"Let's hope they lock the prick up," he muttered.

Frank nodded. "The police have gone to town on the charges. Surely, at least one or two of them will stick."

Over the past couple of weeks, Vaughan had been brought up to speed by his father about what had gone on during the months he'd been away. He was familiar with the details surrounding Evan Wilson's death. That had happened more than a year ago. But the spate of incidents that had put the mine under threat of closure were a surprise. To discover the incidents had been deliberately engineered by Nathan Garcia filled Vaughan with anger.

"Can we tie any of this back to Joseph Rodriguez? I'd love to see that asshole in jail."

Frank shook his head. "No. The old prick's too cunning for that. He made sure there was nothing connecting him to any of the incidents, apart from being Garcia's uncle."

"And Ruby's father," Vaughan added with a meaningful look.

Frank nodded briefly. "Yes. It's a good thing we discovered what she was up to before she did any damage. To the company, at least."

Vaughan grimaced. It still pained him every time he thought about Ruby's deceit. That he'd been taken for a fool so easily, rankled. He'd spent the past forty years evading the advances of predatory women keen to align themselves to a wealthy Barrington heir. Yet Ruby Ashworth had laughed and smiled and jiggled her breasts and he'd fallen right into her trap.

He put his poor judgement down to the fact he'd still been reeling from Elizabeth's revelations and hadn't been thinking straight. But he'd been with Ruby for months. It appalled him that, in all that time, he hadn't once suspected she was anything more than what she purported to be. The whole thing left a sour taste in his mouth. The worst of it was, he'd never trust a woman so easily again. His walls were most definitely up. Who knew if he'd ever feel comfortable letting them down again?

He swallowed a sigh. None of that mattered anymore. He'd put the whole sorry episode behind him. He was there to work and to help continue to build on the success his father had started with Barrington Mining. Beginning with doing a complete audit of all employees right across the board. He was determined to root out each and every one of Rodriguez's former employees and ensure none of them ever worked on a Barrington mine site again.

"How are you feeling?" his father asked.

"Not too bad. I still get headaches every now and then, but I'm getting stronger every day. I went for a run this morning." He grimaced. "The ribs aren't quite as healed as I thought. It knocked me about a bit and took me almost twice as long to do the distance, but I did it."

Frank nodded, his expression filled with relief. "Good. That's good. I'm glad you're getting back into the swing of things, but don't overdo it. You know what the doctor said."

"Yes, Dad. I won't overdo it. Why do you think I'm in the office instead of being out at one of our mine sites?" He smiled.

His father offered him a reluctant grin. "All right, wise guy. But your mother and I didn't hightail it over to Bali the moment we heard about your accident so you could suffer a relapse trying to prove how tough you are." He paused. "No one's going to think less of you if you aren't quite firing on all cylinders yet. We'd much rather see you taking it easy until you're completely recovered. Got it?"

Vaughan sighed dramatically, but softened his reaction with another smile. "Yes, Dad. I've got it. And I'm grateful you care. That you and Mom hightailed it to Bali and brought me back here. I appreciate it."

"Of course," Frank replied, his voice gruff. "You're our son. When Ruby told us you were badly hurt, we didn't hesitate to get on a plane. Your mother spent the whole time praying you'd be okay."

Vaughan grimaced at the mention of Ruby. "I wondered how you'd found out. I assumed it was Ruby who'd raised the alarm, but..." He frowned. "How did she contact you?"

"By email. It came from your address."

"She must have known my password..." he mused.

Yet another surprise. Just like the discovery that she'd known all along who he was and that getting close enough to him to spy on his family's business had been her sole purpose for being in Bali. The same familiar feeling of betrayal filled his belly with lead. Something of his hurt and anger must have shown on his face. His father's expression filled with concern.

"Are you okay, Vaughan?"

"Yeah," he managed.

"I'm sorry for how things worked out with Ruby. It must have come as a shock. To realize she was in cahoots with her father… That she deceived you all that time… I'm sorry, Vaughan."

Vaughan's throat went tight. Being reminded all over again how Ruby had taken him for a fool was difficult. So was the fact he still had feelings for her. Given what she'd done, he ought to hate her for destroying what they'd had together, and a part of him did. But the part that had fallen head over heels in love with her; the part that had driven him to getting down on one knee; the part that thought they'd be together forever… That part was finding it harder to accept that what they'd had together was gone; that they'd never be a couple again.

That knowledge still hurt. He truly missed her. He ought to cut himself some slack and just accept that getting over Ruby would take time. Feelings that ran that deep wouldn't dissipate overnight. But he was determined to get over her. To put her firmly in his past. It helped being back at work. It also helped that she'd never stepped foot in his apartment. Not like the house they'd shared in Bali.

They'd moved in together about three months after they met. It had made sense at the time. They'd both been paying rent for separate accommodations, but had spent the majority of their time at one place or the other. Getting a place together had been a no brainer. Especially when they were well on the way to falling in love. At least, that's how he'd felt. Now it was clear that for Ruby, her love had been nothing more than an act.

He was glad she hadn't invaded every inch of his apartment in Bondi. He loved his sprawling bachelor pad with its large, comfortable furniture and panoramic views of the ocean. It had always been a place where he could relax and unwind and get over the day's events.

There were no memories of Ruby there and that was something he was grateful for. She hadn't spent time out on the balcony, sharing a bottle of wine and enjoying the sunset. Her clothes had never filled his wardrobe. The bathroom vanity hadn't been overrun with her toiletries and cosmetics. Her perfume had never lingered on the air. It was bad enough that some of his clothes still smelled of her...

He made a mental note to toss out any of his shirts she'd ever worn.

His father cleared his throat and Vaughan realized he hadn't responded to Frank's last comment. There was no point wallowing in the past. He was done with feeling sorry for himself. He was also done with giving Ruby the power to hurt him. He had no say in her behavior, but he could control how he reacted to it. From that moment forward, she was nothing more to him than a woman he'd once known.

"Will you have to give evidence in the Garcia trial?"

His father acknowledged the not-so-subtle change of subject with nothing more than a slight upward movement of his bushy eyebrows. "I'm not sure. I was interviewed a couple of times by two different detectives during the investigation stage. I told them what I knew. They interviewed Hannah, too. She worked closely with Garcia. I won't be surprised if she's called by the prosecution."

Vaughan grimaced. "Poor Hannah. I bet she's thrilled about that."

"No. But she's pleased Garcia's being prosecuted. She'll do her bit to see him brought to justice."

"I still can't believe he was actively arranging workplace accidents! What an asshole! Someone could have been killed!"

"Yes. I feel the same way."

Vaughan shook his head on a fresh wave of anger. "And to think he's Ruby's cousin! That Rodriguez had both of them working on the inside to destroy us."

"Yes. And not only the two of them. Garcia recruited several of Rodriguez's former employees. They were all working with Nathan at Strathwaylin mine as accomplices."

"I should have been here," Vaughan stated grimly.

"You weren't to know what they'd planned," Frank replied. "When you left, the biggest issue we were dealing with was Evan Wilson's lawsuit and our lawyers had assured us they had that under control. We never employed Wilson. Though we were ultimately responsible for safety at the mine site, any liability for his death fell squarely on Rodriguez."

Vaughan shot his father a sideways look. "You suspected Rodriguez right from the start. Did you ever find evidence of any wrongdoing on his part?"

Frank sighed. "Unfortunately, no. That doesn't mean I'm not convinced he was responsible. Maybe not directly, but that prick didn't give a toss about safety. That was the reason I fired him."

"I hate that he might have gotten away with that."

"Yeah. Me, too. I hired several private investigators. They all came back with scratch. If he was responsible, he did a good job of covering his tracks. The only thing we can take satisfaction from is that the plan he hatched with Ruby didn't work out like he expected."

"Yes. I guess I ought to be grateful Ruby finally came clean." Vaughan made a sound of irritation in the back of his throat. "I can't believe how completely I was taken in by her. It was like she batted those long eyelashes and I lost my mind."

"We've been over this, Vaughan. Don't beat yourself up about it. She was a master at deception. Just like her old man. Hell, I almost fell for her over-the-top, concern-for-you routine. Every time I tried to visit you in the hospital, she was there. All red-eyed and teary. Clinging to your hand. Begging you to wake up. She sure gave a good impression of the worried fiancée."

Frank shook his head in disgust. "Rodriguez was the same. He worked for me as a contractor for nearly a year before I started to cotton on to his total disregard for safety. I was just lucky there was only one fatality. Evan's death was tragic, but if I hadn't woken up in time, there could have been others."

Vaughan compressed his lips, feeling grim. Everything to do with Joseph Rodriguez and his family was bad news. Vaughan was well rid of Ruby Ashworth-Rodriguez. With a bit of luck, he'd never cross paths with her again.

Chapter Nine

Ruby sat at her desk and sipped from her cup of herbal tea. She'd found that it helped to settle her stomach. She prayed that it would work now. Though the morning sickness had started to subside, it hadn't gone away altogether. She was surrounded by her father's employees, including Marnie, who'd been Ruby's secretary for years and had been transferred back to her department now that she'd returned. Marnie was way too observant. If she wasn't careful, her secretary would guess her secret and there would be one more thing to worry about.

She sighed quietly. It seemed like ever since she'd arrived home from Bali, things had gone to hell. It had started with Vaughan's accident and having to return to Sydney before she'd planned. Then Hannah had guessed her identity and despite her resolve to tell Vaughan the truth, the timing of her disclosure was taken out of her hands. The rest was history. Too bad it had taken such a traumatic event for her to realize how she truly felt about him. Now, any hope of them having a life together was over and she only had herself to blame.

At least she'd smoothed things over with her father. Though he hadn't apologized for his threatening outburst, he hadn't said anything about her presence back in the office. Neither had he broached the subject of Vaughan again. For that at least, she was grateful.

Reaching for the morning newspaper, she flicked it open. She froze as she stared down at the picture that almost filled the front page. Her cousin, Nathan, had his face averted as he was led away in handcuffs by the police, but there was no mistaking it was him. She scanned the story.

With growing indignation and a rising knot of dread, she stared at the newspaper in shock. The story gave a brief history of Nathan's association with the Strathwaylin mine. One of several mines owned by mining magnate, Frank Barrington. The article went on to describe a series of accidents that had happened over the course of many months at the mine. The police alleged Nathan was responsible and that his actions had been motivated by a deliberate attempt to have the mine closed. Several workers had been injured. No one had been killed, but according to the journalist, that was more good luck than anything else.

Ruby's disquiet grew. She was struck by a wave of nausea. She took a sip of tea and prayed for the morning sickness to subside. Her father had assured her the charges against Nathan were minor. That he was innocent of any wrongdoing. But the article talked about a trial date and the significant number of witnesses on the prosecution list.

That seemed far more serious than what her father had intimated. The police didn't lay criminal charges against someone without a genuine belief they could secure a conviction. Coupled with the sheer number of witnesses prepared to come forward and give evidence against her cousin... It was obvious there was far more to the story than what she'd been told.

Reaching into her handbag, she pulled out her phone."Daddy. I just saw the morning paper. What's going on?"

"Ruby, I've already told you there's nothing to worry about. Nathan and I have this in hand."

"It doesn't look like that to me. They're talking about setting a trial date."

"They can set all the trial dates they like. That doesn't mean they're going to find your cousin guilty."

"But what about the witnesses? Surely, they all can't be lying?"

"Don't believe everything you read, Ruby. The truth is, Nathan's been set up by that asshole, Frank Barrington. He's had it in for Nathan ever since he found out he's my nephew. He was determined to get rid of him and now he's found a way to do it without incurring an unfair dismissal claim."

She ignored a burst of irritation. "I repeat, Daddy. What about the witnesses?"

"What witnesses?" Her father's tone dripped with disgust. "They're all on Barrington's payroll. No doubt he's paying them extra to give testimony that will support his version of events."

"But—"

"Enough!"

Her father's tone was sharp. He drew in a quick breath. When he spoke again, his tone was marginally softer. "I understand your lawyerly instincts might be humming, but I've already told you, Ruby. There's nothing to worry about. Now that your cover's been blown, you're in the clear. It's too bad you didn't manage to discover anything of worth, but there's nothing we can do about that now. At least Nathan managed to have some impact during the time he was at the mine," he muttered.

Ruby blinked in surprise, not sure she'd heard him correctly. "Daddy? What does that mean?"

"Nothing," he said dismissively. "Forget about it. And do yourself a favor. Stop reading the papers." With that, he hung up.

Ruby stared down at her phone, her mind in turmoil. Her father had assured her Nathan was innocent and yet his final comment cast doubt on that. Or maybe she was overreacting? Maybe the pregnancy hormones were turning her mind to mush. She'd been finding it so much harder to concentrate these past weeks.

Her father was right. She should put the whole sorry episode with Vaughan behind her and concentrate on what was important: the fact she was pregnant and still didn't know what to do about it.

Her hand went reflexively to her stomach. There was only the tiniest, almost indiscernible bump. Nothing anyone else would notice. But as much as she wanted to put the conversation with her father out of her mind, as the day progressed, the things he'd said continued to remain front and center. The thing was, she wasn't sure she believed him.

The suggestion that Frank Barrington was behind Nathan's arrest and prosecution was ludicrous. They didn't live in a country where the police could be bought. That meant there had to be more to this than what her father had said. The only thing to do was some digging of her own. Not just into Nathan's situation, but further back. She was curious about her father's relationship with Frank. When had it started to sour?

Decision made, she collected her handbag and left her office. Taking a moment to let Marnie know she was going out for a while, she headed for the lifts. The city library was about three blocks away. She wended her way through the crowds of pedestrians, taking a moment to enjoy the day.

The summer sun was warm on her face. A faint breeze blew in from the ocean, lifting the ends of her hair and bringing with it the smell of salt. Horns honked and bus brakes squealed, but Ruby was mostly oblivious. She loved living in the city. The noise, the crowds, the traffic... It was all part of the vibe. The fast pace, the sense of urgency, everyone focused on their destination. Though she sometimes missed the laid-back lifestyle of Bali, it was good to be home.

She was a block away from the library when she stopped cold. Vaughan stood in front of her, a mere handful of yards away. He spotted her at almost the same moment and went still. His initial surprise was quickly concealed behind a blank mask.

Her hand went instinctively to her stomach. She briskly removed it, relieved that he didn't seem to notice. "V-Vaughan. What a surprise. What are you doing in the city?"

He scowled. "Not that it's any of your business, but I'm back at work."

She frowned. "Already? Are you sure that's wise?"

He glared at her. "What I do is no longer any of your concern. If it ever was."

The coldness in his tone sent shards of pain through her heart. It was all she could do not to burst into tears. No doubt the hormones rushing through her body had a lot to do with that. Still, she couldn't deny how much she missed him and how she longed for them to reconcile. But from the look on his face, that was a pipedream. He was never going to forgive her.

With her cheeks burning from pain and humiliation, she mumbled a few words of farewell and stepped past him. The crowd surged around her, but she was oblivious. She walked blindly, no longer certain of her destination. The last thing on her mind was the library. Seeing him so cold, the reality that he'd never want to parent with her crashed into her. The man she'd seen on the street, so distant, would never be interested in their child. Would likely think she was trying to trap him…

All she could think about was the baby. She was now ten weeks pregnant. Time was running out. She needed to make a decision.

Vaughan stumbled away from Ruby, his mind in turmoil. He was more rattled by their unexpected meeting than he cared to admit. He hated that his heart clenched with pain at the sight of her. He hated that she still had that kind of hold on him. She looked beautiful in a summery, floral dress that kissed the tops of her knees and drew attention to her long, tanned legs. Legs he'd spent countless hours kissing and caressing; legs that had wrapped around his hips, urging him onward toward completion.

With a groan of despair, he forced the memories aside. He and Ruby were over. It didn't matter how beautiful she was on the outside. It was her character that mattered most and she'd proven herself to be so deceitful and dishonest, the memory of her actions still had the power to cause him to catch his breath. And more fool him, he'd fallen completely for her lies. But from his reaction to her, it was clear he'd take her back in a heartbeat, given half a chance.

At forty, he prided himself on being wise to women on the hunt for a wealthy man. As a Barrington heir, he was recognizable. That was the reason he'd gone incognito in Bali. He thought he'd been so clever, concealing his real identity from Ruby. Turned out, the joke was on him.

Still, there was nothing he could do about that now. No point in castigating himself on being blinded to the faults of a beautiful woman. He needed to pick up the pieces and move on with his life.

Throwing himself back into work was the best way to do that. And the best way to get over a failed relationship was to get right back on the horse. Work hard. Date as many women as he could. Have lots of casual sex. Erase Ruby Ashworth-Rodriguez from his life.

With that thought in mind, when he stepped out of the lift on the top floor of his father's building, he made a deliberate detour to Casey's desk. Ignoring his earlier reservations, he plastered a winning smile on his face and walked right up to her.

"Hi, Casey."

She blinked at his enthusiastic greeting. A flush crept across her cheeks. "H-hi, Vaughan. What's happening?"

He got straight to the point. "Would you like to go out for a drink with me tonight?"

Her eyes widened. Then she smiled. "Sure."

"Great. How about straight after work? I'll stop by and collect you." He winked.

Her blush deepened. She averted her gaze and then looked up at him from beneath her lashes with a shy smile.

"Sounds good."

He smiled again and turned away, headed for his office. He whistled tunelessly under his breath, steadfastly ignoring the warnings that continued to rebound in his head. Erasing Ruby from his life was the goal and this was the best way he could think of to do it.

His father stood in the open doorway of his office. As Vaughan drew nearer, Frank frowned.

"What do you think you're doing?" his father asked without preamble.

Vaughan came to a halt. "What do you mean?"

"Did I just overhear you invite Casey out for a drink?"

Vaughan eyed his father steadily. "Yes. So?"

Frank stared right back at him. "Weren't you engaged to be married only a few weeks ago?"

Vaughan shrugged and looked away. "Yes. So?"

"Sooo..." Frank replied, dragging the word out. "Casey's a great worker. We get along well. I don't want you messing that up."

Vaughan deliberately widened his eyes. "Why would I mess that up?"

Frank's gaze narrowed. "Quit being a smart ass. Casey's been working here for years. You've never once expressed any interest in her. It doesn't matter that she's young, attractive and available. You're on the rebound, Vaughan. If you feel the need to kick up your heels and have some no-strings-attached fun, then go ahead. Just don't do it with my EA."

Vaughan forced a grin and waved his father's words away. "You don't have anything to worry about, Dad. We're only going for a drink. I assure you, I'm not going to break her heart. You have my word."

Frank merely glared at him a few moments longer before turning his back on him and disappearing inside his office without another word.

Ruby had lost all track of time. From the moment she'd spied Vaughan, her intention to conduct research at the library had dissipated like smoke in the wind. The crowd of pedestrians ebbed and flowed around her. She was oblivious to the noise, the traffic, the people who pressed in against her on all sides. Even the salty breeze that drifted in from the harbor failed to ease her distress.

Coming face-to-face with Vaughan had shocked her. He was the last person she'd expected to see. She still trembled all over. The way he'd looked at her; the way he'd spoken...

His coldness had been devastating. After all they'd shared, the months of fun and togetherness, pledging their lives together... His aloofness cut deep.

Once again, her hand went protectively to her stomach. How could she tell him about the baby when he still hated her? She didn't want to guilt him into spending time with her. Attending prenatal appointments; being there at the next ultrasound. The labor ward. She bit back a cry of despair. She didn't want him in her life under sufferance. That would be too difficult to bear. Especially now she realized she truly loved him.

She crossed Elizabeth Street with the lights and walked blindly toward the Botanical Gardens. It was a place she'd always found peaceful; a refuge from the hustle and bustle of the city. But on this perfect summer day, the lush green grounds teemed with people.

Surely it was only a trick of her mind that everywhere she looked there were babies being pushed in prams. Young families seated on colorful picnic blankets, cheering on first steps. Smiling, pregnant women holding hands with their partners. They surrounded her; crowded in on her. Mocked her.

She made a sound of distress in the back of her throat and covered her ears with her hands to block out the sound of happy families. Giving a couple with cute, identical twins a wide berth, she dropped onto a vacant bench and stared out across the wide expanse of gardens.

The sun beat down relentlessly on her bare head. Her heart beat double time. She made a deliberate effort to slow down her breathing. Surely, a racing pulse wasn't good for the baby. She was still so confused about what to do and she had no one to turn to for advice.

Vaughan was out of the question. So were her parents. She'd never been close to her mother and telling her father she was pregnant with a Barrington's baby could quite possibly have detrimental effects on his health. Ever since his heart attack, she'd been very cognizant of the need to keep him calm. The health scare might have happened more than two years ago, but that didn't mean he couldn't suffer another one. That was the last thing she wanted, or needed on her conscience.

The need to acquiesce to his wishes was one of the reasons she'd agreed to take part in his scheme to bring the Barringtons down. Of course, she'd believed he'd been wronged and Frank Barrington needed to be held to account for his actions, but her love for her father had also played a huge part in her decision. As had Kyle's death. Now she wished she'd never heard of Vaughan Barrington.

Her hand strayed to her stomach again. Depending upon what choice she made, Vaughan might be a part of her life forever. After all, he was the baby's father. From what she knew of Vaughan, he'd do the right thing. They might not be together anymore, but he'd stand by her and support his child.

Is that what I want? Can I handle having Vaughan in my life? Co-parenting, despite the fact he can't stand the sight of me? What am I? A masochist?

The tumult of her thoughts swirled through her head until she almost groaned aloud again in distress. The emotional upheaval couldn't be good for her baby, but right now, she couldn't seem to switch it off. The pressure of having to make a decision, and soon, pressed in against her. Dread weighed heavily in her belly.

Sitting around bemoaning her situation would get her nowhere. She had to calm down and think. Rationally. Logically. Weigh the pros and cons. It all sounded so easy. Too bad she knew from experience it was far from that. Still, the clock was ticking. Soon abortion would be off the table. She wasn't sure if she was relieved by that, or not. Right now, she was too scared and uncertain to analyze how she felt.

She stood up and headed with determined strides to the bus that would take her home. She was no good to anyone in the office in this state. What she needed was a distraction. She remembered she planned to visit the library and then lit on the idea of calling her brother, Matthew.

Before his death, Kyle had been her confidante. He'd had the right mix of common sense and sensitivity that encouraged heart-to-hearts. He would listen to her problems and dish out loads of good advice. She'd come away from talking with him feeling better. That was only one of his gifts.

But Kyle also had his share of issues. She couldn't argue when her father reminded her that Kyle wasn't as emotionally strong as she was, or Matthew. He'd entered the cutthroat world of business working beside their father, but Ruby had never thought he was right for that kind of job. He'd lamented to her in private about the pressure he was under to keep the company afloat. Though he'd never gone into details, she'd gathered that working so closely with their father hadn't been easy for him.

Then there was the fact he was gay. Though she'd guessed that reality long before he'd come out to her, she'd been proud of him for having the courage to say it out loud. But he'd sworn her to secrecy, extracting from her a promise that she wouldn't breathe a word to anyone—especially not to their father.

Ruby understood. Joe Rodriguez was a hard man. Though Ruby hoped he loved Kyle enough to accept him, no matter his sexual orientation, she had agreed to remain quiet about it.

Now Kyle was dead and the whole issue was moot. Ruby felt sad for her brother that he'd never gotten to live his life freely and openly in the way that he should have been able to.

Her brother, Matthew, also worked closely with their father, but Matthew and Kyle were polar opposites. Where Kyle had been sweet and sensitive, Matthew was hard as nails. He took his cues from their father and had emulated Joseph to such a degree, there was little difference between them. Especially in how they went about making decisions.

Matthew was quick to lay blame and slow to forgive, but his grit and determination had helped make Rodriguez Contracting a force to be reckoned with in the earthmoving industry. At least, it had been headed in that direction before the fallout with Frank Barrington.

It was because of Matthew that Joseph had known Vaughan was headed for Bali. If anyone knew what had gone on before between their father and Frank Barrington, it would be Matthew. Though he wasn't normally the brother she went to for answers, he was her only option now. Besides, given his background of working closely with the Barringtons, he was the perfect person to ask. Better still, going out with him for a drink would take her mind off Vaughan and their baby and that had to be a good thing.

Chapter Ten

Vaughan bought another round of drinks and returned to their table. The upmarket bar on busy George Street was crowded with patrons enjoying a drink after work. The sound of laughter, conversation and the tinkle of glassware competed with the upbeat, modern music that came from the speakers in the ceiling.

The clouds had rolled in just as they'd left their building and he and Casey were forced to make a run for it to avoid getting wet. They'd arrived at the bar laughing, relieved to have beat the summer storm that lasted about as long as it took for them to secure a table by a window. Outside, the streets glistened from the sudden downpour.

Vaughan didn't fail to notice that Casey had taken the time to freshen her makeup and run a brush through her long hair. Instead of the customary bun she usually wore to the office, her hair now hung in soft, shiny waves around her shoulders. He was pricked by a stab of guilt and hastily pushed it away. The relaxed hairstyle made her look younger and even more attractive.

He reached across their table and handed her the glass of white wine she'd ordered. Their fingers brushed. He heard her sharp intake of breath and wished he felt an answering response. His lack of immediate physical attraction to her was downright annoying. She was attractive, smart and funny. Many of the qualities he looked for in a woman.

They'd spent the past hour on office talk and then the conversation switched to their hobbies. He discovered she was a thrill-seeker, like him. Fast cars, motorbikes, water skiing. Mountain climbing, white water rafting, snowboarding. They had so much in common. She was also easy to talk to. Apart from her occasional blushes, there were no uncomfortable moments. He certainly didn't regret asking her out.

The only thing holding him back was the fact he wasn't instantly burning to take her to bed. In fact, right now it felt like he was spending time with a co-worker, or perhaps the girlfriend of one of his friends. Someone he could engage in casual conversation, knowing it wouldn't go anywhere.

He scowled at the direction of his thoughts. Casey reached over and touched his arm. "Is everything all right?"

Once again, her touch left him unmoved. He forced a smile. "Of course. Just thinking about work."

"Hey," she chided. "You're off the clock, remember? Relax. Let your hair down." She flicked her long locks and winked.

He gave a halfhearted grin in response, determined to try harder. Not everyone fell instantly in lust with their life partner. Not every relationship had to be built on the white-hot lust he'd felt for Ruby. In fact, a slow burn was better than combustible heat that burned out all too quickly, right?

He was sure he'd heard that somewhere. Or maybe he'd read it. Whatever. It didn't matter that he wasn't quite feeling it with Casey. It was early days. He needed to give it some time. That's all.

Ruby sipped from her Diet Coke and listened to her brother as he regaled her with stories about his latest adventures in India. She'd never been there, but from what Matthew told her, it sounded like a place she'd like to visit.

Right now, he was on a mission to expand their father's earthmoving business ventures and with mining contracts drying up for Rodriguez Contracting in Australia, he'd been forced to look overseas. He was currently involved in discussions with Adani Mining and was quietly confident he might be able to secure a lucrative contract.

"It's a good thing not everyone has Dad blacklisted," Matthew said dryly.

Ruby grimaced. Her brother's comment reminded her of what Frank Barrington had done and then she recalled her concerns. Now that the moment was upon her, nerves danced in her belly. Determined to get to the bottom of things, she took a sip of her Diet Coke and cleared her throat.

"I never really heard why Dad was fired. Do you know anything about the accidents he was supposedly involved in?"

Matthew's eyes flashed. Unlike her, he'd taken after their father and was almost a mirror image of him. Thick dark hair, dark eyes, and olive skin that were testament to their Spanish heritage. She noticed for the first time gray flecks at his temples.

"What accidents? Dad wasn't involved in any accidents."

She kept her voice calm. "I read the paper this morning. Nathan's face is splashed all over the front page. He's been indicted for causing several accidents at one of the Barrington Mines."

"That has nothing to do with Dad. He wasn't even working at that mine when those accidents are alleged to have happened."

"The paper said that Nathan's been charged. He's going to trial. They must have some evidence against him."

Matthew waved away her words with an angry slash of his hand. "Don't be obtuse, Ruby. Frank Barrington is the richest man in Australia. He *owns* the police. One word from him, and they're running to do his bidding. They've got nothing on Nathan and I'm confident the jury will find him not guilty on all charges. It's the same with Dad."

Matthew's gaze narrowed. "Frank Barrington wanted to get rid of him, so he set about doing whatever he could to make that happen. The easiest way to send someone packing off a coal mine is to make it look like they're a danger to themselves and others. Safety on a mine site is paramount. No one messes around with that. One word from old man Barrington that our father was a safety risk and that was enough to cancel Dad's contract. Then he bad-mouthed us all over the place and made sure we wouldn't get another contract with anyone else."

Matthew shook his head in disgust and then buried his nose in his beer. He emptied the glass in three swallows.

Ruby stared at him. Though her brother had no reason to lie, he was fiercely loyal to their father. She wasn't sure if he'd admit to anything that reflected badly on the man he'd put on a pedestal. She sipped from her drink before speaking again.

"So, you think Daddy was fired for no good reason?"

Matthew's expression remained dark. "That's exactly what I think. Dad's contract with Barrington Mining was terminated without notice. Millions of dollars in lost revenue. Our reputation in shreds. Poor old Kyle, hanging from the rafters. Frank Barrington destroyed our brother and our business. All because he took a dislike to Dad."

Ruby chewed her bottom lip. "Daddy seems to think it's because Frank Barrington's a racist. That he was fired because he's an immigrant. Do you think there's any truth to that?"

Matthew shrugged. His expression remained disgruntled. "Who knows? That could have had something to do with it."

Ruby pursed her lips. She was still uncertain about where the truth lay. She hated herself for not being able to believe her father and brother without question; that knowing Vaughan had put doubts in her mind.

Her shoulders slumped on a sigh. The crowd had grown bigger. She nearly had to shout to be heard over the din of laughter and conversation. She started to ask Matthew to tell her more about his travels through India when the crowd suddenly parted and she froze.

Vaughan was seated at a table across the room. A drop-dead-gorgeous woman sat opposite him. Black shiny hair, ocean-blue eyes, a smile that could have been used in a toothpaste commercial. She looked younger than Ruby by a decade. In her mid-twenties at most. They were laughing together.

Jealousy stabbed through her, hot and piercing, followed quickly by a rush of hurt. Not so long ago, he'd declared his undying love and asked her to be his wife. Now he was out with another woman and by the look of things, having a wonderful time. It was all she could do not to rush out of there and find somewhere dark and quiet to hide.

She cast a frantic glance toward her brother. "Matthew, I'm not feeling so well. Do you mind if we call it a night?"

Vaughan pushed his chair away from the table and half-stood before being stopped cold. Ruby sat close to a man, talking over drinks. Barely three weeks had passed since he'd broken off their engagement and already, she was out on the town with another man. He squashed the immediate surge of guilt. He was also out on the town. He'd deliberately invited Casey out hoping their time together would lead to something else and help him forget about Ruby.

People in glass houses... I'm just as bad as her...

That knowledge didn't ease the tumult of emotions that coursed through him, leaving him shaken. He wasn't sure if she'd seen him, but just in case, he wanted to put on a good show. He wanted her to know he wasn't sitting at home pining for her; lamenting over everything he'd lost.

With that thought overtaking everything else, he regained his seat and deliberately shifted closer to Casey. So close, that their shoulders touched. Casey's eyes widened in surprise, but she gave him a smile of encouragement. From the corner of his eye, he saw Ruby and the other man leave. When the crowd closed behind them and they'd disappeared from sight, he quietly swore.

Fuck.

Unable to help herself, as Ruby squeezed out between her seat and the people who stood next to their table, she glanced across at Vaughan in time to see him snuggle up close to his date. That was enough to rock her world off its axis all over again. Beyond caring whether or not Matthew followed her, she pushed her way through the crowd and stumbled outside. She dragged in a fortifying breath in a desperate attempt to slow her racing heart.

The evening air was crisp and cool after the earlier short, sharp shower of rain that had left the streets damp and the pavements smelling of wet concrete. It was a smell Ruby usually found pleasing, but tonight, it left her feeling sick. Anger and hurt and jealousy swirled inside her, turning her inside out.

She and Vaughan were over. It was ridiculous to feel so distraught, so betrayed by the sight of him with another woman. He'd made it clear he was never going to forgive her. She needed to accept that and move on with her life, whether or not that included a baby.

With haste, Vaughan escorted Casey out of the bar. They came to a halt on the footpath.

Casey shot him a quizzical look and he fought back an embarrassed blush. The truth was, from the moment he spied Ruby, he regretted inviting Casey out. Ruby had left with her date not long after he'd spied them. But that didn't make it any easier to get her off his mind. She was all he could think of.

He'd wanted to dash over to her table and snatch her away. She was his woman. He couldn't bear the thought of her seeing other men. But that wasn't fair. He was the one who'd sent her packing. He was the one who'd told her he never wanted to see her again. She had every right to be dating other men. It annoyed him how much he hated the idea.

What he did know was that spending time with Casey wasn't going to cure him of his affliction and it wasn't fair to pretend there could be anything between them. She was a beautiful, intelligent woman and they shared many common interests. On paper, she was a perfect match. But there was no spark.

It's all Ruby's fault. She's spoiled me for other women. Damn her!

He should have known he wouldn't be able to erase Ruby's memory so easily. Not so long ago, he'd pledged his life to her. Feelings that strong couldn't just disappear overnight, no matter how much he wanted them to. He'd been foolish to think he could rush recovery by dating other women.

Too late, his father's words of warning came back to him. He cursed silently under his breath. Pursuing any kind of relationship with Casey was doomed to failure. Even worse, if he persisted, there was a good chance things would end badly. And if she turned in her resignation, his father would be pissed, and rightly so.

Casey deserved better. It wasn't fair to lead her on. She wasn't Ruby and never would be and that was okay. He needed to face the reality that expunging Ruby from his heart would take more than a night or two in someone else's arms.

There was nothing more for him to do but leave. Letting Casey down as gently as he could, he offered a heartfelt apology and with his face burning from embarrassment, he turned and strode away.

All he could think about was Ruby. She consumed him like an addict was consumed by a drug. No matter how hard he tried to get her out of his mind, out of his system, she found her way back. He looked around, hoping to see her. And then he did.

She stood with her date about fifty yards away, waiting for a cab. A taxi pulled up and her date stepped forward and opened the back door. Ruby climbed into the car and then turned to look at him. Vaughan held his breath. The man merely lifted his hand in a casual wave and then closed the cab door. A few moments later, the cab pulled away from the curb.

Vaughan let out his breath on a quick sigh. It seemed her night was over. Vaughan watched for a few moments longer. Long enough to see Ruby's date flag down another cab.

He shouldn't be so relieved she was going home alone, but he couldn't deny the truth. He was desperate to talk to her, to hear her voice again. It was embarrassing how much he missed her. How much he hated what she'd done to them. How much he wanted her back.

Without thinking, he pulled out his phone and dialed his sister's number. Hannah answered on the second ring.

"Vaughan. What's going on?"

"Don't ask. You wouldn't happen to know Ruby's address, would you?"

"What? Why would you want Ruby's address?"

"I just told you not to ask. Do you have it, or not?"

"Of course I do. Where do you think I confronted her about her deception?"

Vaughan ignored her pointed comment. "Can I have it please?"

"But—"

"Please, Hannah. I need to see her."

Some of his desperation must have seeped into his tone. Without another word, Hannah read off the address.

"Thank you," he said.

"I hope you know what you're doing," Hannah muttered.

"So do I," Vaughan replied. "So do I."

Chapter Eleven

Ruby rested her head back on the seat of the cab and swallowed a weary sigh. Seeing Vaughan with another woman had been a shock. Now that they were no longer together, she guessed she ought to get used to the idea that he'd start dating again. She just hadn't expected it to happen so soon or that she'd witness it.

No matter how he felt about her, that didn't put a dent in her love for him. It was the worst irony ever that over all the months they'd been together, when Vaughan had continuously assured her and shown her the depth of his love, she'd kept a wall around her heart. Now, when she'd finally lowered her defenses and accepted that she loved him with everything she was, he wanted nothing to do with her.

The cab pulled up outside her building. After paying the fare, she opened the door and stepped onto the footpath. She'd only taken a couple steps toward the entry door when she pulled up short. Vaughan stood a few feet away, his arms crossed over his chest. He looked so handsome in his business suit. His charcoal-gray striped tie had been loosened and his hair was a little askew. The combination made him even sexier than usual.

He must have gone to the bar straight from work...

The random thought barely registered before Vaughan opened his mouth and spoke.

"Ruby."

That single, solitary word, spoken just above a whisper, had the power to send a ripple of desire down her spine. His husky tone, filled with need, instantly hardened her nipples. The chemistry between them had always been instant and despite their estrangement, it seemed her body hadn't got the memo to stop.

"Vaughan." Her voice was just as husky as his. She flushed and cleared her throat and then remembered he'd been out on a date. Her tone hardened. "What are you doing here?"

"I need to see you."

Despite her best attempt to remain unaffected, her stomach somersaulted at the yearning in his gaze. With a gargantuan effort, she reined in her burgeoning desire. She gave him a pointed look. "So? Are you going to tell me who you were with? One of your sisters, perhaps?"

Ruby was well aware the woman she'd seen with Vaughan wasn't one of his sisters. She'd done plenty of research on the Barrington family on the plane to Bali. She was familiar with how each of his three sisters looked.

A stain of embarrassment spread across Vaughan's cheeks. He averted his gaze. "Her name's Casey," he mumbled. "She's my father's EA."

Ruby froze. Some of the turmoil inside her must have shown on her face. Vaughan's face filled with remorse.

"I'm sorry, Ruby. She means nothing to me. It was a first date."

A date! Oh, God. It's just what I thought. He's dating again.

It was as bad as she'd feared. Hurt pulsed through her, choking her with emotion. Useless tears burned behind her eyes. She blinked furiously in an effort not to cry.

"I see it didn't take you long to move on," he said, his tone censoring.

As Vaughan's words registered, fury ignited inside her. Tears forgotten, she glared at him, incensed. "I beg your pardon! For your information, I was out with my brother."

He had the decency to look embarrassed. "Your brother?"

"Not that it's any of your business, but yes. Matthew's my older brother. I had two. Kyle died last year." She gave him another pointed look. "Perhaps you've forgotten that."

Vaughan's expression filled with remorse. "Oh, Ruby. I'm so sorry. I'm an idiot. I... I think I lost my mind a little when I saw you with that guy. Which was totally stupid. And unfair. You're entitled to see whoever you like." He paused. "I ought to go home and leave you alone."

She stared at him. He looked so sad and dejected, she softened. "It's good to see you again," she whispered. "You're looking well. Almost as good as new. I like the outfit. It suits you."

All the time they'd spent together in Bali, she'd never once seen him in a suit. His usual garb was shorts and T-shirts or casual, linen button-downs and chinos. The business attire was so much more formal, but he wore the clothes well. For someone so tall and perfectly proportioned, that didn't come as a surprise. Neither did the way her body reacted to him and from the tension in Vaughan's body and the heightened awareness in his eyes, it was obvious he felt the same.

Hope sprang to life inside her, but she immediately tamped it down.

This is crazy... We're not together anymore... He hates me...

But the way he was looking at her, it didn't look like he hated her. His lips had parted slightly. His chest rose and fell in rapid succession. He devoured her with his eyes.

"Vaughan..." Her tone was half pleading, half warning.

In an instant, he was beside her, enveloping her in his arms. His lips found hers and familiar heat ignited between them. She swallowed a gasp. His lips were firm and supple, sensuous, and achingly familiar. It had been so long since they'd made love.

Her arms crept up around his neck and she fitted herself against him. His arms tightened around her, crushing her breasts against his chest. He cupped her ass and pressed her against his erection. She couldn't contain a groan.

"Let's go inside," he murmured against her lips.

Beyond words, all she could do was nod. Taking his hand, she led him into her building and up to the ninth floor. They'd barely made it through her doorway before Vaughan took her in his arms once again. With lips locked together, he walked her backward.

The brief storm had blown offshore and bright moonlight now flooded the room through the windows. It gilded Vaughan's caramel-blond hair, making it almost appear that he wore a halo. She cupped his beloved cheek and continued to kiss him. When they reached the couch, they toppled together onto the cushions, laughing like teenagers.

A little voice in the back of Ruby's head sounded a warning, but it was far too late for that. Her body was on fire, demanding the kind of release only Vaughan could give her. Impatient now, she sat up and fumbled with the buttons that ran down the front of her dress. When she'd unbuttoned enough of them, she moved until she could shimmy it down her hips. She stood before him in nothing but lacy, black underwear and matching bra.

Vaughan stared at her, his eyes glittering like emeralds with desire. He reached out and caressed her hip. "You're so beautiful."

The raw emotion in his voice sent another wave of desire crashing through her. Her nipples hardened in response. Working quickly, Vaughan tore off his jacket, his tie, his shirt. Next came his boots, his socks, his belt and pants, until he was naked, except for his boxers. Her gaze roved over his body, the perfect pectorals, the bulging biceps, the washboard stomach that would put any professional athlete to shame. Though he'd spent weeks in a hospital bed, it didn't show on his body.

The only visible evidence of his injuries was a small white bandage wrapped around his ribs. She reached out and lightly touched the fabric with her fingers.

"Does it still hurt?" she whispered.

He shook his head. "Not too much."

She looked up, suddenly concerned he might not be well enough to make love. As if reading her mind, he grinned.

"Don't worry. I'm definitely capable of *that*. In fact, if I don't get my cock inside you soon, I'm going to explode. Now, *that* might do some damage."

She returned his grin, feeling more carefree than she had for a long time. "Well, I can't be responsible for inflicting more damage on you."

With that, she reached behind her and undid the clasp of her bra. With her teasing gaze locked on his, she flung the bra away. Next, she slowly eased down her panties and kicked them out of the way. Vaughan's gaze darkened with desire. Reaching out, he trailed the back of his fingers down one breast, grazing her nipple, before moving lower.

As his fingers teased over her stomach, she tensed, recalling too late the baby that lay beneath. But he merely glided over the smooth skin of her belly and then continued lower until his fingers were stroking the soft folds between her legs. As sensation after sensation rocked through her, all thoughts of

Vaughan discovering she was pregnant now firmly thrust from her mind.

"You're so wet, so silky," he murmured.

With his eyes locked on hers, he continued to stroke her. It was the most erotic thing she'd ever experienced. Unable to stand a moment longer without touching him, she reached out and pressed her hand against his cock. Thick and hard, it strained against the cotton fabric of his boxers. Needing to feel his skin, she dipped her hand under the waistband and encircled his cock.

He gasped. "Oh, Ruby, that feels so good."

And then even touching wasn't enough. In quick succession, Vaughan shucked off his boxers, bent and lifted her in his arms and started striding down the hallway. At the same time, he nuzzled her neck, driving her wild with his lips.

"Which room's yours?" he asked, his voice muffled against her skin.

"Second on the left," she managed on a gasp.

His long strides ate up the short distance. In no time at all, he deposited her on her king-sized bed and followed her down, covering her body with his. Their lips met in another searing kiss. Ruby's heart pounded. Need rushed through her, flooding her veins, centering in her core. She moved restlessly against him, silently urging him on.

His cock nudged at her entrance. Her legs fell apart in response. Needing no further encouragement, with his glittering green eyes locked on hers, Vaughan thrust his hips forward and plunged into her warmth. She gasped from the impact. It had been so long since they'd been intimate. He stretched her wide as her body adjusted to him, becoming familiar with him once again.

Clinging to his shoulders, she stared up into his eyes. They were bright with desire, love…and something else. Something that looked very much like regret. An answering response rose up inside her, but it was too late to go back. Her body was on fire, crying out for release. So she did the only thing she could do. She closed her eyes and concentrated on the exquisite feelings Vaughan stirred up inside her—had always been able to stir up inside her.

His thrusts became more urgent as his own need reached its peak. She dug her nails into his shoulders, her breaths coming fast. They reached the pinnacle at the same time and climaxed together. Vaughan collapsed against her, panting hard. It was a long time before they both caught their breath enough to speak. Vaughan was the first one to break the silence.

"Ruby, I…"

She pressed a finger against his lips. "*Shh*. Not now. Please, can we just enjoy this moment, call a temporary truce?"

He looked like he wanted to argue, but in the end, he merely sighed and gathered her into his arms. With her head on his chest, she allowed herself a sad, trembling smile. There was so much left unsaid between them. This wasn't a reconciliation. She couldn't expect him to forgive her that easily. But it was a start. She clung to that thought and fell asleep feeling more at ease than she had since the day they'd met.

When Ruby woke the next morning, she was alone. Stifling the burst of disappointment, she climbed out of bed and padded to the bathroom. She found a note from Vaughan on the sink.

I'm sorry, Ruby. I guess I'm not yet ready for this... I'm sorry.

She stared down at the note and fought back a rush of tears. She'd already suspected Vaughan was far from being in a place where he could accept the things she'd done. But she refused to regret the night they'd spent together. She loved him with everything she had. A night spent with him was something she'd cherish forever. And one day, who knew? She refused to give up hope that they might get back together. Not after last night.

Maybe it was foolish to cling to that kind of hope, but she couldn't help it. A saner, more sensible, Ruby would dismiss that kind of silliness out of hand and force herself to come to terms with the fact that Vaughan was lost to her forever and the sooner she accepted it, the better. But right now, she didn't feel like being sensible and the hormones that flooded her veins held her captive on a rollercoaster of emotions. Every time she thought about Vaughan, she wanted to cry.

She grimaced at her reflection in the mirror. Her face was pale and dark shadows were visible beneath her eyes. On top of that, her hair was a tangled mess. With a weary sigh, she took a shower and dressed for the office. She smoothed her skirt over her slightly protruding bump, grateful Vaughan hadn't noticed.

She was immediately beset by guilt. He was the father. He had a right to know. Except she still didn't know what she planned to do about the pregnancy. Was it fair to tell him about the baby when she might opt for a termination?

She closed her eyes briefly against a wave of despair. If only she had a magic wand to wave that would miraculously give her the answers she needed and take all the uncertainty and turmoil away. She was so tired, so lethargic. So fuzzy about everything. At least the nausea of the past ten weeks had finally eased. She might even be able to hold down some breakfast.

The streets outside her apartment were crowded with people heading to work. She wondered what time Vaughan had left and whether he'd had time to return to his place in Bondi, or whether he'd gone straight to the office. And then she silently castigated herself.

I need to stop thinking about him... One night together doesn't mean anything... He's not ready... He might never be ready... I need to give him space...

The distressing thoughts circled through her mind, driving her crazy. With a sound of impatience, she squeezed her eyes tightly shut for a moment and then opened them again. She tilted her head and peered up at the bright blue sky. It was clear and cloudless. The kind of perfect summer day Sydney was famous for.

The sun sparkled like diamonds off Sydney Harbour, putting on a spectacular show for the tourists that were already filling the boardwalk that ran along Circular Quay and all the way to the Opera House. They were iconic Sydney landmarks and Ruby didn't blame the tourists for wanting to get up close to them. The views of the harbor from both places were stunning.

But even the magnificent day couldn't dislodge the dread and foreboding that continued to weigh her down whenever she thought about her baby. As much as her instinct was to keep it, she had to be sensible and canvass all options. With Vaughan out of the picture, perhaps a termination was the best way to go? He need never know about the baby. They could both get on with their lives. It sounded like the most logical decision. So, why didn't she feel ready to accept that option?

Sighing quietly, she shifted her handbag to a more comfortable position and began to walk to the nearest bus stop. While she waited for the next one to arrive, she pulled out her phone and started checking emails. She glanced up idly at one point and her gaze became riveted on a sign that hung from a building on the opposite side of the road.

Women's Health Medical Clinic.

The glass frontage was covered in colorful posters depicting all aspects of women's health, including reproductive issues.

It was possible they also provided support for women in her situation. She checked for an oncoming bus, but there were none to be seen. The traffic lights changed, bringing a halt to the traffic. Making a spontaneous decision, she gripped the straps of her handbag more tightly and crossed over with the other pedestrians.

A few yards down the street and she was there. Outside the clinic. Her heart pounded. Her chest went tight. But she held on to her courage and pushed open the glass front door. A middle-aged woman with gray hair and kind eyes smiled in greeting from her position behind a reception desk.

"Good morning. Is there anything I can do for you?"

Ruby managed a semblance of a smile. "I... I'm not sure."

"Do you have an appointment?"

"No. I... I'm after some information. On pregnancy terminations," she said in a rush.

The woman's kindly expression didn't change. "Of course." She pushed away from her chair and opened the door to a cupboard that stood behind her. She reached in and drew out a handful of brochures and then passed them over the counter.

"Here you go. Hopefully you'll find answers to your questions in there. If you'd like to talk to someone about it, I can make an appointment for you to see one of our staff."

Ruby took the brochures and blindly shoved them in her handbag. Her heart still thumped. Breathing remained difficult. She wasn't sure she was ready to talk to anyone.

Somehow, telling someone she was pregnant and actually having a conversation about her options made the situation much too real. It was cowardly to continue to put off the decision, but right now, anything more was beyond her.

"N-no. Thank you. I... I'll see you later."

With face flaming, she turned abruptly and pulled open the door. She stepped out onto the footpath and started to walk blindly through the crowds. A bus pulled up and people streamed through its doors. Pedestrians pushed and shoved, all in a hurry to reach their destination.

"Excuse me. I'm sorry. Please, let me through."

The words fell from her lips like she was on autopilot. Her mind rocked with thoughts of the clinic and the brochures that now seemed to weigh like a ton of bricks in her handbag. As the crowds swelled around her, she was overcome with panic. Spinning on her heel, she abruptly changed direction and collided with a warm, hard chest.

"Oh, I'm sorry. Are you all right?"

The deep voice was pure male and strikingly familiar. With foreboding sinking like stones in her stomach, she looked up and gasped in shock.

Vaughan.

Oh, no. Not again. I don't think I can handle seeing him again so soon. Not after last night...

Vaughan looked just as surprised as she was. Heat burst across her face. For an instant, she was tempted to brush past him and continue on her way as if she hadn't noticed it was him, but that would be childish. Besides, there was no way she could pretend she hadn't seen him or that they hadn't been together the night before.

She shot him a nervous smile. "Vaughan." She prided herself on her steady tone.

A flush stained his cheeks. He shifted uncomfortably. His gaze glanced off hers before it landed somewhere over her shoulder. Her heart sank.

He can't even look me in the eye...

"Ruby. I... I didn't expect to see you again so soon."

She merely shrugged. "I got your note."

His blush deepened. His gaze shifted to his feet. "Yes. Um... I'm sorry. I..."

She reached out and touched his arm. "It's okay, Vaughan. I understand."

He cursed under his breath. "Hell, Ruby. I should never have come to your apartment. It wasn't fair. On either of us. I miss you, want you, but then I think about what you did, how you deceived me for so long, and I don't know that I can ever trust you again. Without trust, we have nothing."

His words came out in a rush, as if they'd been holed up inside him for too long and now that they'd been given release, there was no way to stop them. Though every word he uttered only served to drive even more nails into her heart, she understood. She'd hurt him deeply, inflicted so much pain there was a very real chance he might never get over it. And that was on her. She was overwhelmed with regret.

Her chest went so tight it was difficult to breathe. Tears burned behind her eyes. Any moment, she would lose it.

I need to get away from here, from Vaughan...

Oblivious to the people passing by, she spun on her heel and stepped away. Almost immediately, someone collided with her shoulder, half dislodging her handbag, which she hadn't bothered to close properly. Brochures scattered all over the footpath. She gasped aloud. The faceless stranger muttered an apology and kept going. She squatted and hurriedly began picking up the pamphlets.

"Here. Let me help you."

Vaughan was there beside her, crouching low, his expression resigned. She snatched up the brochures, wanting desperately to keep them away from his prying eyes. And then he had one in his hand and as he glanced down at it, his eyes widened with shock.

Her stomach dropped. She trembled, unable to look at him, willing silently for him to just let it go. She should have known better. When she finally found the courage to look at him, his furious eyes bored into hers.

"What the hell? You're *pregnant?*"

Chapter Twelve

Vaughan's mind momentarily went blank with shock. He'd only caught a glimpse of one of the brochures, but it was enough for him to register the content and from the look of guilt that swiftly flooded Ruby's face, his guess had been correct. His heart hammered. He stared at her in disbelief.

With eyes downcast, she nodded. His gut somersaulted in response. Then anger took hold.

"When were you going to tell me?" he rasped. And then another thought took hold. "*Were* you going to tell me, or were you just going to get rid of it without saying a word?"

Ruby's cheeks were pasty. She looked like she was going to be sick. "Not here," she croaked.

Ignoring a burst of concern, he kept pace with her as she pushed her way through the crowds and made a beeline for a nearby café. She half-stumbled into a seat at an outdoor table and set her handbag by her feet with the brochures out of sight. He sat down opposite.

After a moment, he allowed himself to ask. "Are you all right?"

She drew in a shaky breath. She still looked way too pale for his liking, but he was relieved when she nodded.

"I'm fine."

With an effort, he reined in his shock and anger. Neither would help him right now. He pitched his voice low and cast around for some calm.

"Talk to me, Ruby."

Ruby closed her eyes to ward off a wave of emotion. Her nerves were stretched beyond tight. Never in her wildest imagining could she have envisioned Vaughan finding out this way. It was obvious he was shocked and angry. She understood his response. As she'd stumbled toward the café, she'd braced herself for his onslaught. Instead, he'd enquired after her. The tenderness in his gaze put her off-kilter. She didn't know what to think.

Drawing in another deep breath, she eased it out on a weary sigh. Her shoulders slumped in defeat. It was probably for the best that he'd found out accidentally; that the decision whether to tell him or not was out of her hands. She was actually a little relieved that the truth was out there and they could discuss it.

She dragged in a ragged breath and looked at him. "I'm ten weeks pregnant. It must have happened when I was taking antibiotics for that flu I had. They can interfere with the pill's effectiveness. I'm sorry. I didn't plan for this to happen."

Vaughan waved away her words with an impatient movement of his hand. "Of course you didn't plan it. That thought never entered my mind. But, Ruby... Hell... Ten weeks? You've known for ten weeks? When were you going to tell me?"

"I haven't *known* for ten weeks. I only found out a couple of weeks ago. I guess with everything that's been going on, I wasn't thinking too much about myself. I hadn't realized my period was so late. When I did, I took a test. I've also had an ultrasound that confirmed I was eight weeks pregnant."

Vaughan stared at her, his eyes wide with shock. The tenderness disappeared from his eyes and anger flickered back to life. "You've already had an ultrasound? And you didn't tell me? Were you *ever* going to tell me?"

She fought back a rush of tears. She hated that she was so emotionally fragile. Normally she was the strong one in difficult situations. Cool, calm and collected. Able to keep her head. But the hormones were wreaking havoc and there was nothing she could do about it.

She shook her head. "I don't know! I don't know if I was going to tell you, okay? It's all I've been able to think about these past couple of weeks. I've gone back and forth over all the options, including whether or not to tell you. It's been driving me crazy! I still don't know what I'm going to do."

Vaughan opened his mouth and looked like he was about to say something. His expression was a combination of anger and disbelief. He gripped the table, his body tense. She could see the effort it took for him to hold on to his temper.

Then he drew in a deep breath. When he finally spoke, his voice had an edge to it but was calm.

"Can we at least talk about it? This is my baby, too."

She shook her head in confusion. "We're no longer in a relationship, Vaughan. Put aside last night. Whatever that was. You hate me. You told me you never wanted to see me again. What would be the point of bringing a baby into that kind of situation? A baby deserves better than that."

A waitress appeared to take their order, but one dark look from Vaughan and she made a quick retreat. His gaze returned to Ruby. He pitched his voice low.

"I never said I hated you. And just because we aren't together doesn't mean we can't raise this baby as co-parents. It's not ideal, but people do it all the time."

She looked at him. "So, you wouldn't want to get married for the sake of the baby?"

She held her breath as she waited for his answer, even though she was pretty sure what it would be. Vaughan had been raised with old-fashioned values. He'd also spent the first eleven years of his life as an orphan, being moved from one foster home to another. From the little he'd told her about it, that time had been terrible. A nightmare that had only ended when he'd been adopted.

He'd want his own child to know both of its parents and he'd want to provide a safe and secure home for it. But she didn't want him to stay with her out of obligation. She couldn't bear knowing he was by her side only because of the baby.

A raucous seagull squawked nearby, startling her from her reverie. She blinked and drew in another shaky breath. Vaughan cursed softly and scrubbed his hands through his hair.

"Of course, I'd want to get married. You know about my past. Having a child growing up without me, or sharing custody, only being able to spend time with my own kid on allotted days... I hate the very thought of all that. But I'm very aware I might not get a choice. After all, I can't force you to marry me."

She pressed her lips together in an effort to hold back a rush of emotion. It was exactly as she'd thought. Vaughan would marry her out of a sense of obligation. He might not hate her, but he didn't love her, either. He was prepared to do the right thing and stand by her for the sake of their child. She could imagine how miserable they both would be, knowing that was the only reason they were together. There was no way she could live like that, and she suspected Vaughan couldn't either.

He hadn't been given enough time to process everything. He was merely acting out of instinct. Though she loved and admired him for wanting to do the honorable thing, when he took the time to think things through, he'd see how impossible it was to marry only for the sake of their baby. He said he didn't hate her now, but over time he'd end up resenting her for putting him in that situation and then the hate would come and the love she felt for him now would slowly, but surely die. That wasn't a good future for anyone.

No, all she could do was to try and convince him that the only sensible thing to do was for her to either go this alone or terminate the pregnancy. Taking hold of her courage, she looked him in the eye.

"I need more time to think about everything. Decide what I'm going to do."

His expression turned earnest. "I understand how difficult this must be for you, Ruby, and I hate that you've had to deal with this alone. For what it's worth, I want to keep the baby. I really do. Somehow, we'll figure things out."

"But your note. You said—"

"I know what I said, but that was before I knew about the baby. Please, Ruby. Don't say anything else right now. This is a big decision. I don't want to put any pressure on you, but please, promise me you won't make any decision about this alone."

She held his gaze for a long moment. Hope that maybe they could raise the baby together flared briefly inside her, followed almost immediately by common sense. She already knew the reasons why that wouldn't work. Still, he was the father and the least she could do was to keep him informed.

"Okay. I promise. Whatever I decide, I'll talk to you about it before I make any final decision."

Some of the tension left his face. He nodded. "Thank you."

Ruby chewed on her bottom lip. The fact Vaughan wanted to keep the baby filled her with a spark of hope, but was that the best thing for everyone, including their unborn child?

Once again, she wished for someone or something to step in and make the decision. While the commonsense part of her brain told her the most logical thing would be to terminate the pregnancy, knowing how much she loved Vaughan meant that she wasn't sure she could bring herself to end the part of him that was growing inside her. And there was always the tiny chance that one day Vaughan would find it in his heart to forgive her and they'd reconcile.

The more she thought about it, the more she realized she wanted to keep the baby, too. Women raised babies on their own all the time and this baby's father was interested in being around, at least some of the time. At least he didn't hate her. Or said he didn't. That was a start, but she'd always thought a baby needed two parents who loved each other. Security, safety, all the things she and Vaughan didn't have. Things she'd lately discovered she wanted. Badly.

A surge of pain and yearning washed over her. She'd royally messed things up. She wanted nothing more than to turn back time and shower Vaughan with all the love and devotion she now felt for him. She wanted desperately to regain his love; to share a future with him. If only she knew how.

Vaughan passed by Casey's desk on his way back to his office. Thankfully, she'd greeted him with her customary friendliness when he'd arrived earlier that morning. He was glad there were no hard feelings or that things weren't weird between them.

"Vaughan! In my office."

His father issued the order in a no-nonsense tone. Vaughan frowned, wondering what had happened. He didn't have to wait long to find out.

"What the hell were you thinking, taking Casey out on a date? I thought I made it clear she's off limits to you."

Nerves fluttered in Vaughan's stomach. He stepped farther into the room and closed the door behind him. "What did she tell you?"

"Everything! She's my EA. We're close. Aside from your mother, she knows me better than anyone. We don't keep secrets from each other."

Vaughan drew in a breath and sighed. "First of all, it wasn't a date."

Frank eyeballed him. "You asked her out for a drink. What else would you call it?"

Vaughan lowered his gaze. "Okay, it was a date. But so what? She's single and so am I. I don't see what the problem is."

"The problem is what I told you yesterday. A few weeks ago, you were in love with someone else; engaged to be married, no less. You're on the rebound, Vaughan, whether you're smart enough to recognize that or not. I won't have you messing with my EA. Not only is she a valuable asset to this company, I care about her. She's like a daughter to me. I don't want to see her get hurt." His gaze bored into Vaughan's. "Do you understand?"

Vaughan stared right back at him, refusing to be intimidated. "Yes, Dad. I understand. But there's no need for you to worry. There's nothing going on between me and Casey. She's a great girl, but... She's not for me."

His father eyed him speculatively. "I see. Still hooked up on the Rodriguez girl."

"No!" Vaughan's response was instant. Then his shoulders slumped on another sigh. "Fuck. I don't know. I loved Ruby with every fiber of my being, Dad! I wanted to spend the rest of my life with her. And all the time, she was deceiving me. She never loved me at all." He blew out his breath. "Now she's pregnant."

"*What?*"

Vaughan looked up. His father appeared just as shocked as Vaughan had felt when he'd realized. He nodded grimly. "Yep. Ten weeks, apparently."

"Is it yours?"

Vaughan gasped, appalled. "Dad! How could you ask such a thing?"

Frank merely shrugged and crossed his arms over his chest. "We both know how dishonest she can be. How do you know she wasn't cheating on you with someone else?"

Vaughan shook his head. "No. There's no way she'd have done that. You don't understand. We lived together for months. We'd pledged our lives to each other. The only reason we didn't make it official in Bali was because Ruby wanted to wait and get married in Sydney, so her family could be there to help celebrate."

His father's expression turned thoughtful. "Do you really believe that?"

Vaughan frowned, remembering his earlier reservations. "I don't know."

"Maybe she kept putting off the ceremony because she never intended to marry you and she merely agreed to your proposal to buy herself time. After all, she was there on a mission to get close to you in the hope of eliciting family secrets that might help her father in some way. She admitted that, didn't she?"

Vaughan nodded reluctantly. "Yeah. She did."

The more he thought about it, the more Vaughan realized his father was right. During all the time they'd been together in Bali, Ruby had never once told him she loved him, not even when he proposed. She'd thrown herself in his arms and had kissed him senseless and then they'd ended up making love, but those three words hadn't escaped her lips, not even when he said them.

He hadn't thought too much about it at the time. He was in love and he was certain she was too. What did it matter that she hadn't said the words? Not everyone demonstrated their feelings that way. He could tell from the way she smiled at him, touched him, made love to him that she had deep feelings for him. That had been enough. Now he saw things all too clearly.

She'd never been in love with him. That's why she'd never said the words. The first time he'd heard them had been in the hospital in Sydney when he'd told her they were over. No doubt she'd panicked, realizing the plan she'd hatched with her father was about to unravel. Vaughan didn't know what kind of a reward she'd been promised if she came up with the goods, but no doubt it had been worth her while. No wonder she'd gotten desperate when he'd called things off.

He didn't want to consider the possibility that she'd cheated on him, but how could he know for sure? Though everything inside him rebelled at the thought, it was now clear that the Ruby he thought he'd known in Bali wasn't that woman at all. He hated that his father had planted the seed of doubt, but now that he had, there was nothing Vaughan could do to dislodge it. He had to know for sure.

"What are you going to do about the baby?" his father asked gruffly.

Vaughan compressed his lips, filled with determination. "First, I'm going to make sure it's mine. After that, I guess I'll have to let Ruby decide. She knows I want to keep it. We've talked about it. She promised not to make any decision without me."

Frank nodded. "I guess that's the best you can hope for."

Chapter Thirteen

Ruby took the rest of the day off. As much as she wanted to stay busy to keep her mind off Vaughan and the decision that continued to weigh heavily on her mind, her emotions were in so much of an uproar she could cause her co-workers alarm. After leaving the café, she walked the short distance back to her apartment. Letting herself in, she kicked off her shoes and made her way down the hallway to the open-plan kitchen and living room.

The marble tiles were deliciously cool beneath her bare feet. It was barely nine o'clock, but already the day held the promise of summer heat. Thank goodness for the ocean breeze that blew in across her balcony through the open sliding door.

She dropped her handbag on the kitchen counter and caught a glimpse of the offending brochures peeking out as she did so. If only Vaughan hadn't come along at that exact moment. He'd have never been any the wiser. But she couldn't bring herself to feel disappointed that he knew. He was the baby's father. Though some people might disagree with her, he had a right to know.

He'd told her he wanted to keep it. That somehow, they'd work things out. She ought to be thrilled he felt that way, and she would have been if his feelings for her hadn't changed from when they were together. At thirty-six, her biological clock was ticking. It wasn't that she'd never wanted to have kids, but bringing a child into the world under these circumstances... Was it fair to any of them?

Before her thoughts could do that circle once again, she pulled open the fridge and reached for a bottle of chilled white wine. Her hand hovered over it and then she opted for a bottle of water instead.

What does it matter if I'm getting rid of it?

The fact that she'd chosen to avoid alcohol was telling. She'd done the same thing the night before, with Matthew. She didn't have to be a genius to understand what her subconscious was telling her: She wanted to keep the baby.

It was as if a burden had been lifted off her shoulders. Just like that, she was lighter, happier, more at ease. Her hand cupped the small bump in her abdomen and she was flooded with warmth.

My baby. I'm going to be a mom...

During the occasional times over the years when she'd given parenthood a thought, she'd always imagined raising a child with the man she loved. That she'd be safe and secure in a committed relationship, preferably marriage. She might have been raised in modern times, but she had a great deal of respect for the institution.

Though her parents' marriage was less than ideal, they were still together and had been that way for more than forty years. Vaughan's parents were also good role models for marriage. He'd told her they'd been together a long time. Could co-parenting with Vaughan actually work?

Twisting the cap off the bottle of water, she took a couple of sips and then headed for the balcony. Stepping outside, she lifted her head and breathed in the clean, salty air. The balcony was her favorite spot in the apartment. It was large enough to fit a couple of deck chairs and a small drinks table and afforded a spectacular view of the Harbour Bridge. With a sigh, she dropped into a deck chair, took another sip of water, then closed her eyes.

The sound of her phone ringing disturbed the silence. With a groan, she stood and slipped back inside. She'd left her phone in her handbag. By the time she reached it, she'd braced herself for it to go to voicemail and was almost tempted to let it do so. Then she checked the screen and her heart skipped a beat.

Vaughan.

What now? I told him I need time to think... It's barely been an hour...

She groaned under her breath and answered the call.

"Ruby."

His curt tone took her aback. She frowned. "Vaughan?"

He cleared his throat. "I'm sorry, but I have to ask. Am I the father?"

Her shock almost rendered her speechless. Surprise was quickly followed by anger. "*What?*"

"Given your art for deception, I need to be sure."

Heat infused her face, setting her cheeks on fire. Any moment, she could combust. "How *dare* you, Vaughan Barrington. Go to hell."

With that, she stabbed at the phone, ending the call. Then the hurt set in and the tears fell in earnest. She made it all the way to the couch before she collapsed on it and curled up in a ball.

Damn you, Vaughan Barrington!

If only she hadn't fallen in love with him! Then his insinuation wouldn't hurt so much. Okay, so she'd deceived him about a lot of things in Bali, but the idea she might have cheated on him... It was the biggest insult he could have leveled at her. So what if she'd been less forthcoming about who she was and what her real reasons were for being in Bali. That faded into insignificance when compared to his implied accusation.

How could he have spent all those months with her, been as intimate with her as anyone could be, profess his love for her, propose marriage, and yet not know her at all? She was incapable of two-timing him. He should know that, at least.

Yes. I lied to him about who I was... Yes. I wasn't upfront about my reasons for being there...or that our meeting in Bali was anything but chance...

But then she'd gotten to know him. She'd spent all those wonderful months in Bali, hanging out together, having fun, making love...

No. As painful as the situation she now found herself in, she wouldn't regret an instant of her time with Vaughan. She'd fallen in love with a good, kind, and caring man. A man who made her laugh. A man who could make her pulse leap with nothing more than a look. It was too bad that by the time she realized how much he meant to her, it was too late.

Staring down at the phone in his hand, Vaughan cursed. He wasn't surprised at Ruby's reaction to his question. After all, he'd accused her of cheating. The woman he'd fallen in love with could never have done such a thing.

But that's the problem. I don't know who the real Ruby Ashworth is. Everything I thought I knew about her turned out to be a lie...

Except, there were some things she couldn't have lied about. Her kindness, her goodness, her compassion. He recalled many times in Denpasar when they'd go to the markets, or just out for a walk. Inevitably, they'd come across groups of rag-tag children playing barefoot in the streets. Ruby never failed to stop to talk to them. She'd urge him to go and buy food from a nearby vendor and then she'd offer it to the kids.

It happened so often, they used to wait for her, calling out her name when they spied her coming toward them, following her around. She never once lost her patience with them, or told them to go away, and she always left them a little better off, mostly by giving them food, but sometimes she'd buy them clothing or shoes, or toys.

She'd done that the entire time he'd known her. Small acts of kindness, offered freely to strangers. There'd been nothing in it for her but the satisfaction of helping someone in need.

Maybe she was trying to impress me? Another way to get closer to me, to get me to drop my guard...

The insidious thought crept in, but he irritably pushed it away. If her decency and kindness had all been an act, he would have seen cracks in the façade. They'd been together for months and in all that time, she'd never given him cause to suspect it was all smoke and mirrors; that none of it was real. No one could be that good of an actress. And he refused to accept he was that bad a judge of character.

Yes. Ruby had her flaws—lying to him about who she was and her reason for being in Bali—but that didn't negate all her good qualities. No one was perfect. Certainly not him. She'd lied to help her father. He could understand that motivation. Family was important to him, too. It wasn't her fault that her loyalty toward a snake like Joseph Rodriguez was misplaced. He was her father. Naturally, she'd trust his word.

Now she was pregnant. Deep down, Vaughan was certain the baby was his. It had been churlish of him to even ask the question. If the thought hadn't been put into his head by his father, it would never have occurred to him to ask.

Not that he blamed his father. He understood Frank's concern, but his father didn't know Ruby. Not like he did. That's why he'd fallen in love with her.

Unbidden, his thoughts turned to Elizabeth Craigdon. He'd been so quick to judge her for putting him up for adoption, he hadn't stopped to really consider all the circumstances or to put himself in her place. She'd been young and single. Back then, single mothers were frowned upon, judged; many were cast out by their families. She'd told him her parents had refused to let her keep him and he'd dismissed her words as if they didn't matter.

But they did matter, and it shamed him to admit he should have held on to his temper and invited her to tell him more about that difficult time.

Ruby was pregnant with his baby. He now realized what that meant to him. How much he wanted her to have it. How powerless he felt knowing the ultimate decision was hers.

What about his biological father? The man must have known about the pregnancy. How had he felt about it? Had he urged Elizabeth to go through with the pregnancy, or had he abandoned her in her hour of need? Vaughan couldn't imagine giving up his child, no matter what.

Everything was so unclear. He wanted to talk to Elizabeth again. Get the full story. Refrain from judging her—or his biological father—until he knew everything. Nothing was as black and white as he'd thought. She could have chosen to abort him, and yet she hadn't. Getting a termination back then wouldn't have been as easy as it was today, but the practice had gone on. Okay, so she hadn't kept him, but she'd given him life. That meant something.

With a sigh, he leaned back in his chair and scrubbed his hands through his hair. When had his life gotten so complicated? He had to talk to Elizabeth again and this time, he needed to come with an open heart and truly listen.

Elizabeth sipped from her tall glass of iced tea before relaxing back against the pool lounge. Summer was in full swing and the mid-afternoon sun had a decent sting to it. In fact, she'd not long climbed out of the pool. The crystal-clear water had been cool and refreshing and just what she needed to lighten her low spirits.

She'd been feeling down ever since her visit from Vaughan. She'd suspected from his silence over the past year that her revelation she was his biological mother hadn't been met with enthusiasm. Having that suspicion confirmed in such a harsh way had been difficult. His out of hand dismissal of her efforts to explain had been worse, and she was now at a loss about what to do. Archie had urged her to let things lie and hope Vaughan might come round, but not knowing if he was ever going to get to that point was distressing.

Setting the glass aside, she closed her eyes and sighed. A wide-brimmed, floppy hat and sunglasses protected her face from the worst of the sun's harsh rays. Her one-piece bathing suit was still damp from her recent dip, but it wouldn't be long before it was dry and she'd be forced to dive back into the pool again to stay cool.

Not that she minded. She'd always loved to swim. It was one of the things she did regularly in order to stay trim and fit. At her age, swimming was the perfect exercise. It didn't put any strain on her joints and yet, was an excellent source of cardio. Archie also enjoyed the pool.

Right now, he was in the city, going over the details of a new investment opportunity with his sons, Logan, Noah, and Flynn. As it turned out, Logan was the biological son of Archie's brother. That recently discovered, shocking revelation hadn't changed the way Archie thought about Logan. As far as Archie was concerned, Logan was and always would be his son.

Logan felt the same. It gave Elizabeth hope Vaughan might also come around in his thinking and that somehow, he'd find it in his heart to forgive her and accept the role she'd played in his life. She never wanted to try and replace his mother. It was obvious Evelyn Barrington had done a wonderful job raising him. But she longed to have some small recognition; a tiny acknowledgement that he was grateful for her decision to go through with the pregnancy, despite the fact she hadn't kept him. She hoped he'd eventually make a miniscule place in his heart for her.

No, that was too much to ask. She couldn't realistically expect him to accept her and open his heart to her as the woman who'd given him life, but she wasn't yet ready to give up all hope. He'd come to her, after all, to raise the issue of his birth. He could have stayed away forever, never acknowledged the truth of what she'd written him; never allowed himself to even think about it again. And yet he had come to her. She clung to that. A foolish hope it might be, but it was hope, just the same.

"Elizabeth?"

At Amy's call, she sat up with a start. "I'm beside the pool, Amy."

The housekeeper appeared a few moments later. "You have a visitor. It's Vaughan Barrington."

Elizabeth's heart stuttered in shock and then raced away, pounding so hard she thought it might leap right out of her chest. She pressed a hand against her breastbone in an effort to contain it.

"Vaughan's here?" she croaked.

"Yes. Would you like me to show him in?"

"Y-yes," Elizabeth stammered, still filled with disbelief. Though she'd longed to see him again and be given another opportunity to explain, she hadn't imagined he might return so soon. She looked briefly heavenward.

Thank you, God...

Scrambling off the lounger, she reached for her towel and wrapped it around herself. She patted her still-damp hair.

I look a mess...

She thought briefly of taking a few minutes to hurry upstairs and change and tidy up, but didn't want to risk Vaughan leaving. She had no idea why he'd returned so soon after his last visit and she wasn't going to take any chances that he might suddenly change his mind.

"Show him into the music room please, Amy."

The housekeeper nodded and disappeared on silent, rubber-soled feet. Elizabeth drew in a deep breath and took a moment to settle her equilibrium as best she could. She didn't want to read too much into Vaughan's unexpected appearance, but she couldn't help the burst of hope that filled her with warmth deep inside.

Careful... I don't want to get my expectations up or put any pressure on him... Cool, calm and collected. That's the way to approach this. Deep breaths. Cool and calm. Now, smile...

Vaughan stood with his back to her. He'd lifted the lid on the black baby grand piano and idly ran his fingers over the keys. She cleared her throat to get his attention. He turned immediately.

Her heart clenched. Her smile widened. "Vaughan! It's good to see you again!"

Chapter Fourteen

Vaughan frowned momentarily at Elizabeth. Her face was alight with hope and expectation. He cursed silently under his breath for arriving unannounced. Though he'd gone there in order to smooth things over, he had no intention of letting her into his life. But neither did he want to hurt her.

Damn it! I should have done this over the phone. That way I could have kept the conversation short and to the point and I wouldn't have to look at her and feel guilty about not giving her what she wants...

It was too late now. He was already there. The only thing to do was to get it over with as quickly as he could and leave.

"Hello, Elizabeth. You're looking well."

He grimaced at the inane comment. In fact, she looked a little bedraggled. She wore a plain black swimsuit and had wrapped herself in a striped towel. Her damp hair hung limply around her face. She looked nothing like the well-groomed, elegant older woman he'd met the first time.

She offered him a wry smile. "We both know that's not true. I've been swimming. It's so hot outside. Still, you have the most immaculate manners. A testament to the wonderful job your parents did on your upbringing. You're a credit to them. They must be very proud."

Her voice was thick with emotion. He caught a glimpse of a tear in her eye. He swallowed. It couldn't be easy for her to face the reality of all she'd given up when she signed the adoption papers. All the milestones she'd missed. Still, that wasn't his problem. She'd been the one to make the decision, no matter what led her to make it and what she said about not having any choice.

"Please, take a seat," she said, indicating the pale blue, velvet-upholstered three-seater.

He did as she asked. She dropped carefully into the matching armchair opposite. She offered him another over-bright smile. "So, what brings you here?"

"I want to apologize," he said without preamble.

She blinked in surprise. Once again, hope flared in her eyes. He reflexively held up a hand in an effort to ward it off.

"Don't get me wrong. I'm not here to get into another discussion about why you gave me up. It's just that... I found out something recently. The details aren't important, but it made me think differently about a few things." He dragged in a breath. "You didn't have to go through with my birth. You had other options. You might not have wanted to keep me, but at least you gave me a chance at life. I... I want to thank you for that."

Elizabeth swallowed and then teared up. She pressed a wrinkled hand against her mouth, as if trying to hold her emotions in. Vaughan wished he could remain unmoved by her response, but he wasn't made of stone and the woman seated across from him was the reason he was alive.

"Th-thank you," she stammered, her voice hoarse. "You'll never know how much I regret bowing to the pressure from my parents and giving you up." She paused and then added, "You look so much like him. Your father. David Mason. Your blond hair, albeit a little darker. Your green eyes, your strong jawline... The moment I saw you in Christopher's hospital room all those months ago, I knew you were my son. It was like I'd been transported back forty years." She let out a shaky breath and slowly shook her head. "It still spins me out to look at you."

Vaughan tried hard to tamp down his interest, but it was impossible. "Tell me about him."

Elizabeth was quiet for a while. She clasped her hands together, then tucked them into her lap. Her face took on a faraway expression. Finally, she spoke.

"I was nineteen when I fell pregnant. David was twenty-two. I think I mentioned before that we were both studying at the Conservatorium of Music. I played the piano. David played the violin." She sighed softly. "He was a maestro. It was like listening to angels sing.

"You can probably imagine my parents' reaction. Or maybe you can't. Things were different back then. Single mothers were shunned. Good girls from good families didn't have babies out of wedlock. It's just the way it was."

"Did you ever consider an abortion?" Vaughan asked. He held his breath while he waited for her answer.

She emphatically shook her head from side to side. "No."

He gave her a skeptical look. "Not once?"

"Never. I was raised a Catholic. An abortion was out of the question and even if it wasn't, I'd never have considered it. I loved you from the very first moment I realized I was pregnant. I loved your father with all my heart and soul. Okay, so I was nineteen and innocent. He was my first boyfriend. What did I know of love? But at the time, I thought he'd hung the moon and stars. Though I understood the difficulties confronting us, in particular having to deal with the disapproval of my parents, I was ecstatic we were going to have a baby."

Vaughan grimaced. Elizabeth could talk about how much she'd loved him as long as she liked, the fact was she'd given him up at birth. Nothing changed that.

"What did my father think?"

Elizabeth's face fell. She averted her gaze. "Unfortunately, he wasn't quite so enthusiastic about the idea. I had to leave the conservatorium, of course, and that was my only way to see him. My parents wouldn't allow him to come around and there was no other way for us to meet."

She smiled wryly. "You have to remember, there were no mobile phones in those days and only one phone in our house. David didn't have a phone at all. I sent him a few letters, but

I never received a response. The one and only time he wrote to me was to tell me he was breaking things off. His workload at the conservatorium was demanding. He couldn't afford the distraction of fighting for me and our love. He made no mention of you."

She twisted her hands in her lap. Her breath caught on a soft sigh. "I didn't blame him. I understood exactly how demanding a position at the conservatorium was."

Anger stirred inside Vaughan. "You're letting him off too lightly. He was as responsible for your pregnancy as you were."

Elizabeth looked at him. She compressed her lips and shrugged. "I understand how you might feel that way. Over the years, there have been times when I looked back and realized David could have tried harder, proposed—anything to fight for us. But he was young and completely invested in his career and, dare I say it, selfish and weak and obviously not as in love with me as I'd thought."

Vaughan fought against a wave of compassion. He didn't want to feel sorry for this woman, but it was hard not to commiserate with her circumstances. She'd been young and naïve; unceremoniously dumped by a man she'd been in love with; a man she'd entrusted with her heart. A man she'd thought loved her enough to protect her, take care of her, and their unborn baby. Him. It was slightly surreal to realize they were talking about *him*.

"Did he ever come and see me?"

Elizabeth sighed quietly and slowly shook her head. "No. I'm not even sure he knew you'd been born. By that time, it had been months since I'd seen him. I assumed he was still at the conservatorium, but I didn't know for sure. I asked my mother to send word to him, but I don't know if she did. Not that it would have made much difference. I was only given an hour alone with you, and I was your mother. An hour! The time went by so fast!"

Elizabeth's voice cracked. Vaughan's thoughts were in turmoil. His anger found its head. "You talk about how much you loved me; how an hour wasn't enough. But you signed the papers that meant I was out of your life forever. You didn't want the responsibility."

Elizabeth's eyes filled with tears. She nodded sadly. "You're right. Though everything about that time is hazy and I remember everything happening in a rush – being pressured to sign the papers by my parents; being told by the nurse that it was for the best, not only for me, but for my baby.

"But I've had forty years to think about my decision; to turn it over and over in my head. To wonder if I could have done things differently; kept you and raised you on my own." She lifted a tortured gaze to his. "And the truth is, perhaps I could have. I was twenty. Like you said, hardly a child, despite the fact I'd been protected and coddled all those years and had never lived on my own. I didn't know the first thing about raising a baby. I had no money, no job."

Vaughan opened his mouth, but she waved his words away.

"Of course, I could have overcome those obstacles. I was young and healthy and smart. I could have made it work. But I was scared and weak and a coward. I took the easy way out." She gave a humorless laugh. "Oh yes. It was so easy. I spent the next forty years mourning your loss. Thinking about you every day. Praying you were happy. Thriving with a family that loved you. I couldn't bear to think that things might not have worked out for the best for you, like everyone had promised."

She cleared her throat, her voice hoarse. "You were taken away from me and I never saw you again. It felt like you'd died. In some ways, it might have been easier if you had."

Vaughan made a sound of distress. Elizabeth hurriedly reassured him.

"I don't mean for that to sound offensive. It's just the way I felt. If you'd died at birth, at least then I would have had closure, a grave to visit. The way it happened, I had nothing. I wasn't allowed to know where you'd gone, or who'd adopted you. All I could do was wonder, and hope and pray. I had to believe you'd been adopted by a loving family. That you were living your best life. That was the only way I survived."

Vaughan shook his head and fought off a wave of bitterness. The first eleven years of his life had been hell and here his mother had been consoling herself that he was living his best life. Tears burned behind his eyes.

As if sensing his distress, Elizabeth looked over at him. Her bottom lip trembled with emotion. He wanted to rail at her, curse her for those awful eleven years, but what was the point?

Nothing would change the fact she'd put him up for adoption and that it had been more than a decade before he was taken in by loving people who provided him with everything he'd yearned for; everything he'd been denied.

In the end, if Elizabeth hadn't signed those papers, he'd never have known his parents. Frank and Evelyn Barrington. The most loving, devoted parents anyone could want. And his brothers and sisters. All eight of them. Not once had they treated him as anything other than a blood relative. That included Christopher.

He'd been twelve when Vaughan joined the family. Old enough to be resentful over an intruder, especially one who vied for their parents' attention. And yet, even Christopher, for all his faults and failings, and with the bitterness and resentment over his own past coloring his every decision, had embraced Vaughan as his brother and welcomed him into the family.

Vaughan had much to be grateful for. He'd been given a life many abandoned children only dreamed of. Okay, so he might not have grown up with his biological parents, but what did that matter in the scheme of things? His adoptive family had been everything he could have hoped. They'd raised him to be the man he was. A man who was good and kind and principled. Who believed in fairness and helping others. Who took people at their word, sometimes to his own detriment.

He thought of Ruby and frowned.

Ruby.

She'd lied to him about who she was and what she'd been doing in Bali, but the truth was, he still loved her. She'd done the wrong thing; betrayed his trust. But who among them was perfect? Certainly not him. Showing up on her doorstep and making love to her not long after he'd told her he never wanted to see her again was testament to that.

His shoulders sagged. It was time to let go of the past. The hurt and betrayal and abandonment by his biological mother. The same hurt and betrayal at the hands of Ruby. If he truly loved her, he'd find it in his heart to forgive her. The same went for Elizabeth. What was done couldn't be undone. All he could do was accept what had happened and move on. If he didn't, he'd be stuck in the past, forever blaming someone else for the fact his life hadn't turned out the way he wanted. He'd grow bitter and twisted and would no doubt end up dying alone.

Is that what I want? Is that the way I want to live the rest of my life?

No!

His response was forceful and immediate. He closed his eyes briefly against that realization and sucked in another breath. He eased it out and slowly opened his eyes. The hurt and pain and anger he'd carried around with him for so long had gone. He was lighter, freer than he'd ever been in his life.

Curious now rather than angry, he looked at Elizabeth. "Why did you wait so long to find me?"

She compressed her lips. "Three years after you were born, I met Henry Craigdon. I never told him about you. I didn't tell anybody. Maybe that was wrong of me, but by then I was doing my best to put your loss behind me. You have to realize, there was no such thing as counseling, no help at all back then. I'd made the decision to give you up and I was never going to see you again. There was no point wallowing in self-pity, although I did that for a while."

She grimaced. "My parents forced me to take a job. It was the best thing they could have done. It gave me a purpose, something to consume my time. I worked in my uncle's accountant's office. That's where I met Henry. We eventually married and had six children. I'm sure you know most of them through Christopher."

Vaughan nodded. "Yes. I'm not sure I've met all the partners, but I know most of your kids. They're good people. You did something right."

He gave her a half-smile, so she understood he bore no grudge against the fact she'd gone on to have other children and had raised them.

Elizabeth smiled softly. "Thank you. I'm very proud of them all." She paused and then added, "As I am of you."

Her gaze was intense and glittered with emotion. He swallowed past the lump in his throat.

"You don't even know me."

Chapter Fifteen

Elizabeth smiled serenely. "That's where you're wrong. From the moment I discovered you were my long-lost son, I was desperate to know everything about you. It wasn't easy getting information out of your family—mostly Christopher—after all, they didn't know why I was making inquiries. I had to be discreet. I didn't know how you would feel about me being your biological mother and I didn't want to make the news public without speaking to you first..."

Vaughan twisted his lips. "And by then I was hiding out in Bali."

Elizabeth winced. "Yes."

"You still haven't told me why you waited forty years to look for me," Vaughan said quietly.

Elizabeth sighed. "I'm sure you're aware, Henry died recently."

"So, then you decided it was time to go looking for me?"

Elizabeth blushed. "Not exactly. Henry died as he lived—selfishly, arrogantly, disrupting as many people's lives as possible. Mine included. I won't go into all the details, but the two years since his death have been difficult. For everyone. A year ago, a man came to my door claiming to be my son. His name was Ashton Walker." She paused and looked at him. "Did Christopher tell you anything about him?"

"No. I haven't discussed any of this with Christopher."

Elizabeth nodded briefly and folded her hands into her lap. "Ashton arrived unannounced and told me he was the son I'd given up for adoption more than forty years ago. He knew enough about me and David that I believed him. He didn't look at all like David, but he had dark hair and blue eyes like me. I just assumed he'd taken after me and not his father."

She paused, as if lost in thought. "The truth is, I wanted to believe him. I was overwhelmed with happiness that I'd finally been given back my son. That I'd been blessed with a chance to get to know him, to be a part of his life. I invited him to stay with me at Craigdon Manor. He moved in that very same night."

"How did your children feel about that?"

She frowned. "Not all of them were so welcoming. A few of them were suspicious. My daughter, Isabella, was especially distrustful." She bit her lip. "I should have listened, but my desperate desire to believe Ashton was my son, blinded me. I treated him like royalty. I showered him with expensive gifts. You don't have to be Einstein to realize I was doing everything I could to make up for putting him up for adoption and to rid myself of forty years of guilt.

"And he was good at reminding me of that fact. Though he said he'd been adopted by a good family and had enjoyed a happy life, he made it clear that didn't make up for not being raised by his biological mother."

"How long was it before you realized he was a fraud?"

She sighed. "I'm ashamed to admit I refused to accept he wasn't the real deal. It was only after some of my children started looking into Ashton's background that I realized I'd been taken for a ride. He was a professional con artist. This wasn't the first time he'd posed as someone's long-lost son." Her voice hitched. "He had no idea, or simply didn't care, how much hurt and pain his actions caused people like me."

Anger flared inside Vaughan. He cursed silently, wishing he could get his hands on this Ashton and give him the thrashing he deserved. To play on the emotions of desperate, guilt-ridden mothers... That was about as low as anyone could go.

"I'm sorry you had to go through that," he said quietly, meaning it. For all the hurt and pain he felt at her abandonment, nobody deserved to be treated like that.

"Thank you," she whispered. "It was a difficult time. I went from the highest of highs, thinking my son had been returned to me, to the lowest of lows when I realized I'd been duped. I felt so stupid. I was devastated all over again. It was like I'd lost my son for a second time and it was almost as difficult as it had been the first time."

She lifted a tear-stained face to his. "But one good thing came out of it. Ashton told me he'd found me by putting in a request through the department of Family and Community Services. I didn't know the laws had changed, making it easier for parents and children who'd gone through the adoption system to find one another. Though I'd suffered a devastating blow with Ashton, I was filled with a determination to find my real son." She looked him squarely in the eye. "*You.*"

"So that's how you found me."

She nodded. "Yes. And I'm so glad I did. When I wrote you that letter, I had no idea how you'd feel. I was terrified, worried about how you'd react. But I had to do it. There was a very real possibility that you wouldn't want to have anything to do with me, but I had to take that chance. And I'm so glad I did."

She dragged in a ragged breath. "I hate that before you were adopted by the Barringtons, your life was miserable, but there's nothing I can do about that except feel guilty. I'm never going to get back all those years I lost, but I'm just so grateful to have met you and I hope and pray that sometime down the track, we might be able to spend more time together and get to know each other. As friends."

Vaughan swallowed against the lump that lodged in his throat. When he'd first read the letter from Elizabeth, he'd never imagined he'd even want to come face-to-face with her again, let alone get to know her. But something had changed and he suspected it had everything to do with the fact Ruby was pregnant. He wanted so much to be a father. To give his child a wonderful life. To smother his baby with love and affection, offer safety, security, and all the other things that had been missing from the first eleven years of his life.

But all of that would come down to Ruby. He hated that it was her decision; that if she decided to go through with an abortion, there was nothing he could do about it. But no matter how difficult it was, he had to accept her decision. He hadn't endeared himself by accusing her of cheating.

He hated that he'd done that. Even as the words came out of his mouth, he'd known he was lashing out at her, saying nasty things, because he was hurting. He couldn't take back the accusation. All he could do was apologize and hope that she'd keep her promise not to make any decision about the baby without consulting him.

Standing slowly, he crossed over to where Elizabeth sat. Reaching down, he took her hand and pulled her to her feet. Slowly, and a little awkwardly, he hugged her. Her arms came around his waist. With her breath hitching on a sob, she clung to him. As the tears coursed down their cheeks, they held each other for the longest time.

For a long time after Vaughan left, promising to stay in touch, Elizabeth couldn't move from her position. So many emotions overwhelmed her. Relief, happiness, regret, joy that they'd found each other and had established a fragile peace. She couldn't wait to tell Archie.

Though he'd been hurt by her decision not to tell him about her first-born son until the arrival of Ashton on their doorstep, he'd since had time to come to terms with her shocking secret and had forgiven her for keeping it from him. He'd known about her decision to search for Vaughan and he'd supported her through these difficult months when she didn't know how her letter had been received.

He'd be elated things had worked out so well. That Vaughan's anger and hurt were abating. That he was willing to spend time with her; get to know her; let her be part of his life. It was all she'd prayed for, but hadn't expected. She was overcome with the knowledge her prayers had been answered.

Coming to a sudden decision, she stirred herself from the couch and went in search of her phone. Archie had told her he'd be spending most of the day in the city with his sons. In the meantime, there was work to be done.

First and foremost, she needed to call a family meeting. It was time her children met her real son. This time, there was no doubt he was hers. She was sure they'd welcome him with open arms, even the notoriously suspicious, Isabella. A wry smile turned up her lips and slowly grew wider. She felt better than she had for a long, long time.

Ruby lay stretched out on the couch. An open book lay across her lap. She'd spent most of the day resting, feeling more tired than she could remember. No doubt the first trimester was taking its toll on her body, but the argument with Vaughan had done little to bring her peace of mind. If he wanted a DNA test when the baby was born, then so be it. She had nothing to hide. In the meantime, she'd block him out of her mind—and her life. Any man who questioned her about the paternity of his baby didn't deserve to have anything to do with her, or the baby. And that was that.

The knowledge that she intended to go through with the pregnancy and raise her baby alone filled her with equal parts fear and excitement. She was terrified of messing up, but she also realized she wanted this baby desperately. Vaughan's love for her might have dried up, but that didn't mean she no longer felt deeply about him. Their life together might be over, but she had a part of him growing inside her; a part of him that would be with her for the rest of her life. That knowledge brought her comfort and sadness at the same time.

In a perfect world, they'd be together, blissfully in love and thrilled about the prospect of raising a child. But the world wasn't perfect and sometimes, love wasn't enough or didn't last. She had to face up to that and get on with it. Forge a life for herself and her baby, alone.

Well, not exactly alone. She had a loving family, a brother and parents who'd be thrilled she was expecting. She wouldn't tell them about the father—at least, not yet. No sense antagonizing her father right now. Better to let some time pass, let him get over the bad blood between him and Frank Barrington before she disclosed the first Rodriguez grandchild came from Barrington stock. After all, she didn't want to be the cause of another heart attack. Or worse.

Thoughts of her family reminded her that she hadn't made it to the library. She was still keen to do some research into what had happened at the mine between Frank Barrington and her father. Something told her there was more to the story than what she knew. After all, the fallout had driven her brother to suicide. She'd always tried to be a fair-minded person and she owed it to herself to get both sides of the story. That way she could draw her own conclusions and not be influenced by those around her, including her family.

With that thought in mind, she swung her legs off the couch and stood. She set her book aside. Taking a few moments, she ran a brush through her hair and freshened her makeup, straightened her sundress, slipped on her sandals, grabbed her handbag, keys and phone and left.

The library was within comfortable walking distance, but the way she felt right now, she opted to drive. She could have taken a bus, but it had been awhile since she'd taken out her Mazda. It needed a run. Joining the stalled rush-hour traffic, she took a moment to peer up at the sky. It was another beautiful day. The sky was once again crystal clear and the most amazing blue. Fluffy white clouds floated high overhead.

She was hemmed in on either side. Ramping up the AC, she switched on some music that was Bluetoothed to her phone. The soft sounds of classical music filled the car. A Strauss waltz, one of her favorites. She drew in a deep breath and eased it out, determined to let her tension go.

The traffic inched forward. She changed lanes and then pulled up at a red light. Pedestrians crossed in front of her, hurrying on their way. Young people, old people, mothers pushing prams. Office workers, tourists, school groups, laborers wearing high-visibility clothing from a nearby construction site.

It never ceased to amaze her that, no matter what time of day it was, there were always people about. No doubt that was part of living in a busy city. The noise, the people, the sheer energy... It all contributed to the vibe. Sydney. The city she was born in. The city she loved.

Just before the light changed, a man darted across the road, dragging a young child by the hand. At the last minute, he picked the child up, swinging him high before settling him on his shoulders. The child laughed and clung to his father. The man turned his face toward the boy and winked.

Ruby's heart clenched with emotion. It was such a tender moment between two people who obviously loved each other. *What kind of father will Vaughan be?*

Instinctively, her hand went to her tiny bump. She cupped it protectively. An increasingly familiar rush of warmth went through her. She was so glad she'd made the decision to keep their baby. She'd promised Vaughan she wouldn't make a decision about the baby without him, but he'd already made his feelings on the subject clear. Despite the hurtful question about the baby's father, she was sure he still wanted to keep it.

At least, she hoped that was the case. Not that it mattered. She'd made up her mind to raise the child on her own. Whether Vaughan was on board with her decision or not didn't change that. As the light turned green, she pressed the accelerator. The car surged forward. Half a block later, the Mazda swerved to one side. Her steering became sticky, hard to maintain, and then she heard a noise.

Great. A flat tire. Just what I need.

With a sigh of resignation, she pulled over to the curb and got out.

As Vaughan left Craigdon Manor behind him and headed back to the city, he selected one of his favorite country music playlists and settled back against the luxurious leather seat of his Porsche Cayenne to enjoy the ride home. He was glad he'd made the decision to visit Elizabeth. Their discussion had helped to process his hurt and anger at being abandoned and he'd learned something about his biological dad.

David Mason might have been a talented musician, but the man was a selfish prick. He'd gotten his young girlfriend pregnant and had then abruptly removed himself from her life. He'd never offered to take responsibility; hadn't been there for the birth. Elizabeth blamed herself and her parents, but Vaughan knew where the real blame lay.

It was the same with Ruby. Okay, so she wasn't a young girl without means to support herself and their baby, but he was the father. It was his duty, his responsibility to take care of the child, and its mother. And he was more than willing to do so. Happy about it, even. He might not have planned to become a father, but now that a baby was on the way, he was ecstatic.

At forty years of age, he hadn't been certain that he'd ever find the right woman, the one he wanted to settle down with, have a family with. Then he'd met Ruby. She'd simply blown him away. It was unfortunate she'd deliberately deceived him about certain things, but he'd had time to think about that.

She was close to her family. Though misguided, she wanted to help them. Most people felt that way about the people they loved. He understood her father had been a big influence on her decision to hide her true identity from him and to deceive him about her real purpose for being in Denpasar. How was she to know her father had lied about what had really gone down at the Strathwaylin mine? Or that her brother's suicide had nothing to do with Vaughan's family? Joseph Rodriguez was her father. She trusted him. Vaughan would have done the same thing if his father had approached him.

The anger and hurt that had consumed him when he'd discovered her treachery had subsided. He might not agree with her decision to deceive him, but he understood it. Besides, those things were less important now. She was having his baby. She needed his support.

He could live with the fact she didn't love him. That wouldn't affect the way he felt about his kid. He needed to call her and apologize for his hurtful accusation, reinforce his desire for her to keep their baby, and hope like hell she kept her promise not to make a decision about it without him. With that thought in mind, he tapped on his phone and dialed her number.

Ruby cursed under her breath as she ended the call to the National Roads and Motorists Association. Though she didn't drive all that often, right now she was pleased she'd kept her subscription to the NRMA current. They assured her they'd send someone to fix her flat tire. Unfortunately, they'd also warned her it would be more than two hours before the repair guy would be on the scene. They were experiencing an unusually high number of callouts and it was rush hour. She'd have to join the queue and wait.

As the sun beat down overhead, she climbed back into her car. No sense in getting sunstroke while she waited. From what she'd been told, she was going to be there for a while. She was tempted to walk back to her apartment and wait there, but the fatigue that had plagued her for weeks made the thought of doing that unappealing.

Blowing out her breath on a weary sigh, she reached for her phone. Maybe her brother was still at the office. Maybe he could come and change the tire. It was worth a shot. She dialed his number and waited for him to pick up.

"Ruby, what's up?"

"Hi, Matthew. I...um... I'm in a bit of a fix. I've got a flat tire."

"Why are you calling me? Haven't you heard of the NRMA?"

His caustic tone irritated her, but she was about to ask him a favor. With an effort, she held on to her temper.

"I've called them already. They can send someone to help me, but there's a two-hour wait."

"So? Wait."

She gritted her teeth and slowly counted to five. "I was wondering if you could come and change it for me?"

"You're kidding, right?"

"I'm not that far away. Only a few blocks from the office. Are you at work?"

"Yes. But I'm wearing a five-thousand-dollar suit. Do you really expect me to get down on the ground and change a tire?"

The incredulity in his voice was almost more than she could take. "Matthew, I need your help. You can always take your jacket off. Hell, take your pants off, too, if it's that important. I don't care."

"I'm going to pretend you didn't say that, Ruby. I'm sorry. I'm not going to be able to help you. You're going to have to find someone else. Or, here's an idea; wait for the NRMA."

Ruby was left staring at a blank screen as the call was brought to an abrupt end. "Damn it, Matthew! How could you be so selfish!"

She thought wistfully of her brother, Kyle. He would never have abandoned her in her hour of need. Okay, so the NRMA were on their way and eventually she'd be back on the road. It wasn't exactly a matter of life and death. But still... Matthew was an asshole.

With a groan of irritation, she threw herself back against the seat and stretched out her legs. She might as well get comfortable. She was in for a long wait. Reaching over, she pumped up the volume on the stereo and lost herself in her music. The volume was so loud, she nearly didn't hear her phone.

It's Matthew... He's realized what a jerk he's been... He's calling to tell me he's on his way...

She dug her phone out of her handbag and checked the screen.

Vaughan.

Her stomach clenched reflexively. Dragging in a fortifying breath, she answered the call.

"Vaughan. What's going on?"

"Ruby. Hi. How are you?"

She grimaced. "I've had better days."

"Me too. I... I've just been to see my biological mother."

Ruby frowned and sat up straighter. "I thought you told me your biological mother was dead?"

"Yes. I did. The thing is, I spent most of my life believing she was. I discovered right before I left for Bali that she's very much alive and living in Sydney."

Ruby recalled how Matthew had overheard a conversation between Vaughan and a check-in attendant at the airport, something about getting away from life as he knew it.

"That's the reason you left, isn't it? That's what you were escaping from?"

"Yes."

Vaughan's tone was equally somber when he spoke again. "Her name's Elizabeth Craigdon. I've just come from her house. We talked about a lot of things and I... I wanted to call you and tell you I'm sorry for the question about the father of your baby. I never believed you could cheat on me. It was a stupid thing to say. I was hurt and angry and wanted to strike out. It was mean and nasty and spiteful and I'm ashamed of myself."

Tears welled up in Ruby's eyes. She swallowed against the lump in her throat. The blast of a horn behind her startled her. She jumped and was even more startled when a man pulled up beside her and started shouting at her to get out of the way because she was blocking traffic. Shaken, she turned her face away and ignored him. With another loud blast of his horn, he drove away.

"Where are you?" Vaughan asked.

"I'm in the city."

"Sounds like you're stuck in traffic."

"Yes. You could say that." She told him about the flat tire.

"Why didn't you say something sooner?"

"Well, I told you I'd had better days."

"Shit, Ruby. I was so caught up in my own drama, I barely listened. I'm sorry. Sit tight. I'll be there as soon as I can."

"That's okay. I've called the NRMA."

"Call them back and cancel. I'm on my way into the city right now. I'm maybe twenty minutes away. Give me your location and I'll put it into my GPS."

A rush of warmth and gratitude flooded through her. Vaughan didn't care that she'd already put in a service call and she hadn't even told him about the two-hour wait. He was on his way to help her and she hadn't even had to ask.

"Thank you. If it's not too much trouble, I'd really appreciate that."

"Of course. No trouble at all. I'll be there as soon as I can. Do you have a useable spare?"

"Yes. At least, I think so."

"Then we're all set. See you shortly."

She ended the call with a smile on her face.

Chapter Sixteen

Vaughan found Ruby without any trouble and immediately set about changing her tire. At first, she stood on the footpath and watched him, but as she grew more flushed from the heat, he insisted she sit in the relative comfort of her car. When the spare tire was fixed in place and the flat in the boot, he opened the passenger side door and leaned in.

"All done. You're good to go."

She shot him a grateful look. "Thank you, Vaughan. You don't know how much I appreciate your help. It's very kind of you."

He waved away her thanks. "It was nothing. You needed help. I would have done the same for anyone."

She pulled a face, but there was a teasing look in her eyes. "And here I thought I was special."

He sobered. "You are special. More special than you can know," he said huskily, overcome with an unexpected surge of emotion.

Her blue eyes darkened. She bit her lip and looked away.

He frowned. "What is it, Ruby?"

She drew in a deep breath and then caught and held his gaze. "I'm going to keep the baby," she said in a rush.

He blinked and then stared at her in amazement. "You're keeping the baby?"

Her lip wobbled. Tears filled her eyes. "Yes. Is that all right?"

He raised his eyebrows. Joy surged through him. "Are you kidding? Of course, it's all right! I want our baby more than anything!"

He jumped in beside her. Unable to help himself, he reached across the gearstick and gave her an awkward hug. Then all the things that still stood between them came crashing in on him and he slowly pulled away.

"Is there anything you need me to do? Do you need money?" he asked.

Ruby shook her head. "No. I guess we still have a few things to talk about, but there's plenty of time, right? I'm only ten weeks in."

"Right." He thought about all the things ahead of them and some of his enthusiasm dimmed. As if sensing the change in his mood, Ruby gave him a tight smile.

"Well, I guess I'd better get going. Thanks again for your help. You're a lifesaver."

He managed to make a semblance of a smile. "No worries. Anytime."

With that, he climbed out of her car and watched in silence while she slowly pulled away and merged into the traffic.

Within minutes she disappeared from view. His shoulders slumped on a sigh.

She was going to keep their baby and he was truly thrilled about that. It was too bad she didn't love him. Oh, she said she did, but that had only been when he'd been in the process of breaking things off with her. People said all sorts of things when they were under pressure and she'd been eager to stay with him in order to see through her plan for revenge.

Her father's plan... Maybe, maybe not.

She'd told so many lies, had lived a life of deceit for months and he no longer trusted anything that came out of her mouth – certainly no basis for a relationship. He was the father of her baby, and he would be there for her and their child, but his support would be from a distance. He still desperately loved her, but he didn't trust her not to break his heart again. Best for everyone that he kept his walls up.

Ruby suppressed a yawn and continued to scroll through the newspaper archives displayed on the microfiche reader in front of her. She'd already been at the library for more than three hours and she was beginning to feel stiff. Her neck was sore and her back hurt from being seated for so long. Her eyes were also starting to water from staring so long at the screen. On top of that, she was finding it hard to concentrate. Her mind kept returning to Vaughan.

She was glad she'd told him about her decision and even more pleased that he'd expressed his support. She was disappointed that he hadn't invited her back into his life, but she hadn't yet given up hope on that front. He'd loved her deeply enough to propose to her. Surely, that kind of love didn't die at the very first hurdle. If it had, she was better off without him. That was the logical conclusion. Too bad her heart wasn't buying it.

She sighed and rubbed the back of her neck and forced herself to focus on the screen in front of her. She'd scrolled through countless newspapers, dating back at least two years. The problem was, she didn't exactly know what she was looking for. Stories on the Strathwaylin mine situated in the Hunter Valley were number one on her list, but she'd barely found anything of interest and nothing that involved her dad.

The only thing she'd discovered so far were a couple of articles, one of which talked about the record high coal prices and how much production at the mine had ramped up in response to the seemingly endless demand from China for Australian coal. The second article talked about the appointment of Hannah Barrington, daughter of mine owner, Frank Barrington, as the senior group safety officer for the Strathwaylin mine.

The story made headlines because apparently, Hannah was the first woman in the country to be appointed to such an important position. Ruby had no doubt the fact Hannah's father owned the mine had played a part in her appointment, but after meeting Hannah, Ruby knew the woman was smart as a whip, confident and self-assured. If anyone could pull off a job like that in a traditionally male-dominated workplace, it would be Hannah.

With another sigh, Ruby leaned back against her chair and stretched her arms above her head. She was fast losing interest in her research project. She'd been hoping to find something that might give her a clue as to why relations had broken down between Frank and her father, but so far, she'd come up empty. Either there was nothing of enough interest for it to have been reported in the papers, or she hadn't looked hard enough.

Determined to give it one last go, she cleared the search box and went with something broader. "Strathwaylin mine" was all she entered. She immediately got several results. As she clicked on each hit and read through the articles, a pattern began to emerge. Some of the stories were weeks apart, others only a few days. Each outlined a series of small-scale accidents that had occurred at the mine. What interested Ruby the most was that all the incidents had involved her father's company.

She frowned. *Is this why Daddy lost his contract? Did he have one too many accidents?*

Though she'd never worked on a mine site, she understood enough about them to know that safety was paramount. Matthew had said as much. A serious accident could see the mine closed for an extended period of time. The price of coal was at a premium. Any down time was costly for the mine operator and would cause stress at the highest levels.

She continued to scroll through the pages, one newspaper at a time, paying much more attention to each story. One headline in particular stood out: *Tragic death of plant operator.*

Ruby's heart beat faster. She scanned the article with a growing sense of dread. Evan Wilson, a twenty-six-year-old employee of Rodriguez Contracting had been killed in a tragic accident at the Strathwaylin mine. The accident had happened more than twelve months earlier.

About the same time Daddy lost his contract...

Though the article didn't state explicitly who was to blame, reading between the lines, she could tell the journalist harbored suspicions against Rodriguez Contracting. Evan Wilson had worked for her father. He'd been operating one of her father's machines, and presumably working under her father's instruction, or at the very least, his foreman's. An investigation had been commenced by the Resources Regulator, the details of which would be made public in due course.

With her curiosity piqued, Ruby began to scroll through the newspapers following that one, in the hope of finding an update on the investigation. Finally, she found one almost six months after the first story appeared. The Resources Regulator had concluded their investigation. Though no criminal charges had been laid, the case remained open.

Barrington Mining and Rodriguez Contracting had copped substantial fines for a number of serious safety breaches.

Matthew and her father had lied. They'd both been adamant that Frank Barrington had terminated the contract without cause. And yet, according to the newspapers, there appeared to be plenty of reasons why her father's contract would have been brought to an abrupt end. A string of less serious incidents in the preceding months, followed by a fatality...

No matter that no criminal charges had been laid, the Resources Regulator had still held Barrington Mining and her father responsible. The fine imposed on Barrington Mining was much higher than what her father had to pay, but the regulator justified that by stating that the mine owner was ultimately responsible for the safety of everyone on the mine site, including their contractors. Ruby supposed that was fair, but it must have annoyed Frank Barrington when he hadn't been directly responsible for the accident that had taken Evan Wilson's life.

Was it enough of an annoyance that he tore up Daddy's contract? Is that the real reason Daddy was booted off the mine site?

It was possible the decision had nothing to do with racism or a petty dislike, like her father had tried to convince her. And what about the accidents that had continued since then, under her cousin's watch? In Nathan's case, criminal charges *had* been laid. The prosecution obviously thought they had enough evidence of intentional wrongdoing that they were willing to take the case to trial.

She needed to talk to someone who was impartial, who could be trusted to tell her the truth, and who had personal insight into the whole sordid situation. She immediately thought of Vaughan and then dismissed him just as quickly. Though Vaughan had worked for his father at and around the time of Evan Wilson's death, he hadn't been in Australia during the ten months after it. He certainly couldn't have direct knowledge of what had happened with Nathan.

But now she'd discovered those articles, she couldn't just walk away. A number of possibilities filled her mind and she had so many questions. She wished Kyle was still around… Her heart ached at the thought of her brother's death.

What about Hannah?

She worked at the mine as the senior safety officer. Who better to talk to than someone who was directly responsible for safety at the mine? She would know about the incidents referred to in the newspapers. As much as Hannah had rubbed Ruby the wrong way, she admired the other woman's grit and determination and obvious intelligence. Hannah didn't suffer fools. Neither did she beat around the bush. Though Hannah was a Barrington and perhaps had cause to lie, Ruby believed the woman would be straight with her and that's what she needed.

Mind made up, she closed down the microfiche reader, gathered her handbag and left the library. Pulling out her phone, she did an online search for the Barrington Mining phone number and put a call into the Hunter Valley office.

Chapter Seventeen

It had taken Elizabeth more than a week to get her family gathered in one spot. With her children now spread out everywhere, including Isabella who'd moved with her new husband, Raine, to live in Brisbane, getting them together hadn't been an easy feat. Having to sit on her news about Vaughan for so long had also been difficult, but now all six of her children, along with her stepson, Christopher, and her husband, Archie, were gathered around the impressive dining room table.

Dinner had been served and eaten and the plates and cutlery cleared away. Most of her guests now sipped from wineglasses or drank from bottles of beer and looked at her with a mixture of curiosity and expectation. Six months earlier, her oldest son, Callum, and his wife, Grace, had welcomed a baby girl. Callum had taken instantly to fatherhood. Not that

Elizabeth had been surprised. He was already a loving father to Grace's two children from her previous marriage.

The stork had also arrived for Elizabeth's son, Nicholas, and his wife, Harper. The two were proud parents of baby Mack. Elizabeth had spent some time with the little boy right before they'd sat down for dinner and he'd charmed her with his shock of blond hair, his bright blue eyes and toothless grin. He was the image of his father.

She'd barely seen Isabella and Raine since their November wedding the year before, but the way the two kept looking at each other with such loving gazes, it appeared all was well in the Fairfax household. Elizabeth didn't think it would be too long before another impending birth was announced.

Her youngest daughter, Sophia, and her husband, Jarrod, had their hands full with a set of identical triplets. The boys were a gorgeous combination of their parents and at three months old, were all giggles and smiles. That is, until they got tired and irritable and then they'd let the whole manor know they weren't happy. Sophia had checked on them during dinner and was pleased to announce they were sound asleep in the crib Elizabeth kept in one of the spare rooms upstairs.

At the far end of the table, Joel and Jett were seated together with their wives, Sheridan and Danielle. Jett and Danielle's oldest had started school a few weeks earlier and they'd regaled everyone with funny stories of Alexander's first day. Though Joel and Sheridan had yet to add to their family with a child, they'd recently told her in confidence that they were looking into IVF. She wished them all the best.

Now that the moment was upon her, Elizabeth was swamped with nerves. Butterflies filled her stomach. She looked at Archie, seeking reassurance. He smiled and nodded, his gaze intent on hers. She took comfort from his silent encouragement and, drawing in a fortifying breath, rose slowly to her feet.

She cleared her throat to gain their attention. Almost immediately, the room fell silent. She smiled. "First let me say how wonderful it is to have you back here under the same roof. There's nothing I love more than having my children and their loved ones here, enjoying family time and family hospitality." She looked around the vast dining room, exquisitely decorated with a mix of modern pieces and priceless antiques. "This house is far too big for just the two of us."

"Maybe Grace and I and the kids can move back in," Callum quipped.

Everyone laughed.

"Or maybe Isabella and Raine can relocate from Brisbane," Nicholas joked.

Joel winked. "That's if she can convince Raine to leave Queensland."

"Not a chance," Raine quipped amid another round of laughter.

Elizabeth waited for the mirth to die down before speaking again. "No doubt you're all wondering why I called you here." She paused. The thought of reminding them about the debacle that was Ashton Walker brought a flush to her cheeks, but she held on to her courage and forged on.

"You might recall the arrival of Ashton Walker about this time last year and how I told you I'd given birth to a son more than forty years ago."

Her statement was met with various cautious nods. Drawing in another deep breath, she continued.

"After that fiasco, I was so embarrassed to have been taken in by a con artist, that I could barely bring myself to think about the whole sorry incident. But after I'd had time to come to terms with my foolish gullibility, I realized that one of the reasons I'd fallen for Ashton's lies was because I so desperately *wanted* him to be my son."

She gazed around the table at her children and their significant others. "I don't expect any of you to understand, but there hasn't been a day that's gone past since the night I gave my son up for adoption that I haven't thought about him. With Ashton's arrival, that whole tumultuous time came rushing back. Even when the Ashton debacle was over, I couldn't stop thinking about my son."

Briefly closing her eyes, she sustained herself with another deep breath and forged on. "In one way, Ashton Walker did me a favor. He made me realize that it was easier than I ever realized to try and find someone who'd been involved with the adoption system. So, I contacted the department of Family and Community Services. Waiting for their response was the most nerve-wracking time of my life."

She shot a sideways glance at Archie and smiled. "Well, maybe not *the* most nerve-wracking time. That would have to be the night Archie was caught in the fire and I didn't know how bad his injuries were. Now, *that* was nerve-wracking."

Her comment was met with gentle laughter. It gave her the strength to carry on.

"I eventually received a response. I was so nervous, I could barely bring myself to open the envelope. But I did. And I was given the name of my son." She paused. Her heart hammered against her chest. The words were suddenly caught in her throat.

"So, who is he?" Sophia asked, her voice tinged with impatience.

Elizabeth kept her gaze steady on those gathered around the table. "His name is Vaughan Barrington."

"*What?*"

The shock in Christopher's voice was reflected on the faces of everyone else at the table.

"Surely you don't mean, my adopted brother, Vaughan Barrington?" Christopher asked.

Elizabeth nodded. Now that the truth was out there, she felt strangely calm. "Yes. That's exactly who I mean." She sighed quietly and then regained her seat at the table before continuing with her explanation.

"The night I signed the adoption papers, I was assured by everyone—my parents, the nursing staff—I was doing the right thing. The best thing for my baby was for me to give him to a loving family who were desperate for a child of their own. There were so many wonderful couples on the waiting list. I was given to believe he'd be adopted right away. Only, he wasn't."

Isabella frowned. "How do you know that?"

"I asked him," Elizabeth replied calmly.

"You *asked* him?" Christopher exclaimed, his tone incredulous. "You've spoken to Vaughan?"

"Yes," Elizabeth replied in the same calm tone.

Her affirmation was met with a flurry of questions, each one speaking over the next. She held up her hand for silence. Gradually, the noise died down.

"About eleven months ago, I wrote a letter to Vaughan. I told him who I was and that I wanted to meet him. I received no response. Months went by. I found out through Christopher that Vaughan had fled to Bali and nobody knew why."

"So, that's why he left in such a hurry, without a word to anyone," Christopher muttered.

Elizabeth nodded. "Yes. No doubt the contents of the letter came as a shock."

"No doubt," Christopher murmured. "The way I remember it, Vaughan grew up believing his mother had died at birth. There was no record of his father."

"Yes," Elizabeth said. "He told me as much, too." She folded her hands in her lap and continued.

"Contrary to the reassurances I'd been given, Vaughan spent the first eleven years in the foster care system. While he hasn't gone into too much detail, it breaks my heart to know those years were far from easy." She looked toward Christopher. "I'll be forever grateful to your mother and father for adopting him when they did. They welcomed him into their family and showed him unconditional love. The kind of love he always deserved. The kind of love he should have had from the beginning."

Her voice cracked with emotion. Her chest was tight with unshed tears. "There's nothing I can do to change the past, but that doesn't mean I won't live with regret for the rest of my life over the decision I made all those year ago. I should have fought harder to keep him. I should have told my parents to go to hell. I should have found some way to raise him on my own..."

She dragged in a ragged breath in the silence. "I was weak. And selfish. And immature. I had no idea the impact such a decision would have on him and on me; how it would weigh so heavily on us both for the next forty years." Her gaze went around the table, touching briefly on each of her children. "If it hadn't been for all of you, I would have surely lost my mind."

"Don't be too hard on yourself, Mom. You did what you had to do," Callum said softly.

She shot him a look of gratitude. "Thank you, Callum. You always seem to know what to say to bring me comfort."

Callum shrugged. "It's true. You were young and unmarried. You had no parental support. The father took off. You were as good as alone in the world, facing the prospect of raising a child." He looked around at his brothers and sisters. "Times were different then. There was no support from the government for a single mother. And the attitude of society was hardly welcoming. We're not judging you harshly, Mom. Just so you know."

She managed a small smile. "Thank you, Callum." Her gaze shifted to encompass all of them. "Thank you for understanding. And thank you to Archie for his unwavering support. This has been such a difficult time. For everyone. Especially after what happened with Ashton."

"How do we know Vaughan Barrington's legit? That this isn't just another trick?" Isabella asked.

Elizabeth gazed at her daughter. "I understand your concern, but Vaughan is definitely legit. For a start, I was the one who made the first contact with FACS. The information about Vaughan came directly from their department. Also, he's the spitting image of his father." She rummaged in the pocket of her skirt and pulled out an old colored photograph of David Mason.

"Here, look at this."

She handed the photo to Christopher. "Who is it?" he asked.

"That's David Mason. Vaughan's biological father."

Christopher looked at the photo. His eyes went wide and he slowly nodded. "Wow."

He then handed the photo to the person beside him. As the photo was passed around the table, there were collective murmurings of surprise. They all agreed he looked like Vaughan.

"You said you've spoken to Vaughan. How did he take the news that you're his biological mother?" Nicholas asked, his eyes wide with curiosity.

Elizabeth compressed her lips. "Well, it took him nearly a year to approach me about it. That should give you some idea."

"So, you hadn't heard from him all this time?" Joel asked.

She shook her head. "No. Like I said, all I knew was that he was in Bali." Her gaze went to Christopher. "Nobody in the Barrington household seemed to know when he was coming back."

"That's right," Christopher mumbled. "Dad received the occasional email from him to let us know he was okay, but that was it. None of us had a clue why he'd left or if and when he planned to return. It was stressful for my parents. For all of us, really."

"I'm sorry," Elizabeth said. "I didn't mean to chase him away from his family. I had no idea he'd react like that."

"It must have come as one hell of a shock," Joel muttered.

"Absolutely," Nicholas added.

"I'm sure it did," Elizabeth agreed. "I debated a long time before I sent the letter. In the end, I just had to do it. I didn't know how the news would be received, but now that I finally knew my son's identity, I couldn't stay quiet."

"Do Frank and Evelyn Barrington know?" Callum asked.

"No," Elizabeth replied. "At least, I haven't told them. I wanted to wait until I knew how Vaughan felt about it all. As you know, he only recently returned to Sydney and for the first couple of weeks, he was in a coma. No one knew if he'd even wake up."

"So, how was he when he finally spoke to you?" Sophia asked.

Elizabeth drew in a deep breath. "He came to visit me at Craigdon Manor. The first time was just over three weeks ago." She grimaced. "To tell you the truth, he was furious about the letter. He was furious I'd made the decision to give him up for adoption. He accused me of not loving him enough to keep him."

Once again, her voice cracked with the force of the emotions that coursed inside her, choking her up. Callum pushed away from his seat and came to stand beside her. He rested a comforting hand upon her arm.

"It's okay, Mom."

She patted Callum's hand and shot him a grateful look. "Thank you, Callum. I appreciate that."

They all gave her a few moments to compose herself. Then Isabella spoke up. "You said Vaughan came here the first time just over three weeks ago. I take it he's been back since?"

Elizabeth nodded. "Yes. Last week, he paid me another visit. I was surprised and a little wary. We hadn't parted on the greatest of terms. Even so, I was very pleased to see him. He's my son! How could I not be?"

"How was he the second time?" Sophia asked.

"Better. Much calmer. I guess he'd had more time to come to terms with everything. Also, he mentioned that something had happened to him recently that had made him think about things a little differently and as a result, he felt the need to apologize."

Christopher's eyes went wide. "He apologized?"

"Yes. He said he was sorry for how he'd reacted the first time. For the harsh things he'd said. He also thanked me for choosing to go through with the pregnancy. He started asking me lots of questions. We talked for hours." She paused and smiled softly. "Though we still have a long way to go, he left me feeling relieved and confident that over time, the two of us might one day be friends."

"Oh, Mom! That's so wonderful!" Sophia exclaimed, brushing away a tear.

Elizabeth blinked back tears of her own and smiled. "Yes, isn't it? I don't expect any of you to understand what it's been like for me all these years... Going through life carrying such a big secret... Always wondering about him... What he looked like... Where he lived... Whether he was happy... Sometimes I thought I'd go mad with all the questions, especially when there was no hope of ever getting any answers.

"When the opportunity presented itself, I just couldn't stop myself from filling in the paperwork and sending it off. I'd spent forty years wondering. I didn't want to spend another minute more."

"Why didn't you tell any of us what you were doing?" Isabella asked.

Elizabeth sighed quietly. "I told Archie. Before we married, I promised never to keep another secret from him. I've honored that promise." She glanced at her husband. The tenderness in his gaze warmed her heart.

"Archie's been a rock. I'm not sure how I would have gotten through this past year without him. He helped me during those long, long months when I hadn't heard from Vaughan and didn't have a clue how he'd reacted to my letter. And then when Vaughan did finally come to see me..." She shrugged. "Archie was there for me once again." Her gaze zeroed in on her husband. "I love you so much."

Archie's voice was rough with emotion when he spoke. "I love you, too, Lizzie."

She looked back at her family. "The reason I didn't tell any of you was because I wasn't sure how Vaughan would react. There was every chance he'd simply ignore my letter; that I'd never hear from him. That was his prerogative. Though a biological parent now has the right to make contact with the child they gave up for adoption, that doesn't mean they have any power to make the recipient respond."

Her shoulders slumped. "After what had happened with Ashton, I didn't want to be put through the wringer so publicly again if things didn't work out like I hoped."

"We wouldn't have done that, Mom!" Isabella protested.

Elizabeth offered a half-smile. "I know. But this was something I needed to keep to myself until I knew how it would develop. As it turned out, Vaughan's now willing to keep the lines of communication open between us. I'm quietly hopeful he'll one day let me be a part of his life." She glanced at Christopher. "I've no intention of trying to be his mother, of course. He already has a wonderful mother who couldn't love him more. I'll be forever grateful to both her and Frank for everything they've done."

Christopher nodded. "You're right. They've always loved him unconditionally. We all do."

"I can't believe you and Vaughan are both my half-brothers," Isabella mused.

Sophia offered a wry smile. "This family just keeps getting bigger and bigger."

Joel winked at her. "Well, you and Jarrod have done your bit. A set of triplets first time round. Are you guys finished, or will there be more baby Sampsons in the Craigdon house?"

Sophia rolled her eyes, but smiled happily. Motherhood definitely suited her. She reached for her husband's hand and pressed a loving kiss against his skin. "Hey! I'm one of six. We're only halfway there right, Jarrod?"

Jarrod grinned. He reached out toward Sophia and pulled her in close for a kiss. "Right."

Elizabeth sighed quietly and smiled. She'd broken the news to her family and so far, everyone seemed to have taken it well. She longed for the day when she could bring them all together with Vaughan and truly have a family celebration. It would happen one day. She was sure of it.

"When will you tell Mom and Dad?" Christopher asked, interrupting her thoughts.

She glanced at Archie. They'd already talked about that. "I'm going to leave that up to Vaughan. He has the right to decide if and when to tell them. In the meantime, I ask for your discretion."

"Of course. I'm sure he'll tell them," Christopher said.

Elizabeth nodded. "I'm sure he will, too. But it's not my place to suggest it or to put pressure on him."

"They were under the same impression about Vaughan's biological parents as he was. That his mother had died shortly after giving birth and his father was unknown. They're going to be shocked."

"Yes," she agreed. "I had no idea they were told this. I hope they won't be too angry that I waited so long to come forward."

"They won't be angry," Christopher reassured her. "I've never met two more loving, forgiving people." He winked. "My mother wasn't always an angel, you know. She had a past of her own."

Elizabeth smiled as the last of her tension eased. She knew very well that Evelyn had given birth to Christopher out of wedlock and that his father was the late Henry Craigdon. The man who Elizabeth had gone on to marry and who she'd remained with until his death more than thirty years later.

Looking around the table at her family, she couldn't help but sigh with contentment. There was so much history between them, so much binding them together. The Craigdons and the Barringtons. It was a little daunting. But it also filled her with hope and anticipation that one day, they'd all come together as one big, supportive, loving family.

Chapter Eighteen

It had been over a week since Hannah had received a surprise call from Ruby Ashworth. Even more surprising was that Ruby wanted to speak with Hannah about Rodriguez Contracting and what had gone on at the Strathwaylin mine. Though immediately suspicious of Ruby's motives, Hannah had agreed to meet. She didn't trust Ruby. The woman had broken Vaughan's heart. Hannah was fiercely protective of her brother. She was also determined to give Ruby some hard truths. She wouldn't sugar coat anything.

Unfortunately, there had been some pressing issues at the mine that same week that had needed her attention and it was only now that she'd found the time to drive to the city to meet with Ruby.

As Hannah pulled into a multi-storied parking station and switched off the ignition, the rain that had been threatening for the past half hour began to fall. Reaching around to the back seat for an umbrella, she pulled it out, slung her handbag over her shoulder and exited her car, heading for the Marble Bar.

Hannah hadn't been surprised by Ruby's choice of venue. The bar was a beautifully renovated, historically breathtaking, heritage-listed venue located beneath the Hilton Hotel and catered for a more mature crowd, especially on a weeknight. With its dark mahogany interior, iconic marble arches and pressed metal ceilings, it exuded old-world charm. It was a far cry from the loud, glitzy nightclubs and bars Hannah usually favored farther north along George Street. Then again, Ruby was much closer to Vaughan's age, than hers.

Making her way down the stairs, she looked around but didn't see Ruby. She glanced at her watch. She was right on time. Making a beeline for the bar, she hopped up on a vacant stool. A cute barman approached and took her order. Once upon a time, she would have encouraged the flirtatious look in his eyes, but ever since she'd fallen in love with Liam, she couldn't summon the slightest interest in other guys. It just went to show how hard she'd fallen. She couldn't be happier about it.

She was curious about Ruby's motives for wanting to meet to discuss the mine. What did she want from her family now? Hadn't she done enough damage already? Vaughan was heart-broken, getting around the office with barely a smile on his face, and that was all Ruby's fault.

Halfway through her glass of Sauvignon Blanc, Ruby appeared. She was soaked to the skin.

"Oh, my goodness!" Hannah exclaimed, momentarily forgetting her wariness and jumping off the stool. She reached out toward Ruby. "Are you all right?"

"I'm fine," Ruby replied, using the sleeve of her blouse to pat her face dry.

"That storm came from nowhere. I had blue sky until I was about a half hour from the city. I'm guessing you were caught without an umbrella." Hannah smiled.

Ruby grimaced. "Yep. I don't know what I was thinking. I left my apartment and got on the bus. By the time I reached my stop, it was pouring." She sighed. "My mind must have been somewhere else."

Hannah sympathized and decided to cut her some slack. From the tone of Ruby's phone call, she had plenty of distractions. Dealing with family was tough. So was the thought that those same family members might not have been forthcoming about past events.

Tugging a clean linen handkerchief out of her handbag, Hannah handed it to Ruby. "Here. This might help."

Ruby took it gratefully. "Thanks." She wrapped the handkerchief around the ends of her loose hair and squeezed out the water that had been dripping on her shoulders. When she was done, she offered the soggy handkerchief back.

"It's fine. Keep it," Hannah said.

"Are you sure you don't want it back?" Ruby flashed a grin. Hannah blinked, momentarily blindsided. Ruby's smile lit up her face and emphasized her stunning good looks.

No wonder Vaughan fell in love with her... It's too bad things didn't work out...

No, what was too bad was that Ruby had lied about who she was and what she was doing in Bali. She'd deliberately sought out Vaughan with the sole intention of causing trouble for Barrington Mining. Hannah needed to remember that Ruby couldn't be trusted. Her earlier good humor disappeared.

"Would you like a drink?" she asked in a much more somber tone.

Ruby's face reflected her tacit acknowledgement that the two of them were far from friends. She nodded just as somberly.

"Thank you. I'd love a house white, but I think I'll stick with a soda water and lime."

Hannah blinked in surprise. "Are you sure I can't get you something stronger? You caught a bus here, after all."

"No, no. Soda water will be fine."

"Suit yourself."

Hannah got the barman's attention and ordered. When the drink arrived, she overrode Ruby's objection and handed over enough money to cover the cost before focusing her attention once again on the woman her brother had once loved enough to ask her to be his wife.

Curious about what kind of woman had managed to capture her brother's heart, even for a few months, she eyed Ruby over the rim of her glass.

"I can't believe you were engaged to my brother. Do you know, we'd all just about given up on Vaughan ever finding love and settling down. We thought of him as the perennial bachelor. I'm curious what it was about you that caused him to fall so hard?"

Ruby's gaze remained steady on hers. "I'm not sure. I guess we just connected and fell in love. There was an instant attraction."

Hannah gave her a dry look. "I'm not blind to your physical attributes, but Vaughan's dated plenty of beautiful women. He's never expressed the slightest interest in proposing to any of them, and yet he proposed to you. Tell me about yourself."

Ruby held her gaze. "What would you like to know?"

"I don't know. What do you do for a living?"

"I'm a lawyer."

Hannah was secretly impressed. She'd dropped out halfway through a law degree. She'd found all that legislation and the case law they'd been forced to read so long and boring. She needed a bit more excitement than being stuck with her head in a law book all day long.

"Do you work for a firm in the city?"

"No. I work for my father in his contracts department."

Hannah tensed. "I see."

"Yes. In fact, I worked on the very contract negotiated between Rodriguez Contracting and Barrington Mining."

Hannah narrowed her eyes. "Then you'd know there were strict safety provisions contained in there and any breach of those clauses would mean severe penalties, including giving Barrington Mining the right to terminate."

To Hannah's surprise, Ruby didn't even flinch. Her gaze remained confident and steady. "Yes. In fact, that was one of the clauses I had no trouble with. A mine site is a dangerous workplace. Safety should be paramount."

"Then I don't understand your opposition to my father's decision to bring the contract to an end."

"Oh, come on. We both know that contract was terminated without cause. Why do you think my family is so angry?"

Hannah's anger stirred. "Without cause? What are you talking about?"

Ruby blinked. "You're saying there was a safety breach?"

Hannah stared at her. "Yes. More than one. They culminated in the death of one of your father's workers."

"Evan Wilson," Ruby stated flatly.

"So, you know about that."

"Yes. I went to the city library last week and read about it in an old newspaper."

"Then you must know, my father had no choice but to terminate your father's contract. The accident that resulted in the death of Evan Wilson was the final straw. It was only one in a string of safety breaches, all of which your father had been reprimanded for and warned that he was putting his contract at risk."

"I'm not sure I believe you."

Hannah glared at her. "You think I'm lying? Just because that kind of deceit comes easily to you, don't think I'm of that same ilk."

Ruby blushed and lowered her gaze. "I'm sorry. I'm not accusing you of lying. Just... Perhaps you haven't been given the full facts. Were you at the mine when my father worked there?"

"No. My first day on the job was the day Evan Wilson was killed. I only had a vague understanding of the arrangement between your father and Barrington Mining. I was aware your father was a contractor and my father told me there had been several safety breaches prior to that tragic accident. My father is a fair man. I didn't question his decision to fire him."

"How do you know your father was telling the truth?" Ruby fired at her.

Hannah opened her mouth, outraged. "How *dare* you!"

Ruby held up her hands in a form of surrender. "I'm sorry. But my father told me something entirely different. You take offense at my suggestion that your father might not have told you the truth, but you expect me to accept my father was lying?"

Hannah's breath came fast. She clenched her fists. Ruby was also breathing hard and her color was high. She reached for her soda water and took several quick gulps. Hannah sipped from her wine. With a concerted effort, she got her temper back under control. In mutual, unspoken agreement, silence fell between them as they took a few moments to regather their thoughts and calm down.

"Out of curiosity, what did your father tell you about why his contract had been terminated?" Hannah asked.

Ruby drew in a breath. "He told me it had been terminated without just cause. All he could think of was that your father had it in for him because he's an immigrant."

"*What?*" Hannah was beyond shocked.

"My father migrated from Spain before I was born, but there are some people who still regard him as a foreigner. He's a little bit sensitive to that. He became a proud Australian citizen more than twenty years ago and takes offense to being treated like he doesn't belong here."

Hannah shook her head. "I don't know what nonsense your father told you, but accusing my father of being racist is a joke! He's the least racist person I know! He couldn't care less where you come from or the color of your skin. He employs people from all walks of life and cultures. Australian-born or immigrants, women or men, young old, Christian, Jew or Muslim. He doesn't care. We're also one of the biggest employers of aboriginal people in the country and we're very proud of that. All my father cares about is employing the best person for the job."

Ruby remained silent after Hannah's passionate speech. Determined to convince her of the truth of what she'd said, Hannah spoke again, albeit in a mollified tone.

"If what your father told you was true, why didn't he sue?"

Ruby stared back at Hannah and then slowly lowered her gaze. She took refuge in her drink and wished, not for the first time, that it was something stronger. The question of litigation had occurred to her before. Way back when her father first told her about the contract being canceled without cause. She had intimate knowledge of the clauses that dealt with the rights of termination and had been justifiably outraged that the contract had been wrongly brought to an end.

In fact, she remembered posing that very question to him, urging him to commence legal proceedings against Barrington Mining. To her surprise, he'd brushed off her suggestion with some vague response that she could barely remember now. Then Kyle had taken his own life and the world had been turned upside down for all of them. A few months after the funeral, Matthew had overheard Vaughan in the airport and in no time after that, her father had urged her to follow Vaughan to Bali and do whatever it took to get close to him and have him take her into his confidence.

"We need to hit them where it hurts, Ruby," her father had said. "Inside information. Anything we can use to disrupt Barrington's bullshit operation. He canceled my contract without cause and now your brother's dead. We owe it to Kyle to get payback."

The reminder of her brother had hit her hard. She'd still been grieving his loss and trying to process what had happened to drive him to his death.

She remembered her father's words clearly.

"Frank Barrington's had it in for me and my business from the start. He deserves to pay for what he did to Kyle. Now, will you help me, or not?"

He was her father. Her brother was dead. How could she have resisted such a plea? She'd gone to Bali all fired up and determined to do whatever she could to make Frank Barrington pay. If that meant cozying up to Vaughan and pretending to be in love, then she'd been prepared to do it.

Only, she hadn't planned on him being so wonderful or that her fake feelings would grow into the real thing… Now it was all too late. Even worse, she had a sneaking suspicion that Hannah was telling the truth. The newspaper articles certainly supported Hannah's version of events. There *had* been a number of safety incidents involving her father's company. And Evan Wilson, her father's employee, *had* been tragically killed.

As if reading her mind, Hannah spoke again.

"I'm not sure if you've heard about your cousin, Nathan Garcia? He's been charged with several criminal offenses. He's been committed to stand trial."

Ruby compressed her lips and nodded grimly. "I read about that in the papers, too." She paused and then added, "When I asked my father about it, he told me Nathan was innocent and dismissed it as nothing more than a witch hunt instigated by your father."

Hannah was silent for a long moment, her gaze fixed on her glass. When she finally looked at her, there was a hint of sympathy in her gaze.

"Given that you've been in Bali most of the past year, you probably don't know Nathan worked at the Strathwaylin mine as my open cut examiner, more or less my second-in-charge. In fact, I was the one who employed him. He supplied an impressive resumé that indicated extensive experience in mine safety. He also interviewed very well. He talked the talk and convinced me he was the perfect person for the job."

Ruby frowned. "But Nathan's spent most of his time working from my father's office. He's spent hardly any time at all on mine sites."

Hannah nodded. "Yes. I know that now. But at the time, I had no reason to believe he was being dishonest. His resumé outlined a good deal of experience in the very role I needed filled. I took him at his word. And before you ask, no, I didn't call all of his referees. That was my bad. If I had, no doubt I would have twigged to his deception a lot earlier. In fact, I would never have put him on."

Ruby stared at Hannah with a growing sense of dread. First, it seemed highly possible her father had lied to her about the reasons behind the termination of his contract. Now she had an awful suspicion that her father's claims about Nathan's innocence were also about to be dispelled. She gripped her glass and wished again that it was something stronger as she willed herself to sit there and listen to what Hannah had to say.

"I've worked at the Strathwaylin mine for a year now. Nathan was my righthand man for most of that time. Almost from the start, the mine was plagued with a series of incidents. Mostly minor, but they all had to be reported to the Resources Regulator and were, to be frank, worrying. They were the kind of basic safety breaches that shouldn't have happened.

"Nathan kept assuring me that my concerns weren't warranted. That he continuously reinforced the need for safety with the men. That sometimes, accidents just happened. But they *kept* happening and a couple of them were quite serious. Fortunately, no one was badly injured, but they were grave enough that we risked getting the mine closed by the regulator.

"My concern continued to grow, along with the frequency of the accidents. Nathan continued to insist I was overreacting and that he had things under control. Then a new investigator at the Resources Regulator began to look into two of the most recent incidents."

She paused and looked directly at Ruby. Ruby's heart sank. From the look on Hannah's face, she knew exactly what was coming.

"The investigator found proof Nathan was involved, didn't he?"

Hannah nodded. "Yes, he did. Not only that, but we also got Nathan on tape admitting it."

Ruby brought her hand up to her mouth in an effort to contain her shock. That information would have formed part of the police brief. Nathan and his lawyer would have been given a copy of all the evidence they had against him in support of the charges. There was no way she'd believe her father wasn't also aware that the police had Nathan on tape making admissions of guilt and given her brother, Matthew, worked closely with their dad, Matthew had to know, too.

I've been lied to by both of them... My father and my brother... My family... People I love and trust... And what about Kyle? What did he know about all this?

She'd never felt so betrayed. Instinctively, her hand went to her stomach and splayed protectively over her tiny bump.

Oh, hell. What a mess I've made of everything... My loyalty to my father's been so completely, incredibly misplaced...

That misplaced loyalty had cost her Vaughan, her soul mate, the love of her life. She bit back a sob.

Hannah gently touched her arm, her face filled with concern.

"Ruby? Are you all right?"

The quiet question tipped Ruby over the edge.

"No!" she cried. "No, I'm not!"

To her horror, tears filled her eyes and began to spill down her cheeks. As if a dam had suddenly been released, she buried her face in her hands and sobbed. Hannah squeezed her arm and murmured words of comfort, but Ruby was largely oblivious.

The pain of her father's betrayal was the worst pain she'd felt. Even worse than when Vaughan had coldly dismissed her from his life. As much as that had cut her heart to shreds, she'd clung to the fact that he'd once loved her with everything that he had and surely, that kind of love couldn't disappear overnight. That faint hope had sustained her.

But right now, there was nothing to cling to that could make this any better. Her father had deliberately lied to her, *used* her, for his own selfish gains. It was a gut-wrenching realization.

She cried for a long time, but when she finally lifted her head, Hannah was still there, regarding her with a mixture of concern and sympathy.

"I'm sorry, Ruby. Finding out this stuff must be difficult."

She nodded and hiccupped. "You could say that."

Hannah offered a grim smile. "For what it's worth, I think you're better off knowing the truth."

Ruby dragged in a shaky breath. "I agree. As hard as it is to accept my father lied to me, I'm grateful that you told me." She ran a hand through her tangled, damp hair. "I just can't believe what a fool I've been. I've ruined everything."

Hannah regarded her solemnly. "You mean, with Vaughan?"

Ruby nodded. "Yes. I lied to him. I hurt him so terribly with my deceit. He was devastated when he discovered what I'd done. The worst of it is, I'm still desperately in love with him and now he hates me."

Hannah grimaced. "Vaughan doesn't hate you. He doesn't hate anyone. He doesn't have what it takes to hate. He had such a terrible early childhood, he was determined never to let that shape him. He's always had a positive attitude toward life. If you know him well enough to be in love with him, you must know that."

"I do. That's one of the things I love about him." Ruby shook her head sadly. "Oh, Hannah! I've made such a mess of everything!"

Hannah compressed her lips. "Don't be too hard on yourself. Does he know you love him?"

Ruby shook her head. "No. Or at least, when I told him at the hospital, he didn't believe me, particularly after he realized the depth of my deception. Not that I can blame him." She grimaced. "And now I've complicated everything with the baby, I don't know where I stand."

Hannah's eyes widened in surprise. "You're *pregnant?*"

"Yes."

"Wow. Does Vaughan know?"

"He knows. He's agreed to support me and the baby."

"You mean, financially?"

"Yes. But that's the extent of it. There's been no talk of us getting back together."

Confusion and wariness flashed in Hannah's eyes. "I see."

"I don't think you do." Ruby dragged in a deep breath and sighed wearily. "When I found out I was pregnant, Vaughan and I had not long broken up. I didn't know what to do. He told me he never wanted to see me again. I could tell he hated me. And there I was, pregnant. The last thing I wanted was for him to stay with me out of obligation. We both know he's exactly that kind of guy. When I first told him about the baby, he confirmed as much. He wanted to get married."

"So, what's wrong with that? You guys had already been engaged once!"

"Yes, but that was before Vaughan found out about my deception. Before everything we had together fell apart. Like I said, I hated the thought that he might offer to stay with me only because of the baby. I selfishly wanted him to be there for *me*."

Hannah nodded. "I understand," she said softly. "You needed that reassurance. After all, anything could happen. Babies don't always make it full term. How would you feel if you got married for the sake of the baby and then you had a miscarriage?"

"Exactly," Ruby said grimly, relieved that Hannah did in fact understand.

Hannah pulled a face. "Boy, what a mess!"

Ruby managed a wry grin. "I told you, right?"

"So, what are you going to do?" Hannah asked gently.

Ruby grimaced. "I don't know. I guess I'll lay it all on the line with Vaughan and see where we end up. I've already told him

I don't want to marry for the sake of the baby. The only thing I can do is apologize again for my actions and offer him an explanation, tell him how much I love him, and hope for the best."

Hannah leaned over and gave her a spontaneous hug. Ruby stiffened in surprise, but then relaxed into the unexpected embrace. It seemed Hannah believed her, and for that she was grateful.

"For what it's worth, I'm hoping my brother forgives you and realizes the difficult position you've been in. Torn between love for your family and love for the son of your father's enemy. I'm sorry that you're having to go through all this. Your family, the baby, Vaughan... It's a lot to deal with."

Ruby teared up again. "Yes, it is. And thank you. I... I really appreciate you taking the time to listen."

"I'm pleased we cleared the air. I understand your motives a little better now. If you need someone to talk to, you can always call me, okay? I wish there was something more I could do to help, but Vaughan's unlikely to take advice from me." An impish expression filled Hannah's face. "Still, that's never stopped me in the past. Maybe it's high time for my big brother to get an earful from his baby sister. What do you think?"

Ruby offered a trembling smile. "Thanks, Hannah. I appreciate the support, but Vaughan's finished with me and it's all my fault. I ruined the only truly good thing in my life and shattered the trust of the best man I've ever known. I now need to pick up those pieces and move on, if only for the sake of my baby."

A determined glint flashed in Hannah's eyes. "Don't give up on my brother yet. There's a new Barrington on the way and the best thing for it is to have its mother and father on the same page. When I'm through talking some sense into Vaughan, I'm confident he'll see things the same way."

Chapter Nineteen

Hannah had planned to see Vaughan right after she'd dropped Ruby off at her city apartment, but a phone call from her fiancé, Liam, had changed her mind. Or, more specifically, Liam had advised her against it.

"It's getting late, Hannah. It's raining cats and dogs down there. It'll take you nearly an hour to get to Vaughan's place in Bondi. Have you arranged for anywhere to stay tonight? Please don't tell me you intend to drive through the storm back to Muswellbrook?"

Hannah sighed. "You're right. So, the storm's hit up there, too?"

"Yes. It's a nasty one. A lot of thunder and lightning and a fierce wind along with the rain. It's pelting down. I'd be far happier if you booked a room in a nearby hotel and waited this one out."

"Okay," she agreed. "You win. I'll check into the Hilton. I'm only a block away from there."

"Thank you." He paused. "How did things go with Ruby?"

"Actually, things went better than I anticipated. It's a long story and I look forward to filling you in on all the details when I see you, but for now, let's just say we had a good talk, cleared the air and... I wouldn't be at all disappointed if she and Vaughan patch up their differences and go through with their wedding."

"Wow!"

Hannah smiled at the surprise in Liam's voice. "I know, right? It was unexpected. I left Muswellbrook feeling decidedly antagonistic toward Ruby Ashworth-Rodriguez and now... Hey, we might even become friends."

"Wow, again," Liam said.

Hannah grinned. She was still a little amazed at how her view of Ruby had turned around. She'd agreed to meet because she wanted to make certain the woman knew the truth about her father. She'd braced herself for a tense conversation and had convinced herself she was probably wasting her time. Ruby didn't strike her as a woman who liked being put in her place—or being told that she was wrong.

But she'd surprised Hannah, as had the realization that Ruby had already been having doubts and doing her own research, despite what Ruby's father had told her. That couldn't have been easy, let alone to accept the uncomfortable truths she'd uncovered. Hannah had come away from their meeting with a grudging respect and admiration for a woman she'd once considered an enemy.

"Listen, babe. I've just arrived at the hotel. I'll call you after I've checked into my room."

"No worries. Talk soon. I love you."

"I love you more." She smiled as she ended the call.

With nothing to unpack, it wasn't long before Hannah was showered and wrapped up in a fluffy robe and sitting cross-legged on the super-king bed. Though she and Liam hadn't yet taken the leap and moved in together, he'd spent plenty of nights sleeping over and the thought of spending the night alone in that huge bed was a little depressing.

After ordering room service and picking at the bowl of chicken and mushroom pasta, she finally set it aside and called Liam again. He answered on the second ring.

"What are you doing?" she asked.

"Lying on the couch watching TV."

"What are you watching?"

"A re-run of last year's rugby league grand final. It's riveting."

She pouted. "It's good to see you're missing me."

"Of course, I'm missing you."

"Where's Jacqueline?" she asked, referring to Liam's sister.

"She's at work."

"So, you're home alone?"

"Yup."

And then Hannah had an idea. She stretched languorously back on the bed. "What are you wearing?"

She heard Liam's sharp intake of breath and smiled. This wasn't the first time they'd engaged in phone sex. Though Liam had been the one to initiate it the first time, it hadn't taken her long to catch on to the idea.

He cleared his throat. "Um... I'm in my boxers and a T-shirt. What about you?"

"I just took a shower. I'm all shampooed up, exfoliated and moisturized. My legs are silky smooth."

"Are you naked?"

"Not yet. But I can be. Give me a moment."

"I'll give you all the time you want. How about you and I get comfortable?"

Hannah grinned. "Oh, I like the way you think, lover."

When it was over, and they were both relaxed and replete, Liam smiled. "That was great, babe. We must do it again sometime soon."

"Better than football?" She smiled sleepily. It was all she could do to keep her eyes open.

"Oh, yeah. I'm not sure I have the energy to get off the couch." He yawned loudly. "'Night, Beautiful. I love you."

"I love you, too. 'Night."

She fell asleep with a smile on her face.

Hannah leaped out of bed the next morning feeling rested and relaxed and even more anxious to get into the Barrington

Mining head office to speak with Vaughan. She'd never expected to find her soul mate and fall in love, but life didn't always go to plan and she, for one, was glad. She was besotted with Liam. She couldn't imagine life without him.

She wanted the same for her brother. He'd once been in love with Ruby enough to propose to her. Hannah was certain those feelings hadn't just up and died. She hoped that he and Ruby could patch things up and get their lives back on track. Together. The fact there was a baby on the way only made it make more sense. She was going to do her bit to make him see that Ruby was worth the trouble.

Her father had told her Vaughan had returned to work after he'd discharged himself from the hospital and he'd always been an early riser. She wasn't exactly sure what she was going to say to him, but she wanted to help in any way she could.

Ruby obviously cared for him. She'd admitted she was still in love with him. But Vaughan wouldn't be easy to convince. He'd been badly hurt and his trust in Ruby shattered. Hannah was counting on the fact that he'd once loved Ruby strongly enough to propose and his love wouldn't easily fade.

She waved a greeting in Casey's direction where she sat at her desk. "Hi, Casey. How are things?"

Casey smiled. "Hannah! Good morning! What a surprise!"

Hannah winked. "I came down to the city last night for a meeting. I thought I'd pop into the office. Is Vaughan in?"

Casey nodded. "Yes, they're both in. Vaughan's in your father's office."

"Thank you. Are they alone?"

"Yes."

Hannah acknowledged her response with a nod and sailed on past Casey's desk.

"Oh, by the way, congratulations on your engagement," Casey added.

Hannah paused. "Thank you. Liam and I are very happy."

Casey winked. "You were the last person I thought I'd see planning a walk down the aisle."

Hannah laughed. "You and me, both."

Casey's laughter followed Hannah down the short corridor to the executive offices. She knocked briefly on the closed door of her father's office and then walked right in. Both men registered their surprise.

"Hannah! What are you doing here?" her father asked.

"Hi, Daddy. Morning, Vaughan. I just happened to be in town, so I thought I'd pay you a friendly visit."

From his position seated behind his carved oak desk, Frank spread his arms wide. "You're welcome any time. Is everything all right at the mine?"

"Yes, of course."

"What brings you to the city, little sis?" Vaughan asked, folding his arms across his chest and propping a hip against Frank's desk.

Hannah smiled. "Ah. Funny you should ask that."

Vaughan frowned, his eyes filling with suspicion. "That sounds ominous. What's going on?"

Hannah forced a laugh and strode casually across the room. She was more nervous than she thought she'd be, talking to Vaughan about his love life. She and Vaughan had always been tight, but he was nearly two decades older than her. He'd already left home by the time she was born.

Still, he'd made an effort to stay in touch and to get to know his younger siblings. As she'd grown older, she'd called on him for advice. He was good at cutting through the nonsense to the heart of the matter. She always came away from their discussions feeling better about herself and whatever decision she'd been pondering.

But on those occasions, she'd been the one seeking advice; it had been *her* love life or business decisions they'd been discussing. She wasn't exactly sure how he'd take having the spotlight on him. She was about to find out.

Sauntering with forced casualness over to the floor-to-ceiling windows that dominated her father's office, she stared out at the impressive view. On a good day, it was possible to see clear out to the Sydney Heads, but the deluge that had saturated Ruby the night before had hung around and had developed into a wet and dreary day.

Right now, the view out the windows was of a dull gray sky, heavy, dark clouds that promised another drenching and a storm-gray sea dotted all over with foamy whitecaps—testament to the strength of the wind outside. Hannah had struggled to hold on to her umbrella on the way over to Barrington Mining headquarters.

Feigning interest in the street below where knots of people scurried like ants on their way to work, she used the time to corral her courage. The silence lengthened. When she couldn't put the conversation off a moment longer, she drew in a deep breath, squared her shoulders, and turned to face them. Her gaze zeroed in on her brother.

"I met with Ruby Ashworth-Rodriguez last night. We had a good talk."

Vaughan's expression darkened with anger and surprise. "What the hell? Why would you do something like that?"

Hannah held up her hand. "Please, Vaughan. Before you jump on your high horse, just hear me out."

"This better be good," he muttered, still looking far from pleased.

Hannah took that as a sign to continue. "Surprisingly, Ruby reached out to me. It seemed she'd done some research into her father's accusations of unfair treatment and wanted to hear my take on what had happened."

Ignoring her father, Hannah watched Vaughan closely. He'd tensed but nodded slightly. She forged on. In a straightforward tone, she relayed what had unfolded during the previous evening's conversation.

"So, you see. She only did it to help her father. You can't blame her for that," Hannah said when she'd finished.

Vaughan's jaw clenched. "She lied about everything for months, Hannah. How can you dismiss that as if it means nothing?"

Hannah's temper flared. "I'm not dismissing anything, Vaughan!" She drew in another breath in an effort to control her anger. "I admit the way she went about things was dishonest and wrong, but she obviously loves her father. He set her up. He told her the kind of lies he knew she wouldn't be able to resist."

"You mean, telling her it was our fault her brother committed suicide?"

Hannah gasped. "What?"

Vaughan shot her a cynical look. "I see she didn't tell you everything."

Hannah frowned in consternation. "Her brother committed suicide?"

"Yes. Apparently in response to the terminated contract."

"Oh, my God," Hannah said dazedly. "Poor Ruby! The lies her father told her were even worse than I thought!" She turned on Vaughan. "How can you stand there and not feel sorry for her? Put yourself in her position. If Daddy had come to you with a sad story of how someone was racially vilifying him and there was nothing he could do about it and it was going to cost him millions in lost contracts, even her brother's life... What would you have done?"

"But it didn't happen to Dad," Vaughan muttered.

"But say that it *did*. How would you have reacted?" Hannah persisted.

Vaughan sighed wearily. "I would have done what I could to help him."

"Exactly!" Hannah was filled with triumph. *So far, so good...*

"I don't understand what this has to do with anything," Vaughan grumbled. "Why are you now taking her side? No one forced Ruby to deceive me like that. Her father might have put the idea in her head, but she was the one who carried through with it...for months and months and months. We lived together, for Pete's sake! At no time did she feel the need to come clean and tell me the truth. If Liam hadn't realized who she was, she might never have confessed. She broke the trust between us, Hannah. That's something that's almost impossible to overcome."

Hannah nodded briefly, conceding the point. "You're right, but I know how much you care for her! You were going to get married! Vaughan Barrington! The perennial bachelor who could have had any woman he wanted and yet no one managed to capture his heart. Until Ruby. You can't just dismiss that like it means nothing."

Vaughan stared at the carpet, his eyes hard, his expression fierce. Hannah was filled with a surge of panic. She played her final card.

"Ruby told me about the baby."

Her bombshell was met with silence. Hannah looked from Vaughan to her father. Her father didn't seem especially surprised by her announcement.

Vaughan must have already told Daddy... That's a good sign...

"You're going to be a father, Vaughan! How amazing is that?" she exclaimed.

Chapter Twenty

Vaughan scowled at Hannah, shocked that Ruby had told her about the baby. "What does that have to do with anything? I already told her I'd support them both."

Hannah's lips twisted into a grimace. "Yes, financially. How romantic."

"What do you expect of me, Hannah?" he cried in exasperation. "She lied to me. She broke my heart. On top of that, she doesn't love me!"

Concern clouded Hannah's eyes. "But, you're happy about the baby, aren't you?"

"Of course, he is," their father said, surprising them both.

Vaughan turned to face him and raised a single brow In silent query. He hadn't spoken to his father about the baby since he'd suggested he make sure the baby was his. But somehow, Frank had already guessed that Vaughan didn't really believe Ruby had cheated on him and was ready to take care of and love his child from the moment he'd become aware of its existence.

In response to Vaughan's silent question, his father merely shrugged. "Well, it's true, isn't it?" Frank blustered.

Vaughan kept his gaze steady on his father's. "Yes, Dad. You're right. I very much want Ruby to have our baby and I'll take care of it and love it for the rest of my life."

"Well, there you go!" Hannah exclaimed. "Oh, by the way, Vaughan. You're wrong about her not loving you. She's head-over-heels, sick-in-the-stomach in love with you."

Vaughan froze. He stared at his sister coldly. "Don't joke about things like that. Ruby never loved me. She pretended to in order to get what she wanted. That's it. All that time we were together in Bali was nothing more than a farce. You'll never convince me otherwise."

Hannah threw up her arms. Anger and impatience flared in her eyes. "For heaven's sake, Vaughan. Wake up. Okay, so maybe Ruby didn't fall in love with you as quickly as you fell in love with her. I don't know all the details. I wasn't there. What I do know is that she's desperately in love with you now and she's scared to death of what lies ahead. She thinks you hate her and she doesn't blame you for feeling that way. Don't you think you owe it to yourself to at least talk to her and ascertain the truth?"

Vaughan stared at his sister, torn with indecision. He'd been thrilled that Ruby wanted to keep their baby, but that didn't necessarily mean she loved him, *really* loved him. She'd told him in the hospital she loved him, but then he'd discovered her treachery and had no longer trusted anything she said.

But if Hannah was correct, Ruby was in love with him. Was this just another ploy to get him on side? Was she really that cold, that calculating? As if able to read his troubled thoughts, Hannah spoke again, her expression intense.

"She's devastated about being lied to by her family. Not only by her father. Apparently, her older brother maintained the same deceits. It was only when she undertook her own research that she started to consider the truth."

Hannah dragged in a breath. "I didn't hold back. It didn't give me any joy to apprise her of all the ugly details concerning her father and how he runs his business, but I didn't sugarcoat it, either. It must have been difficult for her to hear. We're talking about her *family*. The people she loves the most. You can imagine what that's done to her, Vaughan. Her family have turned out to be morally corrupt liars and frauds, and that's destroying her."

Vaughan's mind spun. Each word was like a physical blow raining down on his head. He hated the thought of Ruby feeling so terrible, especially when he wasn't there to comfort her. No matter that they were currently at odds. That didn't mean he no longer cared for her. Hannah was right. The kind of deep feelings he'd had for Ruby didn't dissipate overnight—or even over a few weeks—no matter how much he might have wanted them to.

Some of his inner turmoil must have shown on his face. Hannah stepped closer and touched his arm.

"Call her, Vaughan. Be honest. Tell her how you feel. Listen to what she has to say. Open your heart to forgiveness. None of us are perfect, brother. You never know, you might just need her to forgive you one day."

Her words filled Vaughan with guilt. It was true. He'd judged Ruby and found her wanting; rebuilding the shattered trust between them would be difficult. But in spite of it all, he still loved her. Perhaps that had more to do with the fact that deep down, he agreed with his sister. None of them were perfect. And that included him. People made mistakes. Was it fair that they be made to pay for them for the rest of their life?

It shamed him that he already knew the answer to that.

Ruby rubbed at her gritty eyes. She'd slept fitfully through the night. In fact, she was surprised she'd slept at all after Hannah's revelations the night before. She was exhausted, mentally, emotionally and physically. Everything she'd read about the first trimester and overwhelming fatigue was true. It didn't help that she had so much going on in her head with Vaughan and the baby and her family...

She shuddered. She couldn't bear to think about her family, especially her father. She'd trusted him; believed everything he'd said. Had acted on his urgings and taken up his cause. And for what? All she'd done was betray the first and only man she'd ever loved, and ruined her chances of a future with him.

Heaving a sigh, she pushed back her bedroom curtains and gazed out at the dull, gray day. It perfectly suited her mood. She yearned to climb back under the covers and hide away until the pain subsided, but a day in bed wasn't going to change anything. She intended to confront her father and demand the truth. She was done with listening to his lies.

The things Hannah had revealed about her father... Of course, there was a chance the woman was lying. No, she immediately discounted the idea. The research she'd done backed up Hannah's story. It had shed doubt on her father's story even before she'd spoken to Hannah. And then there was Nathan.

Hannah had worked with Nathan for nearly a year. She was in a perfect position to have firsthand information on what had gone down at the mine. The police investigation which had resulted in charges being laid and had Nathan now having to defend himself in court was real.

Ruby no longer believed her father's protestations that Nathan had been arrested on trumped up charges and that Frank Barrington had paid off the police. They didn't live in the kind of country where corruption easily infiltrated the highest levels and the police could be bought. Hannah's version had been backed by law enforcement. Ruby was going to confront her father about the truth of it all.

That's what she wanted from him: the truth. His lies had set into motion a course of action that had resulted in her losing the love of her life. There would be no apology forthcoming.

Her father was a hard and proud man. He wouldn't seek her forgiveness. She also had questions about Kyle. Her father had insisted her brother had committed suicide as a result of Frank Barrington's actions. Now Ruby wasn't so sure. The thought made her sick inside. What had really gone down to make her brother commit such a final act as suicide?

One thing was for certain, she looked forward to the upcoming confrontation like she looked forward to a root canal. But she'd never been a coward and she wouldn't let fear hold her back now. She needed answers.

After taking a quick shower and dressing in a pale pink linen shirt and a blue, knee-length skirt, she made herself a cup of decaf coffee and then nibbled on a piece of dry toast. The worst of the morning sickness had passed, but she'd discovered that if she ate too much first thing, the nausea would return.

Picking up her phone off the kitchen counter, she stared down at the screen. She wanted to call Vaughan and tell him what she was about to do. Get his advice. Seek reassurance.

No. This was her fight. Best to leave Vaughan out of it. Finishing her coffee, she tossed the leftover toast into the bin and tidied up the kitchen. When she couldn't put off the visit to her father a moment longer, she grabbed her handbag, phone and keys and left.

On the way out to her car, she put in a call to her father's EA. There was no sense in her turning up at the office ready for a confrontation and then finding her father wasn't in.

"Hi, Beth. It's Ruby. How are you?"

"Hi, Ruby! I'm fine. What can I do for you?"

"I need a few minutes with my dad. Is he in yet?"

"I'm sorry, Ruby. Your father's working from home today. I don't expect him in the office until tomorrow."

After thanking Beth for her time, Ruby ended the call. She sighed. Her parents lived in Point Piper, a small but exclusive harborside suburb about four miles east of the city. At that time of day, taking into account peak hour traffic, it would take her at least twenty minutes. More than double the time it would take to get to her father's office. Still, if she wanted to get this over with, there was nothing for it.

She made one last call to her secretary, Marnie, and told her to re-schedule her morning's appointments. Then she pulled out into the busy traffic. Point Piper stretched over just eleven streets. The suburb was renowned for its spectacular views of the Opera House and the Harbour Bridge, and cherished for its privacy and prestige.

Wolseley Road, where her parents lived, was home to a number of celebrities and several billionaire business tycoons. Though Joseph and Maria Rodriguez were not quite in that league, Ruby was proud of what her parents had achieved. The fact that they'd emigrated from Spain with a few suitcases and some meager savings made their current lofty status all the more amazing.

As she joined the queue of traffic heading east, she wondered how their financial position was affected by the loss of the Barrington Mining contract. Her father had hinted that he was in dire straits, but she didn't know if he'd exaggerated, or whether that really was the case.

She'd never asked them about their finances. Though she was employed as an in-house lawyer, she wasn't on the executive and had never been invited to participate in board meetings. When she was growing up, there had been plenty of money. Though her parents weren't millionaires at that time, they'd already started to make a name for themselves in the local earthmoving industry and they'd lived a prosperous life.

She and her two older brothers had been raised in a comfortable, four-bedroom home in Maroubra. It didn't have the multi-million-dollar price tag of Point Piper, but it was in the fashionable eastern suburbs and far from a shabby place to grow up. There had been a nice view of the ocean from the back deck.

In most people's estimation, her childhood had been idyllic. A pleasant home life, a caring family, lazy weekends at the beach. For Ruby, it would have been almost perfect if her mother had made more of an effort to be part of their lives.

Maria Rodriguez gave all outward appearances of being supportive of her husband's ambitions, and in the early days, she was an integral part of the business. She'd worked in the office and managed the accounts while Joe sourced contracts, prepared and submitted tenders and did all the grunt work. As the company grew and expanded, Maria had taken a step back. She'd stopped coming into the office and had spent more and more time concentrating on her own pursuits.

Ruby didn't begrudge her mother having a life of her own, but that life often ran contrary to the rest of the family. More often than not, her mother had been out when she'd come home from school. There were many nights when Ruby had retired for the night not having laid eyes on her mother all day.

Ruby's father had explained that her mother was busy attending meetings of her various charity projects, as well as patronizing art auctions, soirees, and other high-profile celebrity-studded society events. The fact her father mostly chose not to attend those events had confused Ruby, until she'd asked him about it.

"That's your mother's thing," he'd said. "Hobnobbing with all those people. I prefer to stay at home with my kids."

Ruby didn't know if her father had meant to widen the division between his children and their mother, but from that day on, Ruby had begun siding with her father against her mother during arguments and had gone out of her way to make life difficult for the mother she felt had abandoned her for the glitz and glamor of high society.

It meant that at thirty-six, Ruby wasn't close to her mother. Neither were her brothers. Matthew and Kyle had followed in their father's footsteps and gone into the family business, working closely by his side. That was the reason Kyle had been so affected by what had happened when Frank Barrington had turned on them. At least, that's what she'd been led to believe.

Still, until now, Ruby had always regarded her family as close—as close as they could be, her mother notwithstanding—but now she was forced to rethink everything she'd taken for granted. From everything she'd heard and read, it had become clear that her father and Matthew had lied to her.

The family she'd held up on a pedestal, would have defended with her dying breath, had betrayed her. She'd depended upon them to have her back, to give her their loyalty and support, and honesty, as she'd given hers. But they'd let her down; had set her on a course of self-destruction for their own ends. Her belief and trust in them was shattered. She'd lost her anchor, been set adrift. The seismic shift in the world she'd relied on and believed in was devastating.

As she drew closer to her parents' home, her stomach tensed with nerves. Silent tears tracked down her cheeks. The upcoming confrontation would be difficult. She hoped it didn't turn ugly. She hoped her father would own up to his deception and apologize and beg her forgiveness, but she wouldn't hold her breath.

She made the turn into Wolseley Road, barely noticing the stately mansions that stood side by side with modern, architecturally inspired concrete-and-glass structures. All of them commanded prime positions overlooking Sydney Harbour. Her parents' house was no exception.

Gathering her courage, she punched in the code on the keypad that activated the entry gates and drove through. She parked along the paved circular driveway, right outside the house. The heavy clouds of earlier lingered in the sky, adding to the weight on her shoulders. Now that she was here, all she wanted to do was get it over with.

She found her father seated behind his desk in the room he'd claimed many years ago for his office. He'd had it renovated not long after they'd moved in. The dark wood paneling on the walls and the mahogany floorboards complemented the heavy damask red drapes and the carved walnut desk. It was an entirely masculine room with no nod at all to the fact her mother lived there.

"Ruby! Honey, what a nice surprise!"

Her father's affectionate greeting was followed with a hug. Though it took all of her courage to do it, she briefly hugged him back. She wasn't setting out to destroy her relationship with her family. All she wanted was for her father to own up to the truth.

"Ruby. What are you doing here?"

Until then, she hadn't noticed her cousin, Nathan, who stood off to one side, partially concealed in the shadows. She blinked with surprise.

"Hello, Nathan. I could ask the same thing of you," she said dryly.

Though he'd never been as close to her as her brothers, she got on with him well enough. As first cousins, they saw each other regularly at family gatherings and other social events. But knowing what she did now about his behavior at the Strathwaylin mine, having him here while she talked to her father set her on edge.

"Your father and I were just going over the police statements. You heard about my indictment, no doubt?"

"Yes. I read about it in the papers."

Her father waved her words away and returned to his seat. "It's all bullshit."

"Where's Mom?" she asked, looking around reflexively though she didn't expect to see her in her father's office. As far as Ruby recalled, she'd never seen her mother in the room.

Her father's response was curt. "Out. Where do you think?"

Cutting to the chase, she posed the question she'd been dreading. "Why did you lie to me about that mining contract?"

Her father's eyes flared wide with surprise before he quickly concealed it behind a frown. "What are you talking about?"

Fed up with the subterfuge, Ruby advanced on him. She crossed her arms over her chest. "Quit with the games, Daddy. I'm not buying it. You told me Frank Barrington had canceled your contract and turned on you and your business without just cause. That it was because he was racist. That he wanted to be rid of you, no matter what. You told me Kyle took the fall from grace hard. That he couldn't bear to live with the disappointment. You know how I felt about Kyle. How close we were. That's the reason I was willing to help you. In fact, I turned my life upside down for you."

Her father sneered. "Oh, right. Like spending the better part of a year lazing about on a beach in Bali was tough."

Ruby bit back an angry retort. There was no point in trading insults. She was there to confront him with the truth and hope he had the courage and love and respect for her to admit his deception.

"I went there only because you asked me to, Daddy. You begged me to help you; made me believe you and Kyle had been treated abominably by Frank Barrington and yet, strangely enough, you didn't once tell me to prepare a statement of claim or commence legal proceedings. Why not? If Frank Barrington had wrongfully terminated that contract, that should have been your first order of business. Not sending me on a wild goose chase to Bali."

Nathan took a step toward her. An angry flush stained his face. "Just what are you saying, Ruby? Are you accusing your father of lying?"

Her father held up his hand toward her cousin and shook his head briefly. "Thank you, Nathan, but I don't need you to fight my battles." His gaze returned to Ruby's. "You seem awfully confident you know the facts. Tell me, who have you been speaking to?"

"What does that matter? The fact remains you didn't ask me to follow normal procedure and file."

"It matters a great deal."

They eyed each other in steely silence, neither one willing to look away. Ruby finally threw up her hands and rolled her eyes in exasperation.

"I did my own research. I also spoke with Hannah Barrington."

Her father's expression darkened. "A *Barrington?* You'd take the word of a Barrington over your own father?"

"She works at the Strathwaylin mine. She knew all about the safety incidents that had occurred there over the past year or so." Ruby swung around to face Nathan and narrowed her eyes at him. "She also had quite a bit to say about *you.*"

Nathan's lips twisted in a scowl. "Hannah Barrington wouldn't know a digger from a dump truck. The only reason she's in such a lofty position is because her father owns the mine and there's no one who'll disagree with that. Go and ask some of the others who work out there. They'll tell you the same."

Ruby eyed him steadily. "The thing is, Nathan, a short time ago, I might have believed you. But you've been indicted on serious criminal charges. Are you telling me that's all a load of rubbish, too?"

"You have no idea the extent of Frank Barrington's reach, Ruby," her father said. "He has a lot of important people in his pocket. Judges, lawyers, police officers..."

Ruby shook her head, suddenly impatient. "Oh, please, Dad! Stop it! Both of you!" She encompassed Nathan in her glare. "I'm not stupid. As I said, before I spoke to Hannah,

I did some research of my own. I read numerous newspaper accounts outlining a string of safety breaches at the very same mine you worked at. A lot of them mentioned you by name. Are you going to continue to insist that there's no substance to any of it? That even the *reporters* are on Frank Barrington's payroll?"

Suddenly, the mood in the room changed. Instead of admitting to wrongdoing and asking her forgiveness, her father's expression hardened.

"I can't believe I've raised a child who'd take the side of a Barrington over her own family. I've never been so insulted in all my life. I don't care who you've talked to or what you've read. I'm telling you the truth. That contract was pulled by Frank Barrington for no other reason than he hated my guts."

All at once, the fight went out of Ruby. It was clear her father was nowhere near the point, if ever, where he was willing to admit he'd lied to her, let alone man up and apologize for ruining her life. There was nothing more she could achieve here. The best thing to do would be to cut her losses and leave. Her shoulders slumped.

I wish Vaughan was here... I need him... I need him to put his arms around me and hold me close... Reassure me he loves me... That he'll never let anything hurt me again...

She loved him so much. Had probably loved him from their very earliest days together. It broke her heart that by the time she'd realized how deeply she felt for him, it was too late. The damage had been done. They were over.

Still, they'd made a baby together and that would bind them for a long time to come. It was nowhere near the kind of permanent commitment she yearned for, but right now, she was prepared to take any scrap of Vaughan's time that he was willing to give her. She also needed to apologize again for all the hurt she'd caused him as a result of her father's lies. So many lies...

She gazed back at the man she'd once loved and trusted above all others. "What you've done isn't right. I don't care how you justify it. People were injured. Someone was killed! And for what? Money? Power? Prestige? And what about Kyle? Was it really because he was so devastated over losing a contract that he took his own life?" She shook her head, her voice ragged with emotion. "You both disgust me."

Nathan took two quick steps toward her, his expression turning ugly. "Don't you *dare* speak to your father like that," he snarled, getting right in her face. "You're nothing but a spoiled brat. Your father's showered you with everything you could ever want—cars, holidays, a lucrative job. You spent a fucking year on a beach in Bali! And that's the thanks he gets." His lip curled up in disgust. "You sure are something."

Ruby stood her ground, though her heart raced. She flicked a glance in her father's direction. She was surprised to see his face was as hard and implacable as granite.

Ruby went cold.

So that's how it is... He's going to choose Nathan's side over his own daughter... I'm on my own...

Chapter Twenty-One

Vaughan leaned back against his ergonomic, environmentally friendly executive office chair and dropped his boots on his desk. Hannah had left more than an hour ago, but her words kept playing on his mind. He was meant to be working through the latest mining compliance regulations issued by the state government, but his mind kept straying to Ruby.

He was ecstatic she'd decided to keep the baby. They still had a long way to go to repair their relationship, even if it ended up just one of co-parenting, but maybe they could rebuild what they'd once had. The truth was, he still loved her. No matter that she'd lied to him, broken his trust, he still missed her.

Deep down, he still wanted her in his life. He wanted to see if they could work through the circumstances that had torn them apart and start afresh. Especially now that they had a baby on the way. A baby they both wanted.

I need to call her...

It was clear that Hannah was now firmly in Ruby's court, which meant the two must have formed some kind of connection last night. He was surprised that Ruby had told his sister about the baby, especially considering they still had so much to work out about that themselves.

The baby.

His face broke into a smile. *I'm going to be a daddy!*

He opened his briefcase and pulled out his phone. He tapped the screen, entered his password and scrolled through his contacts for Ruby's number. As the call dialed out, his heart leaped with excitement and anticipation.

I can't wait to tell her I love her. That I want us to start over. Take a chance on us and our baby...

Ruby's phone vibrated in her back pocket, indicating an incoming call. With Nathan still eyeballing her and looking like he wanted to tear her head off, she was pleased for the distraction. Pulling it out, she checked the screen.

Vaughan.

Her heart leaped. Though she was still disappointed he hadn't said anything about them getting back together, she wanted to talk to him. She sure could do with a little moral support right now. The aggression rolling off her cousin was enough incentive for her to invite Vaughan to join the fray.

She smiled humorlessly. It would serve her father right to be confronted with the reality that, not only had Ruby believed a Barrington over her own flesh and blood, she was in love with one and having a baby with him. Staring hard at Nathan, she answered the call and spoke in a loud voice, making sure the other occupants in the room heard her.

"Hi, Vaughan. So great to hear from you. I'm at my father's house." She gave him the address. "You ought to come over. Please hurry."

Before Vaughan could respond, Nathan snatched the phone out of her hand and tossed it across the room. She grimaced as it hit the hardwood floors and smashed.

"Nathan! What the hell...?"

His narrow-eyed gaze was dark and furious. Once again, he strode into her personal space, so close she could see the pores of his skin.

"You shouldn't have done that."

The venom in his gaze gave her pause. She'd never had cause to be frightened of him and she wasn't afraid of him now, but there was something in his expression that alarmed her. It was almost like his fury had taken him to another level that wasn't entirely connected to reality.

Her gaze shifted to her father, who remained seated behind his desk.

"Call off your attack dog, Daddy. This is getting ridiculous."

Her father regarded her icily. For the first time, Ruby experienced a shiver of unease.

"No, Ruby. You're the one who's being ridiculous. I'm beyond insulted that you'd take a Barrington's word over mine and now you've rubbed salt into the wound by merrily inviting the enemy into our home." His face turned puce. "You're a traitor of the very worst kind! How *dare* you!"

Vaughan stared down at the phone in his hand, nonplussed. He'd been in the process of responding to Ruby when the call had come to an abrupt end. He'd tried to phone her back, but the call went straight to voicemail.

Strange.

She'd said she was over at her father's place in Point Piper. There shouldn't have been any black spots in the phone service over there and he still had five bars. It was odd that the call had dropped out and now he couldn't reach her.

She'd asked him to come over, which was also strange. There was no love lost between Joseph Rodriguez and the Barringtons.

Perhaps her father isn't home? But why would she invite me over to his house? Why not suggest we meet at her apartment, or at a coffee shop, or in the park?

The last place he expected to meet to talk about their future was in her father's house. Something was awry. He didn't know what, but his instincts urged him to find out, and quickly.

Dropping his phone back in his shirt pocket, he picked up his keys off his desk. As he passed Casey on his way out, he took a moment to let her know where he was going.

"I'll be an hour or so. Maybe a little more, depending on traffic."

Casey's smile was friendly enough. He was glad there were no hard feelings.

"No worries, Vaughan. All good. I'll let your father know."

"Thanks."

Hurrying down the corridor, he took the lift to the underground carpark. The worst of the peak hour traffic was over. Getting to his destination from the city should take him no more than fifteen minutes. Ten if he got cracking and got a good run with the lights. Though Ruby hadn't sounded overly alarmed, she *had* asked him to hurry. Coupled with the strangeness of her request, he didn't want to delay.

As he turned into Wolseley Road, he checked the address Ruby had given him. A hundred yards or so farther down, he came to a paved driveway that was blocked by high, wrought iron gates. There was an intercom off to one side. Winding down his window, he pressed the buzzer and waited for someone to answer.

He was greeted with silence. He pressed the buzzer a couple of more times and got the same result.

Great. She asked me to come over; now she's not around to open the gate. What the hell?

Pulling out his phone, he once again dialed Ruby's number. Yet again, the call went straight to voicemail. A faint stirring of unease filled his gut. The whole scenario was getting stranger and stranger.

Where are you, Ruby? What the hell is going on?

He looked at the gates. They soared more than six feet over his head. They finished with sharp, pointed ends. There was no way he'd make it over them. Refusing to be deterred, he canvassed the solid sandstone fence. It wasn't as high as the gates. Nor did it look as impenetrable. In fact, the natural, slightly uneven surface of the sandstone could provide enough toeholds that he might be able to scale it without too much difficulty.

With no other choice, he shucked off his suit jacket and pulled off his boots and socks. Barefoot, he made his way over to the fence. If he stretched up as high as he could on tiptoes, he could just get his fingers over the other side of the wall. It would have to suffice.

He drew in a deep breath and stepped back a few paces. Then he took a running leap at the fence. And missed.

"Fuck." He grunted as he landed on the grass. But he refused to be deterred.

The second attempt was more successful. His fingers made it over the other side and he clung on for dear life as his toes struggled to find traction on the wall. Gritting his teeth and using his upper body strength, he slowly pulled himself up and over the other side.

He landed hard in the middle of a spiky hedge and cursed again. His cheek stung and his ankle hurt, along with his shoulder. Gingerly, he tried to stand and was relieved when his feet were able to take his weight. He lifted his arm and rotated his shoulder, wincing slightly at the pain. He'd probably pulled a muscle. Reaching up, he pressed his fingers to the wound on his cheek. They came away smeared with blood.

Great. What kind of hero am I? I'm meant to be rescuing a damsel in distress—maybe. The way I'm going, I'll be the one needing rescuing...

His woman had summoned him. She wanted him by her side. That's all the impetus he needed to pull himself together. He straightened his shoulders and limped determinedly toward the house.

Ruby turned her back on her father, still reeling from the vitriol on his face. This whole situation had gotten out of control. When she'd decided to confront her father over his lies, she'd never imagined things would get so ugly. That her father would say such awful things. She wasn't the one who'd caused accidents that had seen workers injured and damage done to equipment that no doubt amounted to thousands of dollars, if not more.

The more she thought about it, the angrier she became. *They* were the ones in the wrong. Nathan was the one facing criminal charges and Ruby was darn sure her father's fingers were all over the plans they'd put in place. They weren't going to turn this around on her. She wouldn't stand for it.

As her fury ignited, she spun on her heel, intent on giving them both a piece of her mind. Before she could speak, the door to the office swung inward and her mother stood calmly in the opening.

Though she was in her early sixties, Maria Rodriguez was still a striking woman. As usual, her dyed-blond hair was perfectly coiffed. Her long, manicured nails were an immaculate scarlet. She wore a full face of makeup and a rich, cream-colored, designer linen suit and matching, shiny leather stilettos that looked like they cost more than what Ruby made in a month. None of that came as a surprise. Her mother had always taken pride in her appearance. No, what was surprising was that her mother was there at all, in her father's office.

"Mom! What are you doing here?"

Her mother's answering smile was so tight and brief, it could barely be called such.

"Hello, Ruby. That's funny, I thought I lived here. What are you doing here?"

Ruby glanced from her father to Nathan and back again. Both men looked flushed and angry. It would take a dimwit not to notice the tension in the room and her mother had never been stupid.

"What's going on here?" Maria Rodriguez asked.

"This is none of your business," her father growled. "Get out of here."

Instead, Ruby's mother sauntered farther into the room. A matching handbag swung jauntily from her wrist.

"Why should I do that, Joe? This is my house as much as yours. And from the look on your faces, it seems like I've interrupted something *very* interesting." She perched on the edge of the cherry-red leather, three-seater couch and elegantly crossed her legs. Then she waved languidly in their general direction. "Please, do continue. Don't stop talking on my account."

Her father glared at her mother with such hatred, Ruby was taken aback. Though her parents had long since lived separate lives under the same roof, Ruby had always been under the impression it was a mutually agreeable arrangement and that there was still plenty of love and respect between the two of them. Now it appeared obvious that wasn't the case. It seemed a lot had changed while she was in Bali.

Her mother shifted on the couch, her eyes narrowed in her husband's direction. Her lower leg swung impatiently back and forth. She crossed her arms over her chest. "What? Nothing to say, Joe? You've never been short of a word before." Her gaze swung to Nathan, who stood off to one side, his expression dark and belligerent.

"You're awfully quiet, too, Nathan. As Joe's righthand man, I'd have thought you'd have plenty to say, especially now that you've been indicted." She looked expectantly at Nathan, but he remained silent.

Ruby frowned. The undercurrent of tension was so thick it was palpable. It was like she'd woken in an alternate universe, where everyone looked familiar, but no one was playing the part she expected. There was more going on there than she knew and there was nothing more irritating than to be left in the dark by her family.

"What's going on?" she demanded, looking from one parent to the other.

Her mother shrugged. "Ask your father," she said in an offhand manner.

Ruby frowned in her father's direction. A fissure of dread iced her veins. "Daddy?"

Her father stared down at his desk and remained stubbornly silent. Her mother made a sound of annoyance in the back of her throat and abruptly got to her feet.

"Oh, for heaven's sake, Joe. If you won't tell her, I will."

The dread morphed into panic. Ruby tensed. "Tell me what?"

Her mother drew in a deep breath and slowly turned to face her. "This has been a long time coming, Ruby. I'm sorry. I should have told you a long time ago. You deserve to know who you've been working for."

Ruby frowned in confusion. "You mean, Daddy?"

"Yes. Of course, I mean your father. I should have warned you off working in the family business right from the beginning, but you were Daddy's little girl. You adored him. He could do no wrong in your eyes. I didn't think you'd believe me if I'd told you all those years ago about the systemic corruption that has followed your father around."

Ruby stilled. "Mom, what are you talking about?"

Her mother looked at her. "Didn't you ever wonder why I stopped working in the office?"

Ruby shrugged. "When the business got successful enough to employ more staff, I just thought you'd lost interest and decided to concentrate on other things."

Maria's laughter was humorless. "Oh, yes. I lost interest all right. I couldn't stand to be around a man who made an art of lying and deceiving people in order to turn a profit. It was always about making more money. If that meant greasing the palms of government officials, then that was just the cost of doing business.

"But it was worse than that. Your father deliberately set out to collect dirt on his competitors. Everybody has secrets. It's just a matter of digging deep enough to find them. And when you're in control of someone's secrets... You own them."

She paused and shook her head slowly from side to side. "And boy, did your father own some people. All very important people, of course. Mostly his competitors. He'd blackmail them into submitting tenders with prices so inflated they never stood a chance. He did it back then and no doubt he's still doing it. That's the kind of man your father is."

Her father's eyes flared with anger. He sneered. "As I recall, you didn't seem to think it was a bad thing when the money started pouring in. Where were your high-and-mighty principals then? You live a life most people only dream of. You were the one who begged me to spend the thirty million it cost to buy this house. And then you spent another million furnishing it. You didn't seem to have a problem spending my dirty money then."

Her mother strode closer to her father's desk, her eyes blazing. "Oh, yes, I was happy to spend your money, just like I've donated millions anonymously to various charities online. Do you know, I trawl through all those crowdfunding pages and randomly select people whose story resonates with me. A hundred thousand here, a hundred thousand there... I realized a long time ago, there was nothing I could do to stop you from lying and cheating your way into a fortune, so I decided to divert as much as I could to good causes; to people who really needed the help."

Joe stood abruptly and leaned across his desk. "How *dare* you! You had no right!"

"I had every right!" her mother snapped. "I helped build this company from the ground up and you turned it into a dirty, disgusting corrupt cesspool of lies that I no longer wanted to be a part of."

She spun on her heel and stared at Ruby, her gaze hot and intense. "You wonder why I quit working at Rodriguez Contracting? Why I disengaged from this family? That's why!"

Ruby stared back at her mother, her thoughts in turmoil. "Why didn't you divorce him then? No one forced you to stay."

"Because your father threatened to sue for custody. He'd already proven how dirty he was willing to play for money. How low do you think he would have stooped in order to get his kids? My reputation, my life would have been ruined. I would have been reduced to seeing my children every other week, if I was lucky. I couldn't take that risk.

"The money meant nothing to me, but I couldn't leave my children behind. You and your brothers meant more to me than anything else in the world. So, I shut my mouth and stayed and I got to raise my children and see you every day. Well, mostly every day. There were times when the whole sordid arrangement got me down. During those times, I had to stay away for the sake of my sanity. But I always came back, didn't I, Ruby?"

Ruby nodded, aghast at all her mother had revealed, and feeling a renewed sense of love and respect for the woman who'd given birth to her.

"Yes, Mom. You always came back," she rasped. She swallowed against the lump that had lodged itself in her throat. "I wish... I wish you'd told me all this a long time ago."

Her mother offered her a brief smile that was gone almost as soon as it appeared. "Better late than never, right?"

Belatedly, Ruby realized her mother was the perfect person to ask about the Barrington contract. Though Maria had long since stopped working in the office, Ruby suspected her mother had kept close tabs on her father's business activities all this time.

She looked her mother straight in the eye. "What happened with Barrington Mining?"

Her mother's gaze flicked to her husband. Seemingly not put off by the ugly glare he leveled at her, she turned back to Ruby.

"The problem with the Barrington Mining contract was Frank Barrington. You see, he wasn't like all the rest. Your father engaged several investigators and spent a small fortune in an effort to dig up dirt on the man, but they came up with nothing. Not to be deterred, your father secured the mining contract in the usual way—lies, deceit, blackmail. His competitors fell by the wayside. The problem was, he got too complacent. He didn't think an accident here or there would matter to anyone. After all, they hadn't mattered in the past. Then again, he hadn't worked for Frank Barrington before.

"The owner of Barrington Mining wasn't too happy about the spate of accidents that continued to happen under your father's watch. Frank started putting pressure on your father to clean up his act; that such flagrant breaches of safety regulations wouldn't be tolerated. When that kind of thing had happened in the past, your father simply revealed some dirty little secret he had on the complainer, but when it came to Frank, he had nothing."

She turned to face her husband, a smug expression on her face. "It made life difficult for you, didn't it, dear?"

Her father growled low in his throat. His face was so crimson Ruby momentarily worried he might be about to have a stroke. Seemingly unperturbed, her mother continued.

"Then Evan Wilson was killed, and all hell broke loose. His death was the final straw for Frank. Your father's contract was terminated, effective immediately, and he and his entire crew were escorted off the site."

"I had nothing to do with that!" her father protested.

Her mother glared at him. "Save it, Joe. I know what you did. Don't you remember? You told me."

Ruby gasped.

"You're lying," her father growled.

Maria's trill of laughter filled the air. "Lying, Joe? I don't think so. How else would I know about the eucalyptus oil you sprayed on Evan's prescription sunglasses? You told me it was your idea. Are you now saying you had nothing to do with that? That you weren't the one who came up with the dirty trick that resulted in a young, innocent man losing his life?"

Joe's gaze turned lethal. Ruby's heart skipped a beat. She stepped closer to her mother feeling an instinctive need to offer protection. But her mother appeared unfazed by her husband's reaction. She continued in a conversational tone.

"Evan kept those sunglasses in the cab of his machine. It was only a matter of time before he put them back on." She glared at Joe. "You knew that when he put them on, he wouldn't be able to see very well. The more he tried to clean them, the more smeared the oil would become. You told me that was all part of the plan, remember?"

Her mother clapped her hands as if in delight. "And what a marvelous plan it turned out to be! It was thoroughly investigated and no one was held to account. A tragic accident, was the official report. There were plenty who couldn't work out how the boy hadn't seen the scraper until it was too late. After all, they're not exactly small pieces of equipment. Alas, no one thought to check that poor boy's sunglasses. The cause of his momentary blindness. Such a clever plan."

She glared at her husband. "So, what do you say, Joe? Are you finally prepared to admit the truth to our daughter?"

Chapter
Twenty-Two

Her father's eyes were cold as ice. Ruby had never seen such a malevolent expression on his face. A shiver of apprehension ran down her spine. She inched herself even closer to her mother. Nathan's expression turned frantic. It was as if he could sense this wasn't going to end well and was now trying to distance himself from the whole sorry situation. Ruby was almost frozen with shock at the revelations.

"I wasn't even working at the mine when Evan Wilson died. I had nothing to do with that." Nathan exclaimed, his eyes wide with fear. "All I did was to set up a few little accidents, just like Uncle Joe told me. We only wanted to cause some trouble for Barrington Mining. Maybe get the mine closed for a while. That was the plan, right Uncle Joe?"

"That's right, Nathan," her father said in a quiet, calm voice that was somehow scarier than if he'd continued to rant.

"That's the least Frank Barrington deserved and it's not like he couldn't afford it."

Ruby's mother narrowed her eyes at her husband. "Your actions cost a young man his life. You might as well have pointed a gun at him and pulled the trigger." She turned her lethal glare on Ruby's cousin. "As for you, you ought to hang your head in shame. You might not have caused anyone's death, but from what I've heard, that was more good luck than good management. You're each as bad as the other."

"No!" Nathan protested. "I was only doing what I was told. I was trying to help out my uncle. I might have done a few shoddy things in the past, but I'm not a murderer! No one's died on my watch."

His breath came fast. His cheeks were flushed. Then he turned on Ruby. "This is all your fault. If you'd done your bit in Bali and gotten close enough to Vaughan Barrington to learn some company secrets, there wouldn't have been any need for me to set up all those random "accidents." We could have taken the Barringtons down from the inside and nobody would have gotten hurt." He stabbed a finger in her direction. "*You're* the one with blood on your hands."

Fury ignited inside her. "Don't you *dare* put this on me! I had nothing to do with your machinations." She turned to her father. "All these years, I loved you, I trusted you. And you repaid me with lies and deceit. Now you've ruined the only good thing in my life."

"Surely, you can't be referring to Vaughan Barrington?" her father continued in that same calm and deadly voice.

Ruby glared at him. "Vaughan Barrington is the antithesis of the two of you. He's good and kind and honorable. He truly cares about other people, even those who owe him nothing and who have nothing to give. He wouldn't dream of having a dirt file on anyone and he wouldn't deceive anyone to get to the top."

Her scathing gaze encompassed the two men. "You disgust me. Don't ever involve me in your underhanded activities again. I want nothing to do with you or your dirty business. From this day forward, we're done. I'm cutting both of you from my life. We don't need you."

Her mother frowned. "*We?*"

Vaughan had knocked several times on the hand carved, double wooden front doors, to no avail. Either no one was home, or they were too far away to hear him. He'd spied Ruby's Mazda parked in the driveway outside the house, so he knew she was there. That meant she couldn't hear him. With nothing else for it, he twisted the knob and pushed open the front door.

"Hello? Ruby? Is anyone home?"

His voice echoed off the vast walls that stretched up to a cathedral ceiling. A magnificent chandelier made up of hundreds of individual pieces sparkled like diamonds overhead. As he crossed the intricate-patterned Italian travertine tile, he gaped at the original artworks that graced the walls. Rembrandt, Van Gogh, Picasso, Storrier. An eclectic mix of styles and colors, but they all had one thing in common: their extraordinary price tag.

He continued forward cautiously and then halted outside the first room he came to. The door was closed, but he caught snatches of conversation coming from the other side. Then he heard Ruby. He couldn't hear all the words, but there was no doubt her voice was raised in anger and it sounded like she had plenty to say.

An extraordinary calmness descended upon Ruby. Now that she'd had her say, it was like a weight had been lifted off her shoulders. She turned to face her mother.

"Yes, Mom. *We.* I'm pregnant. Vaughan Barrington's the father. I love him with all my heart. One day, I hope to marry him. If he'll have me after all I did."

Her father looked incensed. His face turned apoplectic. "You're having a *Barrington's* bastard? How *could* you, Ruby? How could you be so stupid? How could you betray your family like that?"

Ruby continued to regard him calmly. "You're the only one who betrayed us, Daddy. You and Nathan. For nothing more than money and power. I'm going to the police."

Nathan glared at her with a look that was so evil, she genuinely felt afraid. Acting out of reflex, she took a couple of steps backward and came up hard against the couch. Her heart skipped a beat. Her gaze went from Nathan to her father. His face was granite. Her heart clenched. Slowly, Nathan advanced on her. The expression in his eyes grew wild and unfocused. His hands clenched into fists.

Holding onto her courage, she gave him a steely eyed glare, refusing to look away. "You wouldn't dare," she taunted him in a scathing tone.

With a guttural growl, Nathan raised his hand to strike her. The door flew open and hit the wall with a loud bang. Ruby gasped. Vaughan stood in the opening, his breath coming fast. When he spoke, his voice was cold steel.

"I wouldn't do that if I were you."

Nathan stared at Vaughan in indecision. Something in Vaughan's fierce expression finally registered. Slowly, Nathan lowered his arm.

Vaughan wanted to race over to Ruby and pull her into his arms. His heart had nearly stopped at the sight of someone with their fist raised to strike her. But he was wary of the tension in the room and so he advanced slowly. An older woman who resembled Ruby enough that she had to be her mother was perched on a couch. Ruby stood a short distance away. She looked a little shell-shocked, but determined.

With a glare at the man he now recognized as Nathan Garcia, Vaughan stared at Rodriguez. "What's going on? I got a call from Ruby to come over and then nothing." He glanced at the woman he loved. "Are you all right?"

She nodded and opened her mouth to speak, but her father cut across her.

"How *dare* you come into my home uninvited! You Barringtons are lying, thieving murdering bastards! Your father has destroyed my company, my reputation, and my son! He killed himself because of your father's actions!"

Pain and sorrow crossed over Ruby's face. Vaughan advanced toward her, hand out, beseeching. "Ruby, honey. You know that's not true."

Before Ruby could respond, her father exploded. "Bullshit! He's our enemy, Ruby. And you've betrayed this family by laying with him and conceiving his spawn. You're no longer part of this family."

Ruby gasped, her face turning pale. Vaughan reached her side and took her hand. He squeezed it reassuringly before turning toward her father. Suddenly, the woman he presumed to be her mother stood up from the couch, her eyes blazing.

"Enough! Enough of your lies and vitriol, Joe. Tell her the truth."

Ruby's heart pounded. Icy tentacles of fear wrapped themselves around her heart. "Mom? What is it?"

Her mother closed her eyes briefly and drew in a deep breath. "I'm sorry, Ruby. There's something else you haven't been told and...it's going to destroy you."

She gasped. Her heart stopped and then started pounding even harder. Vaughan stepped even closer and drew her tightly against his side. She was grateful for his support.

"W-what is it?" she forced herself to say.

Once again, her mother drew in a ragged breath. Her eyes darkened with pain. "It's about your brother. Kyle."

"Maria..." Her father's voice carried a deadly warning.

Her mother's eyes flashed. "He was her brother, Joe! She deserves to know!"

Ruby's foreboding morphed into a fear so cold and hard it was like she was frozen to the spot. She gripped Vaughan's hand and tried to breathe through the tightness in her chest. Her nails dug into his palm. She looked her father in the eye.

"Tell me."

"There's nothing to tell!" he blustered. "Your mother's trying to stir up trouble between us. She couldn't bear the fact you preferred me over her. She's always been jealous of our relationship. Haven't you, Maria?" he sneered.

Her mother's expression was a picture of icy fury. Her eyes blazed. "I'm done with your lies, Joe. And our daughter deserves better from you. Tell her the truth about Kyle, or I will."

Her parents engaged in a battle of wills as their angry gazes remained locked on each other. Her father was the first to break eye contact. With a muttered curse, he shook his head and turned his back on them. Her mother glared at him and then compressed her lips.

"This isn't easy, Ruby. I'm still struggling with it myself. But you deserve to know what really happened to Kyle and who's responsible for his death."

Ruby brought a hand up to her mouth. Her world had tilted off its axis. She wasn't sure she was ready to hear any more of this. But she had to know the truth. Until she did, she'd never find peace again.

"Tell me," she said quietly, staring at her mom.

"Kyle adored your father as much as you did. He looked up to him, wanted to be like him. That's why he went into the family business. But there was something he couldn't bring himself to tell your father: He was gay."

Ruby gasped again. "You knew?"

Her mother nodded. "Kyle never told me, but he didn't have to. I knew my son. I also knew, as well as he did, that your father would never accept him that way. So, for a long time Kyle kept quiet about it. Until Frank Barrington terminated that contract."

Maria sighed quietly and then continued. "That threw Kyle for six. He was shocked that a contract worth millions of dollars had come to such an abrupt end. You see, he didn't know about your father's shady business operations, or the corruption that had become second nature to him.

"Kyle was always sensitive. Your father made sure to hide from him the less savory ways he did business. Kyle believed your father's protestations of innocence; that Frank had torn up that contract without just cause.

"But, like you, Kyle wasn't stupid. He'd begun to have some doubts. He started to do his own investigation and what he discovered didn't reflect well on anyone connected with Rodriguez Contracting. He also discovered the truth about what happened to Evan Wilson. His lover."

Ruby's stomach clenched. She gaped in disbelief. She had no idea Kyle and Evan Wilson had been a couple.

"You see, Kyle discovered that your father and Nathan had been behind the accident that claimed poor Evan's life. Kyle was devastated. He confronted your father and told him everything, including that he was gay."

"How do you know all this?" Ruby asked, dazed from her mother's revelations.

"I overheard them talking." She paused. "Your father reacted in the way you'd expect. He was shocked and angry and disgusted. He berated Kyle for what he called "a sick perversion" and then disowned him. All in the space of a few minutes."

Bruised and battered, shocked beyond measure, Ruby's head spun. Her dear, lost brother. Poor, sweet, sensitive Kyle. He would have been devastated.

"You heard all this?" she asked, her voice cracking with disbelief.

"Not all of it," her mother said softly. "I caught Kyle on his way out of your father's office. He looked awful. Pale and shaking and talking to himself. I stepped into his path and stopped him. It took him a moment to realize who I was. Then he told me what had happened."

She paused. Her voice caught on a sob. "My poor boy was broken; utterly destroyed. By his own father. I don't know how Kyle would have weathered the fallout over the Barrington contract, but make no mistake, it was your father who's responsible for his death and nobody will convince me differently. Kyle left this house completely devastated. That night, he took his own life."

The pain that ripped through Ruby was like nothing she'd ever known. She clung to Vaughan, who appeared just as shocked as she felt. She looked toward her father, feeling as raw and devastated as her brother had no doubt felt.

"Daddy? Is it true? Is what Mom says true?"

Her father kept his back to her. Throughout her mother's recount, he hadn't said a word. Now he refused to face her and respond to her question. That told her everything she needed to know. She clenched her fists, her breath coming fast. His complete refusal to take responsibility for any of this ignited her fury.

"How could you?" she cried, her voice cracking with the force of her emotion. Tears clogged her throat. "How *could* you?"

Finally, her father turned and looked at her. For a brief moment, she saw what could have been a flash of remorse, but as quickly as it appeared, it was gone, replaced with the unyielding, malevolent mask she'd witnessed earlier. Without a word, he stalked out of the room with Nathan at his heels.

Suddenly, she was crushed in Vaughan's embrace.

"Oh, Ruby! Thank God you're all right. When I couldn't reach you, I was so scared. I didn't know what had happened to you. Your phone call... The locked gates... No one at the front door... Everything was so strange. I'm just glad you're okay."

She pulled back enough to offer him a shaky, teary smile. "I'm okay. Thank you for coming."

He framed her beloved face with his hands. "I love you, Ruby. I love you so much. I'm so glad you're okay."

She stared at him. Tears coursed down her cheeks. "You love me?"

"Yes! With all my heart and soul!" Vaughan hugged her close again. After a few moments, Ruby pulled back again and swiped at her tears with the back of her hand.

"I want to apologize for my part in this whole sorry mess. I was acting under a misapprehension that your father had acted unscrupulously toward mine. Now I know the truth, in no small part, thanks to my mother."

With that, she looked at her mother and offered her an encouraging smile. "Mom, I'd like you to meet Vaughan Barrington." She paused. "Vaughan, this is my mom."

Maria stepped forward and held out her hand toward Vaughan. "I'm pleased to meet you, Vaughan."

"And you, too," Vaughan murmured.

Ruby's heart swelled with love. Though she and her mother had a lot of ground to make up, things were looking up.

"I'm sorry for ignoring you so often, Mom. I thought you no longer cared." Fresh tears slid down Ruby's cheeks. Her mother opened her arms and on a cry of relief, Ruby stepped into them.

"Never that," her mother murmured. "You were always loved, my dearest, beautiful girl. I'm sorry for causing you such doubt and sorrow. I hope we can forgive each other and look forward to the future. I can't wait to get to know your fine young man and hear all about my future grandchild."

Ruby's heart swelled with love.

Chapter
Twenty-Three

Vaughan smoothed the lapels of his designer tuxedo and gave himself a final once-over in the mirror. He and Ruby were on their way to the wedding of the century—or rather, *weddings*. Though his brother, Trace, and his fiancée, Cassie, had been the first ones to set the March date, after a flurry of back and forths between the triplets, they'd agreed that all three of them would get married at once. Not only would that save many of the guests from having to attend on three separate occasions, but it would also be a nice way to recognize the special bond between the three siblings. Besides, it would be fun.

Vaughan couldn't think of anything more exciting than celebrating the marriages of three of his siblings at once. Except, maybe celebrating his own wedding.

Out of the corner of his eye, he spied Ruby putting the finishing touches on her makeup. She looked stunning in a sparkly black, off-the-shoulder evening dress. The stretchy fabric hugged her curves and cradled her tiny bump. At fourteen weeks, she was still barely showing, but that didn't make Vaughan feel any less gooey whenever he glanced at her stomach.

We're having a baby! I'm going to be a dad!

Closing the short distance between them, he moved up behind her and slid his arms around her belly. He cupped their baby tenderly and pressed a soft kiss against the side of her neck. Ruby smiled at him, radiant with love and pregnancy hormones. She tilted her head to give him greater access. He placed another kiss against the soft and sensitive skin behind her ear.

"You look beautiful," he murmured.

"You don't look so bad yourself."

She turned in his arms and straightened his bow tie. "I'd like to kiss you, but you'll end up with lipstick all over your face."

"I could handle that." He winked.

She smiled and shook her head. "No time. We need to get going or we'll be late."

With that, she stepped out of his arms and walked back into her bedroom. They hadn't yet officially moved in together, but he spent as much time in her apartment as she did in his. The commute between their places was only about forty minutes, but Vaughan resented any time they spent apart.

He'd been carrying around the jeweler's box for more than a week now. He was still waiting for the perfect time to get down on one knee. Again. That's why this had to be perfect. The first time he'd proposed, they'd been on a beach in Bali, watching the sunset. That had been romantic, but he wanted to do even better this time.

He'd also waited until she'd had time to come to terms with the devastation wreaked by her father. Though she'd never get over the fact her father had been the reason her brother had taken his life, Vaughan hoped that over time, the pain would ease and that one day she'd find some kind of peace.

That's what made this proposal all the more important. This time it was for keeps. This time it would be the proposal they'd talk about for years to come with their children and grandchildren. But the perfect moment had yet to present itself and he was beginning to wonder if it ever would.

Is it really that important that I pull off the perfect proposal? What does it matter, as long as she says 'yes'?

The truth was, he was growing impatient. He loved Ruby with everything that he was. He wanted to make her his wife. No perfect or imperfect proposal would change that.

"Are you ready?" Ruby asked, interrupting his thoughts.

She held a black sequined evening bag in her hand. He smiled and nodded. "Let's go."

The couples had chosen to hold the combined wedding celebration in the glorious grounds of Sydney's Botanical Gardens with the crystal blue Pacific Ocean as a backdrop. Rows of white chairs had been set out on the green grass.

Vaughan saw Ruby to a seat and then went up to greet the three nervous-looking grooms at the front.

"Trace. How are you, brother?" He and Trace embraced. Then Vaughan turned to Molly's intended, Shane, and Charlotte's future husband, Grayson.

Vaughan was still getting to know his two new brothers-in-law, but from what he could tell, they made his sisters happy and that's all that mattered to him. After wishing them both good luck with the upcoming nuptials, he returned to his seat. Reaching out, he took Ruby's hand and threaded his fingers through hers. They shared a tender smile.

"It's a beautiful day for a wedding," Ruby murmured, tilting her head toward the clear, blue sky.

"It certainly is," he agreed.

The gardens were spectacular and the perfume from the many colorful flowers filled the air with a heavy scent. Ancient Moreton Bay figs, with their twisted roots and majestic, leaf-covered branches cast enough shade over the gathering to take the edge off the early autumn heat.

Vaughan watched as other members of his family arrived and took their seats. He was especially pleased to see Elizabeth and her husband, Archie, take a seat on the Barrington side of the aisle. Though he and Elizabeth were still finding their way, he was confident everything would work out. The anger, the bitterness, the hurt... They'd all but evaporated and he had Ruby to thank for that. Her overwhelming love for him left no room for negative emotions, and that included the way he felt about Elizabeth.

In fact, the triplets and their future spouses had generously agreed to invite all of the extended family, including all of the Craigdons. Vaughan watched as Christopher, whose father had been a Craigdon, and his wife, Lexi, and their tribe of kids filled up two more rows. The rest of the Craigdon clan arrived together. Callum and Grace and their three children. Joel and Sheridan took a seat beside them. Nicholas and Harper, with their young son, Mack, who was the image of his father. The impish grin and cheeky chuckle brought a smile to Vaughan's lips. Isabella and Raine, who'd only tied the knot the previous spring and still looked like they were in the honeymoon phase.

Sophia and Jarrod and their adorable triplets took a seat behind him. He turned and murmured a greeting. Ruby had told him the scan had showed they were only having one. He was secretly glad. He wasn't sure he was up for an instant family. Still, Sophia and Jarrod looked happy enough and the babies were beyond cute in their identical wedding outfits.

Even the Craigdon cousins had been invited. Flynn and Jayde. Noah and Ayla. Logan and Mia. They all looked striking in their wedding finery. All pleased for the brides and grooms.

Then there were the rest of Vaughan's brothers and sisters and his parents. He hadn't yet told them about Elizabeth, but he would. They'd grown closer these past weeks and he was finally at peace with his past. His parents would be as shocked as he'd been when he shared Elizabeth's secret, but they were kind and compassionate people and he was sure they'd welcome her into the family and accept her into their lives, just like he had.

His brother, Lincoln, and Zoe arrived hand in hand. Gone was the haunted look in his brother's eyes that had been there for a long time after Lincoln's return from Afghanistan. In fact, he'd never looked happier. Vaughan guessed that had a lot to do with the woman beside him, who looked like she was ready to give birth any moment. Vaughan hoped she at least got through the day.

Wade and his wife, Alice, were also there, along with Alice's two boys. Behind them came Zac and Emily. Vaughan recalled it was Emily's brother who'd been killed at the mine more than a year ago. He wondered if she knew about Evan's connection to Ruby's brother. He was glad she appeared to hold no ill feeling toward the Barringtons.

He wasn't sure how she felt being at a function that was also attended by a member of the Rodriguez family, but no doubt Zac had warned her of the connection. Vaughan hoped with all his heart that Emily would be just as forgiving toward Ruby as she was toward his own family. After all, what had happened to Evan wasn't Ruby's fault. Knowing that Joe Rodriguez and Nathan Garcia would most likely face criminal charges for causing Evan's death would no doubt bring the Wilson family, including Emily, a little comfort. At least justice would be served.

The last Barrington to take their seat was Hannah. She hurried as quickly as her four-inch heels on soft grass would allow and sat down with her fiancé, Liam. She looked across at Vaughan and caught his eye. She glanced from him to Ruby and back again and then gave a cheeky wink.

Vaughan smiled. He wouldn't be surprised if another wedding announcement was forthcoming. That reminded him of the ring in his pocket and the fact he hadn't yet asked Ruby again for her hand. He vowed silently to attend to that before the night was out. Who needed a perfect proposal anyway?

As the string quartet struck up the wedding march and the guests rose to their feet, Vaughan turned to watch his sisters, Charlotte, Molly, and Trace's fiancée, Cassie, walk down the aisle. The women looked radiant in their gorgeous white dresses, sparkling jewelry and brilliantly colored bouquets.

His heart swelled with love and pride. He hoped one day soon he'd be the groom waiting at the end of the aisle for his beautiful bride. His Ruby. Tightening his hold on her hand, he looked down at her tenderly and smiled.

Elizabeth's heart had never felt so full. Having all seven of her children in one place was more than she'd ever imagined. Knowing Vaughan was slowly warming toward her filled her with overwhelming peace and gratitude. She'd never felt so blessed.

After years spent trapped in a loveless marriage, the days she spent with Archie were bliss. Though their path to love had been rocky and each had been married before, the fact they were finally able to be together while they were still relatively young and in good health had been a miracle. Sometimes she had to pinch herself to remind herself it was all real.

"How are you doing?" Archie said, coming toward her. He handed her a glass of punch.

She'd taken refuge from the heat of the afternoon on a bench beneath one of the stately Moreton Bay figs. The ceremony was over and smartly dressed waiters and waitresses were now attending to the guests, offering them appetizers and other finger foods set out in such fancy displays on platters that they looked way too good to eat.

"Can I get you something to eat?" Archie asked, settling beside her.

She smiled. "No, thank you. I'm all good. Just enjoying the beautiful day surrounded by my beautiful family."

Archie's eyes filled with tenderness. He leaned in and kissed her softly on the lips. "*You're* beautiful. The most beautiful woman here."

Her heart swelled with love. She reached up and cupped his beloved cheek. "I love you, Archie Craigdon. I'm so lucky to have you in my life."

Archie winked and pulled her close. "Right back at you."

Ruby had never felt so much love in one small space. The three weddings had gone off without a hitch. Each couple had penned their own vows and there wasn't a dry eye in the congregation when they were finished speaking. No one could doubt the love each one had for their respective spouses. It gave Ruby hope that some marriages were made to last.

Her parents had finally given up all pretense of playing happy families. The façade of a happy marriage had been completely stripped away. Her mother had moved out to a much smaller, but equally stylish apartment a couple of suburbs away. She was closer to Ruby's place now and Ruby was glad. They had a lot of years to make up.

She hadn't spoken to her father since that fateful day when her world had been torn apart. Every time she thought about Kyle, she teared up. It would be a long time before she could think of what had happened without feeling angry, without wanting to rage at her father, hurt him as badly as he'd hurt Kyle. But he was likely to face criminal proceedings and hopefully some justice would be served. The only thing that brought her a modicum of comfort was knowing that her brother, Matthew, had been just as unaware as she was of the part their father had played in Kyle's death.

She swallowed a sigh. Her fingers momentarily clenched into fists. She forced them to relax. For now, she was at a wedding. No, three weddings. It was a time to set aside her hurt and pain for the evening and enjoy the celebrations.

From the corner of her eye, she spied Frank Barrington heading toward her. Vaughan had excused himself to go to the bathroom. She was alone.

"Ruby. It's good to see you again. Do you mind if we have a word?"

A rush of nerves clogged her throat. She and Frank had gotten off on the wrong foot back in Bali, when he'd muscled in and taken over Vaughan's care. She'd understood that he'd been just as concerned as she was about his son, but she'd resented his arrogance just the same. Things hadn't improved when they'd arrived in Sydney. She was certain he'd been told about her deception and that his attitude toward her would have cooled even more.

That's why she was surprised when he greeted her with warmth. She blinked and stammered a response. "Y-yes. Of course."

Frank took her by the elbow and guided her to a quiet spot off to one side. She looked at him, wondering where this was headed, trying to gauge his mood.

"I'd like to apologize for my earlier behavior," he said, surprising her yet again. "I kind of took over in Bali and again at the Sydney Harbour Hospital and that wasn't fair."

"It's fine," she murmured. "I get it."

He shrugged. "Anyway, Hannah told me what happened with your father and what motivated you to deceive Vaughan in the way you did. I'm not condoning your actions, but I just want you to know, I understand."

Some of her tension eased. She drew in a steadying breath. "Thank you. That's very gracious of you."

Frank shrugged. "I'm sorry. No one should have to suffer like that at the hands of their family."

Ruby swallowed. "It's not for you to apologize. You did nothing wrong. If anyone should be apologizing, it's me."

Frank smiled softly. "Loyalty to family is an honorable thing. It's not our fault that some family members don't deserve that loyalty. How about we call it even and put all this behind us. I can tell from the way my son looks at you that he's head over heels in love. I couldn't be happier for you both." Frank paused. "Welcome to the family, Ruby."

As the sun began to set, the wedding party and guests drifted indoors to a function room in the Park Hyatt Hotel. The soft gray furnishings and yards and yards of bunting and white lace, coupled with the large and extravagant urns overflowing with gorgeous, fragrant flowers set the mood for the reception. As the band struck up a lively tune, Ruby turned to Vaughan and smiled.

"Would you like to dance?"

He grinned. "You read my mind."

Together, they walked to the dance floor and Vaughan took her in his arms. She leaned into him and he rested his chin on her head. Some of the tension she'd noticed earlier eased from his shoulders.

She wasn't sure why he'd been so nervous. It wasn't like he was one of the grooms. He'd appeared to be happy for his siblings.

So, why is he so jittery?

Refusing to dwell on it any longer, she draped her arms around his neck and pulled his head down for a kiss. Their lips met. The passion between them was instant. It had always been like that. Even when she thought she was only in it for the short term, she couldn't deny the instant physical connection they'd had right from the beginning.

As she pressed closer against him, the unmistakable feel of his rigid erection made her smile. He might be feeling edgy about something, but it definitely wasn't her. The music changed to a slow dance and they stared into each other's eyes. Their feet were barely moving as they drank in each other's presence.

"What do you say we get out of here?" Vaughan rasped against her ear.

She shivered with desire from the touch of his lips and nodded. "That sounds like a fine idea."

With that, Vaughan took her hand and led her off the dance floor.

"Your place or mine?" she asked with a smile.

"Neither." His hand went to his pocket and he pulled out a room key. "I made the arrangements earlier."

She grinned, delighted. "I love a man who can plan ahead."

The look he gave her was a mixture of nerves and excitement. "You have no idea."

They caught the lift up to the top floor. Ruby was impressed. "You booked the penthouse?"

"Only the best for the woman I love."

The heat in his gaze scorched her, but some of the tension was back. She wondered at it briefly, then dismissed it from her mind. Whatever was going on with him, no doubt he'd share it with her when the time was right. He was learning to trust her again, one day at a time.

The closer they got to the room, the more Vaughan's nervousness increased. Worry poked at her. She shot him a concerned look.

"Is everything all right?"

He gave her a tight smile that barely made it to his eyes. "Yes, of course."

Then they were at the door and Vaughan passed the keycard over the sensor. It beeped and flashed green. He drew in a deep breath and pushed the door slowly open with his shoulder. Ruby gasped.

The room was filled with lighted candles covering every available surface. They made the room look like a magical fantasy land. They scented the air with something that smelled divine, a mixture of vanilla, caramel and spicy cinnamon. The super-king bed was covered in red rose petals that had been scattered in artful disarray. A bottle of expensive champagne stood nearby in an ice bucket, along with two crystal champagne glasses on the bedside table.

She turned to Vaughan in surprise and delight. "You planned all this?"

He grinned nervously. "Yes."

Her chest went tight with emotion. Tears welled up in her eyes. "Oh, Vaughan! It's...beautiful."

He stepped closer and drew her in his arms. He pressed a soft kiss on her lips. She drew slightly back and framed his head with her hands. The candlelight played over his face.

"I love you so much," she whispered.

"I love you, too."

And then, before she knew what was happening, Vaughan went down on one knee. In his hand was the most beautiful diamond and sapphire ring she'd ever seen. Though she hadn't been able to bring herself to part with the first engagement ring, she'd stopped wearing it weeks ago. She would have been happy to put it back on again with the slightest encouragement from Vaughan, but it seemed he wanted a fresh start.

He stared up at her with eyes filled with love. "Ruby Ashworth-Rodriguez, will you marry me?"

"Yes!" she cried, as tears of joy overflowed and ran down her cheeks. "Oh, yes!"

In one fell swoop, he slid the ring on her finger and dragged her into his arms. He lifted her off her feet and swung her in his arms.

"Mind the candles!" She laughed and cried, all at the same time.

He slid her slowly down his body until her feet were on the carpet again. Then he kissed her so long and thoroughly, getting naked with him was the only thing on her mind. They undressed each other slowly, though both of them were breathing hard. The light from the candles surrounded them in a soft, golden glow.

When they were naked, they took a moment to stand there and look their fill. Almost reverently, Vaughan reached out and cupped his hand over her burgeoning belly. Then he slid his hand upward and scraped his fingers across her nipple. It hardened instantly. Need pooled in her core. His erection brushed her stomach and it was all she could do not to groan.

Together, they fell on the bed among the rose petals and explored each other's bodies. The peaks and valleys. The taut muscles. The scattering of dark blond chest hair. She loved everything about him and was so grateful to have him in her life.

To think how close I came to losing him...

No, she refused to think like that ever again. They were together now. They loved each other. The promise of their future together burned brighter than any candle.

Once again, Vaughan's hand crept down to her belly and cradled their unborn child. The tenderness in his eyes stole her breath.

"I love you so much," he rasped. "My love, my life."

She stared at him, her heart swelling with emotion. "You're my soul mate. My one and only. I'll love you until the day I die."

THE END

If you've enjoyed Vaughan and Ruby's story, please take the time to leave a review. That way other readers can find and enjoy my books. Every review is greatly appreciated.

Get a free book when you sign up for Chris Taylor's newsletter. Go to www.christaylorauthor.com.au to claim your book.

Other books by Chris Taylor

CHRIS TAYLOR

The Sydney Harbour Hospital Series (in order)

The Perfect Husband
The Body Thief
The Baby Snatchers
The Final Bullet
The Debt Collector
The Lab Test
The Stolen Identity
The Cliff-top Killer
The Likeable Fraudster

The Sydney Legal Series (in order)

An Accidental Murderer
At the Hand of her Father
A Woman Scorned
Lies and Deception
Ordinary Evil
The Ties that Bind
The Perfect Crime
A Toxic Inheritance
Malicious Love

The Craigdon Family Series (in order)

Callum
Joel
Isabella
Nicholas
Sophia
Flynn
Noah
Logan
Elizabeth

The Barrington Family Series (in order)

Broken Lives
Broken Promises
Broken Bonds
Broken Spirits
Broken Minds
Broken Vows
Broken Hearts
Broken Dreams
Broken Homes

The Fairfax Family Series (in order)

A Cattleman in Disguise
A Cattleman's Quest
A Cattleman's Daughter

A Cattleman's Secret Baby
To Catch a Cattleman
The Doctor and the Cattleman
To Rescue a Cattleman
A Cattleman's Heart
For the Love of a Cattleman

Bachelors and Brides Series (in order)

Matilda
Austin
Farrah
Benjamin
Verity
Denver
Ebony
Tyrone
Willow

Books by Chris Taylor
Writing as
Bella
Christian

This Is Where It Ends Series (in order)

Jessie's Story

Ryan's Story
Holly's Story
Sarah's Story
Veronica's Story

Love audiobooks? Check out Chris Taylor Books on audio
iTunes   Amazon   Audible

Join Chris Taylor's Facebook reader group/fan page and be
among the
first to receive news of book releases, read and review books
prior to release
and other amazing offers.

Join Now!

Acknowledgments

As usual, no book comes into being without a lot of help and support by my friends and family. A world of thanks must go to my wonderful editors, Nancy Cassidy and Pat Thomas. Thank you for everything that you do to make my stories even more amazing than I could ever dare to dream. To former Detective Superintendent Michael Kilfoyle, thank you for lending my story credibility. Any mistakes are wholly my own.

To all of the team at 100 Covers, thank you for the fantastic book cover. To my sister, Nicole Guihot and to my friends, Ally Thomson and Sue Ricardo, thank you for your excellent editorial comments, proof reading skills and suggestions. I hope you like the final result.

To the fantastic writer organizations such as Romance Writers of Australia, Romance Writers of America and Romance Writers of New Zealand for all the help, support and encouragement they offer new and aspiring writers, including me.

To my readers, thank you for your support and love for my stories. Your encouragement and enjoyment of my humble stories make this journey all worthwhile.

And lastly, to my friends and family, especially my husband and children. Thank you for putting up with late dinners and even later conversations as I've emerged day after day from the sometimes scary but always enthralling world I've created on my computer.

About the Author

Chris Taylor grew up on a farm in north-west New South Wales, Australia. She always had a thirst for stories and recalls writing her first book at the ripe old age of eight. Always a lover of romance and happily-ever-afters, a career in criminal law sparked her interest in intrigue and suspense. For Chris to be able to combine romance with suspense in her books is a dream come true.

Chris is married to Linden and is the mother of five children. If not behind her computer, you can find her doing the school run, taxiing children to swimming lessons, football, ballet and cricket. In her spare time, Chris loves to read her favorite authors who include Richard North

Patterson, Sandra Brown, Kathleen E Woodiwiss
and Jude Devereaux.

You can find out more about Chris and get a free
book when you sign up for her newsletter at her
website:
http://www.christaylorauthor.com.au

Join Chris on Facebook at:
https://www.facebook.com/christaylorauthor/